W9-CXS-621

D1636268

PRAISE FOR T.J. NEWMAN

FALLING

"*Falling* is the best kind of thriller (for me as a reader, anyway). Characters you care deeply about. Nonstop, totally authentic suspense."
—James Patterson, #1 *New York Times* bestselling author

"T.J. Newman has taken a brilliant idea, a decade of real-life experience, and crafted the perfect summer thriller. Relentlessly paced and unforgettable."
—Janet Evanovich, #1 *New York Times* bestselling author

"Attention, please: T.J. Newman has written the perfect thriller! Such a cool, high-concept idea: commercial airline pilot forced to make the ultimate life-or-death choice. Newman's background in the air grounds the story in reality, while her writing amps up the suspense to unbearable levels. Terrific and terrifying, a true page-turner. A must-read for summer vacation—but my advice is, don't start this book until you've gotten off the plane."
—Gillian Flynn, #1 *New York Times* bestselling author of *Gone Girl*

"Heart-pounding. Heart-wringing. Heart-*stopping*! A great book! One of those where you're afraid to turn the next page, but you can't stop."
—Diana Gabaldon, #1 *New York Times* bestselling author of the Outlander series

"Amazing...intense suspense, shocks, and scares plus chilling insider authenticity make this one very special."

—Lee Child, #1 *New York Times* bestselling author

"Think *Speed* on a passenger jet—with the cockpit dials turned up to supersonic."   —Ian Rankin, #1 internationally bestselling author

"One of the year's best thrillers...Newman keeps up an extreme pace from the first page."   —*Library Journal* (starred review)

"Brilliant...incredibly suspenseful...With abundantly human characters, natural dialogue, and a plot that unleashes one surprise after another...the novel that everyone is talking about this summer."

—*Booklist* (starred review)

"A superlative debut...This tense, convincing thriller marks the arrival of an assured new talent."   —*Publishers Weekly* (starred review)

"The frenzy for *Falling* is understandable: At every turn, Newman cranks the tension in unexpected ways that still satisfy the thriller lust. Her insider's knowledge comes through in details that not only bolster the book's credibility but also catalyze the plot."

—Margaret Wappler, *Los Angeles Times*

"An unputdownable thriller that will take you on a wild ride full of twists and suspense."   —*Good Morning America*

"A white-knuckle thrill ride."   —*Newsweek*

"A rich and assured debut...Emotionally complex in surprising and refreshing ways...*Falling* is expertly paced—if you were to begin reading this book at LAX, you'd finish it right as you began your descent into JFK." — *USA Today* (3.5 out of 4 stars)

DROWNING: THE RESCUE OF FLIGHT 1421

"*Drowning* is the first terrific thriller of the year. Honest. It has at least a dozen legit cliff-hangers and a dozen huggable characters you can't stop rooting for. T.J. Newman has the goods. Make that the *greats*!"
— James Patterson, #1 *New York Times* bestselling author

"A stunningly vivid tour de force! Gripping. Shocking. Heartbreaking. You *will not* be able to come up for air until the very last page!"
— Brad Thor, #1 *New York Times* bestselling author of *Dead Fall*

"Stunning, emotional, and unforgettable. *Drowning* reads like *Apollo 13* underwater." — Don Winslow, *New York Times* bestselling author of *City on Fire* and *The Border*

"Masterful."
— Patricia Cornwell, #1 *New York Times* bestselling author

"*Drowning* is *The Poseidon Adventure* meets *The Martian*. It is another can't-put-down, edge-of-your-seat thriller from T.J. Newman, one of our most exciting new authors." — Adrian McKinty, *New York Times* bestselling author of *The Chain* and *The Island*

"*Drowning* is pure adrenaline and all heart. Gripping, relentless, effortlessly assured, T.J. Newman's thriller is tense and moving. You'll be grabbed from page one as the crew and passengers of a downed airliner fight for survival and rescuers race to reach them. *Drowning* is an incredible ride — strap in, brace, and remember to breathe." —Meg Gardiner, #1 *New York Times* bestselling author

"Riveting...T.J. Newman is back with another blockbuster, proving that *Falling*, her lights-out debut, was no fluke, but just the beginning of what should be a long, stellar career...*Drowning* is the book that everyone will be talking about...Each page is dripping with a plethora of emotions — ranging from fear to claustrophobia — all of them palpable and real, creating a reading experience that is truly unlike anything else in print today. And as you experience that rising crescendo of tension and suspense, two things become crystal clear: T.J. Newman is for real, and she's here to stay." —*The Real Book Spy*

"*Drowning* by T.J. Newman is a remarkable novel with extraordinary writing, story, and characters. Newman is a gifted writer and I stayed up all night reading." —Dervla McTiernan, #1 internationally bestselling author of *The Murder Rule*, a 2022 *New York Times* Critics Choice Best Book of the Year

"*Drowning* is a full-throttle adrenaline rush, a relentless, full-speed thriller that will keep you riveted and breathless. Hang on tight for what's sure to become a classic summer smash hit." —Eric Rickstad, *New York Times* bestselling author and author of *I Am Not Who You Think I Am*, a 2022 *New York Times* Critics Choice Best Book of the Year

"The world of airline thrillers belongs to Newman in this follow-up to *Falling*, and it's even better. The story has the beats for the perfect summer action film, let alone a beach read. Expect Newman to be drowning in sales and accolades." —*Library Journal* (starred review)

"A taut, gripping yarn. Not for the weak-kneed."

— *Kirkus* (starred review)

"This is a thriller to the core, one that readers will want to finish in a single sitting. The readers who took a chance on Newman's debut will find much of what they loved in this follow-up—brisk storytelling, masterful suspense, and the chance to vicariously peer into a nightmarish situation from which heroes emerge." — *Washington Post*

"Its own new genre—the disaster procedural. The pace is blinding, the suspense electrifying, the human drama impassioned."

— *Los Angeles Times*

WORST CASE SCENARIO

Also by T.J. Newman

Falling

Drowning: The Rescue of Flight 1421

WORST CASE SCENARIO

A Novel

T.J. NEWMAN

LITTLE, BROWN AND COMPANY

New York   Boston   London

Copyright © 2024 by T.J. Newman

Hachette Book Group supports the right to free expression and the value of copyright. The purpose of copyright is to encourage writers and artists to produce the creative works that enrich our culture.

The scanning, uploading, and distribution of this book without permission is a theft of the author's intellectual property. If you would like permission to use material from the book (other than for review purposes), please contact permissions@hbgusa.com. Thank you for your support of the author's rights.

Little, Brown and Company
Hachette Book Group
1290 Avenue of the Americas, New York, NY 10104
littlebrown.com

First Edition: August 2024

Little, Brown and Company is a division of Hachette Book Group, Inc. The Little, Brown name and logo are trademarks of Hachette Book Group, Inc.

The publisher is not responsible for websites (or their content) that are not owned by the publisher.

The Hachette Speakers Bureau provides a wide range of authors for speaking events. To find out more, go to hachettespeakersbureau.com or email hachettespeakers@hbgusa.com.

Little, Brown and Company books may be purchased in bulk for business, educational, or promotional use. For information, please contact your local bookseller or the Hachette Book Group Special Markets Department at special.markets@hbgusa.com.

Book interior design by Marie Mundaca

ISBN 9780316576796 (hardcover) / 9780316578851 (large print) / 9780316579988 (B&N signed edition)
LCCN 2024936454

Printing 1, 2024

LSC-C

Printed in the United States of America

For Grandaddy and Gpa,
Marion Newman and Tim J. Mullet—the original T.J.

AUTHOR'S NOTE

THE IDEA FOR my first novel—*Falling*—came to me when I was working as a flight attendant and I asked a pilot I was flying with: "What if your family was taken and you were told to crash the plane or they would die? What would you do?" The look on his face terrified me. I knew he didn't have an answer. And I knew I had the makings of my first book.

While writing that book, I had many conversations with pilots about the nuts and bolts of flying procedures and protocols—and also about the emotional and psychological side of being a pilot. *What is your biggest fear as a pilot?* That's the one question I kept asking.

Pilots told me that they feared uncontrolled fires in the cabin or cargo bays. Getting hooked in power lines. Making the wrong call in an emergency. Freezing up and not being able to make any call at all. They worried about turning their spouses into widows or widowers.

The answers started to blur together. I kept hearing the same things over and over until I finally got a response that stopped me in my tracks:

"My biggest fear is a commercial jet slamming into a nuclear power plant."

I wasn't sure if this pilot was being serious. I sort of laughed it off, saying that nuclear power plants—like dams, like any critical infrastructure—were safe in a post-9/11 world. Officials had already worked this out. They had already done whatever was needed to ensure that all nuclear power plants were safe from attack.

As I said this, the pilot just listened. When I finished, he smiled and replied: "And that's exactly what they want you to believe."

T.J. Newman

WORST CASE SCENARIO

The International Nuclear Event Scale has seven levels.

Level 1: Anomaly
Level 2: Incident
Level 3: Serious incident
Level 4: Accident with local consequences
Level 5: Accident with wider consequences
Level 6: Serious accident
Level 7: Major accident

There are only two INES level 7s on record: Fukushima and Chernobyl. There has never been a level 8.

Yet.

TWO HUNDRED AND NINETY-FIVE lives were in the hands of a pilot who was having a widow-maker heart attack at 35,000 feet.

There was no time to tell his copilot to get out of the bathroom and come fly the plane. No time to teach the flight attendant standing at the back of the cockpit how to work the radio. No time to declare an emergency to air traffic control. No time to warn the passengers and crew in the cabin to hang on. There was no time to do anything because he never even realized what was happening. He simply felt a sudden tightness in his chest—and a split second later, his dead body slumped forward on the yoke, and the plane went into an uncontrolled nosedive.

Instantly, everything in the cabin shifted forward. Sodas and bags of pretzels slid off tray tables. Cell phones flew out of hands. Passengers in line for the bathroom fell into one another. And anyone not buckled in found they were no longer in their seats.

Doors to the carts and carriers stretched across the back galley swung open in unison. Sleeves of cups, packets of sugar, plastic-wrapped cookies, pots of hot coffee, heavy pallets of soda—everything was dumped out, crashing onto the floor and spilling out into the plane.

The flight attendant mid-cabin lunged after the cart, but the aisle was clear for the fully stocked beverage trolley to barrel toward the front of the plane. Eight rows up, the four-hundred-pound cart ran over a man's foot, crushing his bones, before lodging itself tenuously between rows.

Every seat in the plane was filled. But in that first moment, that first drop, the cabin was completely silent. No one screamed. No one made a sound. There was no fear, only surprise. Because just like the pilot—unaware of what the pain in his chest meant—the two hundred and ninety-four other souls on board Coastal Airways Flight 235 hadn't figured it out yet either.

Moments later, once they realized they were about to die, the screaming began.

Push the yoke forward, the plane goes down. Pull the yoke back, the plane goes up.

That was the extent of what the flight attendant in the cockpit for the bathroom-break security procedure knew about the controls. That and if she didn't pull the pilot back off the yoke, he would send them straight into the ground.

Her positioning could not have been worse. She was five one and barely a hundred pounds; the captain was well over six feet, pushing three hundred, and she had no leverage. She could only reach him at an awkward angle from behind and to the side of the chair.

Stepping into a wide straddle between the seat and the center control panel, she wrapped her arms around his shoulders and pulled back with a grunt.

His body barely moved. The yoke stayed pushed forward as far as it would go.

At the front of the plane, the flight attendant on the floor in the forward galley crawled toward the lavatory. Breakfast entrées squished under her hands as broken first-class china bloodied her knees. Reaching the bathroom, she pounded on the door.

"Greg," she cried, her voice barely audible over the passengers' screaming. She stopped to listen for a response from the copilot inside—but there was nothing.

When the plane first dove, she'd heard a loud *slam* in the lav, followed by breaking glass. Since then—nothing. The flight attendant didn't know what was happening in the cockpit, but she did know the only other person on board who knew how to fly the plane needed to get out of the bathroom and back up there.

"Greg, *please*! Help!" she pleaded, pounding the door with both fists.

There was no response.

The arms of the flight attendant in the cockpit were shaking. Her hold on the dead pilot was weakening. Nearly all his weight continued to press the yoke forward.

The plane was headed straight down.

"Good morning, Minneapolis center. Delta heavy two-two-four, checking in at flight level three-four-zero."

The routine squawk from a pilot talking to air traffic control coming in over the cockpit speaker startled the flight attendant—but then it hit her.

Air traffic control…

Air traffic control!

"Good morning, Delta heavy. Maintain three-four-zero."

If she could talk to ATC, they could tell her what buttons to push to give the first officer's side control. Then she could pull up on the yoke on *that* side, the right side. She could get the plane out of its nosedive, and from there, ATC could talk her through what to do.

The plane's cabin shook violently as the uncontrolled free fall stressed the airframe. Passengers got out their phones to record the moment or send messages to their loved ones. The lead flight attendant pretended she didn't hear the crying babies or the loud praying as she reached up and lifted the silver placard labeled LAVATORY to expose the door's hidden locking mechanism. She slid the lever to the right; it unlocked.

"Greg," she called, pushing in on the center of the folding door—but it barely budged, stopped by something wedged against it from the inside. *"Greg!"* she said, pushing harder.

Angling her head at the opening, she pressed on the door and peered with one eye through the crack into the lav.

The copilot was crumpled on the floor. Eyes closed, unmoving. Bright red blood streaked down his face from a gash on his forehead. Broken shards of the shattered mirror covered his body.

She couldn't tell if he was alive or not.

If he wasn't, then they were already dead.

"Greg," she barked, her mouth pressed against the crack in the door. "Greg, *get up.*"

Up front, the flight attendant reached around the far side of the captain's seat, feeling for the radio. Panic began to take over when she couldn't find it—until her fingers touched a plastic spiral cord.

Heart thumping, she snagged the cord, pulled it up, and took hold of the mic she'd seen the pilots use countless times. Deep breath. She pushed the button.

"It's Coastal...we...please help," she stammered in a rush, not knowing what to say. "He's dead. The captain's dead. He had a medical, I think a heart attack. The FO's in the lav. He's not here. He's... the pilots are gone! We're going down. Please help us!"

Her voice was loud and trembling and for the first time the fear was coupled with emotion as she stifled a sob...at hearing the sound of her own voice echoing out in the cabin.

It wasn't the radio.

It was the PA system.

The lead flight attendant stared at the locked cockpit door as the sound of her colleague's ragged breathing continued over the plane's speakers.

So that was it. The captain was dead. They were going down.

As she kicked at the lav door, her own tear-soaked sobs joined the passengers'. "Get up! Get *up!*"

* * *

Greg's eyes fluttered open to a hazy view of...where was he?

Everything hurt. Nothing made sense. It was all fuzzy—until he saw the broken mirror.

Woozily scrambling to his feet, he heard someone shrieking his name. He opened the door and found the lead flight attendant on the ground, covered in blood and food.

"He's dead," she said, sobbing. "The captain's dead. *Do* something."

Shock froze him in place. As he blinked, a noise in the cabin grew louder and closer until—*bam*—the cart rammed into the flight attendant, pinning her against the cockpit door and snapping him back to reality.

If he didn't get back in the cockpit, they were *all* going to die.

Now barricaded in the bathroom, Greg clambered to the top of the cart, spilling cups and napkins and stir sticks into the lav. He pounded on the cockpit door.

"Tim!" he called out. "Open up! Tim, open up!"

As blood poured from her facial gashes, the flight attendant moaned in pain, still pinned between the cart and the door. Greg looked around from his perch atop the cart, trying to figure out what else he could do. He glanced over his shoulder back into the plane—and regretted it instantly.

There were two hundred and ninety-five souls on board. Nearly three hundred lives *he* was responsible for.

And they were all looking at him.

"*Tim!* Open the fucking—"

The cockpit door flew open.

In that split second, the image in front of him was frozen in time. The wide-eyed terror of the flight attendant inside who was about to be crushed by a four-hundred-pound cart. The body of the captain slumped forward in his seat. The flashing buttons on every panel in the flight deck. The incessant, robotic voice warning them: *Pull up. Pull up. Pull up.*

And beyond all that...

Was the ground.

CHAPTER ONE

COUNTDOWN TO ZERO HOUR
16 HOURS AND 38 MINUTES

UNITED GRACE CHURCH served not only as a community center, but as the center of community for Waketa, Minnesota.

"You belong to each other, and you are responsible for each other. That is what community means. And that is what Waketa is about."

The congregation nodded.

"We are always told that family is everything," Reverend Michaels continued. "But family's not just your blood. Family is your friends. Your neighbors. Family's your coworkers. And family is everyone in this church today. We are family."

In the last pew at the back of the small church, Steve Tostig listened without hearing.

If Reverend Michaels was responsible for safeguarding Waketa's soul, Steve was responsible for protecting its body. He was the guy who'd be on the town's postcard if there were one: tall, broad chest, flannel shirt, five-o'clock shadow. The type of guy who was popular in high school, mainly because he stood up to the bullies. The kind of person who you hope your child will one day end up with.

Steve sat alone in "widowers' row," as he'd taken to thinking of it, staring out the stained-glass windows at the cemetery down the hill. He'd brought carnations this time, blue ones. At least, the little sign on the bucket at the grocery store said they were carnations.

Claire Jean Tostig

1975–2023

Beloved teacher, daughter, wife, mother.

It wasn't long enough, but it never is.

He hadn't wanted that last part on there. It felt too...woo-woo. Too kumbaya and circle of life. Claire would have liked it. But to Steve, it should have said: *It wasn't long enough*—period.

No acceptance, no meaning. Only injustice. Just sheer, unfair bullshit.

"You know," continued the reverend, "I couldn't help but notice the parking lot has a lot of open spots today."

The sparse congregation mumbled in agreement.

"I'm not concerned," he said. "People are at work. Kids are in school. And Good Friday, the day when we mark the Lord's crucifixion...well, it's not exactly a real crowd-pleaser."

The congregation gave a collective chuckle.

"But you better show up early on Sunday," he continued, wagging his finger. "Boy, that parking lot will be full then. Because on Easter, we celebrate! Sunday we will come together as a community in a moment of joy and light to declare as one: He lives! *We* live."

Reverend Michaels paused. That perfect length of a pause that's not taught in seminary but discovered Sunday after Sunday, season after season, year after year, as you feel out the needs of your flock. Those aching, human souls that once a week came to this place to ponder or discover or wrestle with or be reminded of the whys and hows and whats of existence.

"But you're here today."

He paused again, looking around the chapel, holding eye contact with members of his congregation. When his gaze reached the back of the church, Steve looked away. He had come in after the service started; he would slip out before it ended, and he would not be here on Sunday. Reverend Michaels knew Steve came only on the days when the congregation was light because that meant there wouldn't be as many people asking him how he was doing and if he and his son, Matt, needed anything.

"You showed up *today*," said the reverend. "This day when our Savior was killed. This day when all hope seemed lost. This day of darkness when we had absolutely no assurance that the light would come again…"

He paused.

"You showed up."

People nodded in agreement.

"You know, there's a reason we come on…"

He trailed off, pausing again—but not for dramatic effect or to give time for reflection. He paused because they were all trying to figure out what that noise was. That distant rumble. A rumble that was growing louder with each passing moment.

The walls of United Grace began to shake. The floor beneath the congregation's feet vibrated. Reverend Michaels looked down to the Communion chalice. The surface of the dark red wine rippled.

Suddenly a shadow passed quickly through the church as something flew low overhead. Everyone was immediately up and looking out the stained glass on the west side of the church. Reverend Michaels stayed where he was, three steps up on the altar, hands gripping the sides of the pulpit. From there, he was the only one with a view through the window above the stained glass. He alone saw clearly the enormous commercial airliner streaking low across the sky.

Moments later, the entire church shook in the *boom.*

Screams filled the room as the congregants clutched one another. A framed picture fell off the wall; glass shattered as it hit the floor. At the back of the church, a flash of light grabbed Reverend Michaels's attention. It was the door opening.

The reverend watched Steve sprint through the door and across the parking lot to his truck. While everyone else cowered in the fear and confusion of the moment, Steve was already in action.

Joss Vance sat at her kitchen table a few miles away in a state of shock as hot coffee dripped from her fingers onto the morning paper. Her heart pounded with adrenaline as she looked around the room wondering what the hell that had been when suddenly—the lights flickered.

Joss looked up.

"No. No, no, no..." she whispered to no one but herself as the lights flickered again. But by then, Joss was already on her feet and moving.

She knew what was about to happen. She knew what it meant. And then, just as she'd expected—the power went out completely.

CHAPTER TWO

COUNTDOWN TO ZERO HOUR

16 HOURS AND 37 MINUTES

FIFTY-FIVE MILES SOUTH of the town of Waketa, every office building in downtown Minneapolis went black. Every traffic light blinked off. Every supermarket freezer stopped humming. Every heater in every house in the surrounding suburbs clicked off.

A man at a gas station heard the pump shut off but his truck's tank was only a third full. A kid at recess pushed the silver button on the drinking fountain and ran off, still thirsty, after nothing came out. People in an elevator fell into one another as the cab jolted to a stop. The couple in the front row of a roller coaster looked down the steep drop, wondering if the long pause was part of the ride. A surgeon stayed his hand, the scalpel hovering over the patient's chest cavity, no longer able to see in the pitch-black OR.

As the nearly three million residents of the Minneapolis–St. Paul area looked at one another in that first moment, wondering aloud, "What happened?," most were curious but not terribly concerned.

It was the first misjudgment of the day.

In Waketa, the impact had been less subtle.

A woman flinched as a neighbor's front window shattered at the *boom*.

Her arm shot out, yanked forward by her dog's leash as the golden retriever took off down the road. Running after him, she lost control and fell forward, slicing open her knee, as the dog dragged her onto her back, where, looking up, she watched in disbelief as an aircraft engine dropped from the sky, headed straight for her.

Flames roiling out the back, fan blades still spinning, the engine whistled in its incoming approach. The woman closed her eyes and curled into a ball, and moments later, she felt the heat as it passed overhead before crashing into a neighbor's mailbox, sending catalogs, bills, and torn metal in every direction.

Half a mile away, a farmer bouncing along in his tractor watched a burning chunk of metal sail through the sky and smash into the side of his barn, sending cows running and splinters of rust-red siding high in the air. Distracted, he jammed his foot into the brake pedal at the last second, cranking the tractor wheel to the right in a desperate attempt to miss the single row of aircraft seats that crashed into the freshly tilled soil in front of him.

The seats were not empty.

In the center of town, the water tower stood tall, WAKETA declared proudly in faded green across the front. No rebellious teens were up on the platform scratching their names into the paint as generation after generation of young Waketans always had, which was a stroke of luck, as that was the exact point where a four-hundred-pound beverage cart impaled the bulbous metal tank. Water exploded into the air and began pouring out the side as the most recognizable landmark of the town bled out, splashing mud and grass up onto its rusty, weathered supports below.

Not far away, a section of fuselage hurtled into the center of Main Street with such impact that two manhole covers shot into the air like steel Frisbees. When they fell back down to earth, one crashed through the bank's front window while the other landed on top of a pizza delivery car. The owner of the pizza parlor and the bank's secretary both rushed out to see what had happened. All they could do was gape at each other and the destruction all around them.

Fishermen standing in their waders on the banks of the Mississippi River flinched at the big *boom,* wondering aloud: "What the hell was that?" Moments later, they ducked for cover, pelted from above by falling objects smacking into the river. The fishermen watched charred debris float downstream around them, everything from a suitcase and a coat to tiny bottles of Jack Daniel's and a still burning book. But it was a shoe bobbing past that stopped the men cold.

The foot was still in it.

A grazing herd of white-tailed deer suddenly took off, startled, not knowing what the hissing whistle of the incoming metal shrapnel was. Leaping through the trees and brush, they fled out of the forest, into the open area beside the highway, directly in front of the oncoming headlights of a semitruck.

The driver slammed on the brakes but didn't cut the wheel—unlike the two-door Honda beside it. The car swerved to the right, missing the deer but clipping the semi's back wheels. Spinning around, the car became lodged under the truck, pancaked flat as the semi dragged it down the highway, sparks erupting from the undercarriage.

Brakes locked, the semi's driver struggling to maintain control, the truck jackknifed, twisting perpendicular to the road. The box tipped and rolled forward—one, two, three times—flattening four cars in its path while its cargo rolled out the back. Wood pallets splintered into pieces as cardboard boxes filled with bottles of olive oil burst on the highway. Broken glass and thousands of gallons of oil covered the asphalt in every direction.

A family sedan rear-ended a pickup truck full of yard equipment. The tailgate dropped, and rakes, leaf blowers, and a riding lawn mower scattered across the highway as bags of lawn clippings burst, sending grass and leaves into the air and onto windshields, making the cars' disoriented drivers swerve.

A large SUV lost control and dropped down into the grassy median, where it hit a boulder, flipped up on its nose, and somersaulted end over end into oncoming traffic on the other side of the highway.

A car full of college kids heading home for the weekend didn't see the vehicle in front of them brake until it was too late. The one who wasn't wearing a seat belt was violently ejected, his body landing fifty yards away at the edge of the forest where the deer had first appeared.

In less than a minute, the traffic on I-35, the primary route in and out of Waketa, Minnesota, came to a complete stop in both directions as seventeen vehicles piled up in a tangle of twisted metal and broken bodies. By the time it was done, the only things moving were the few surviving deer leaping awkwardly around the mangled, burning cars and injured, bloody humans as they made their way to the woods on the other side of the road.

Carver Valley Elementary School's playground was buzzing, the kids sugar-rushing from their class parties on the last day of school before the Easter weekend.

Legs pumping, fourth-graders on the swings went higher and higher. A group of second-graders were on a ladybug hunt under the tall oak tree. The sixth-graders, the big kids on campus, played soccer; the game was tied, two to two.

Miss Carla knelt beside one of her first-grade students, who was crying loudly, sand stuck to his scraped knee.

"It's okay, Leo," she said. "Let's get you to the nurse. She can—"

A loud *boom* sounded. Everything halted.

The swings went back and forth, propelled by gravity and

momentum, no longer the pumping kicks of nine-year-old girls. A ladybug crawled out from under a leaf and no one noticed. The soccer ball rolled to a stop on its own. Miss Carla instinctively pulled Leo in close as both their gazes rose to the sky.

Every student, every teacher, the crossing guard, the janitor—they all looked up in awe as an aircraft wing, fully intact but separated from the plane, careened over their heads like a flying saucer. They watched as the wing disappeared over the line of trees beyond the parking lot, and together, they waited for what came next—a deafening crash followed by a roiling cloud of orange flames and a plume of black smoke rising up into the clear blue sky.

The church long behind him, Steve dropped his speed to eighty-five and gawked at the mushroom cloud rising into the air to his left. He instinctively wanted to turn the wheel toward it as he wondered, *Is that...the school?*

Matt.

Adrenaline shot through Steve's system. Was Matt okay? Should he go to his son? His mind flashed to Claire's fourth-grade classroom, even though it no longer belonged to her. If she were there, Matt could have run to her. He could have been safe with his mom.

But not now. She was gone. And Matt was alone.

Steve rode the brakes, coming to a stop in the middle of the road, his heart pounding with parental worry. *Either figure it out and fix it or keep going.* Steve took a deep breath, forcing himself to look at the big picture—clearly, not through a distorted lens of fear and grief.

He could tell the billowing black smoke was actually on the far side of the tree line, the river side. It *was* in the general direction of the school, but it was not coming from the school itself. Carver Valley Elementary was fine. Matt was fine.

Steve nodded and told himself that he was doing the right thing as he accelerated the truck back up to felony-level speed, racing away from the area. Matt was okay and Steve had to get to work. Because damage *there* was a far greater threat.

As he tore down the single-lane dirt road, taking in the smoke plumes large and small that rose across the whole valley, Steve shook his head. Things like this didn't happen in a place like this, a place this quiet. And Steve knew that disbelief coupled with the kind of confusion and terror he'd felt in the church was being felt right now all around Waketa, including at the school. It couldn't get any more horrific than a plane crash like that, he knew they were all thinking.

He knew they were wrong.

He turned at the sign that proudly declared CREATED TODAY TO POWER TOMORROW and came to a stop at the main entrance to Clover Hill nuclear power plant. Holding his badge out the window, Steve was surprised when the door to the security shed opened and an armed guard in a full-body hazmat suit came out. The man scanned the badge, and Steve's face popped up on the computer in the guard shack.

STEVE J. TOSTIG—FIRE CHIEF
CLOVER HILL ON-SITE FIRE DEPARTMENT
FULL OPERATIONAL CLEARANCE

"Bill, is it that bad?" Steve asked, motioning to the hazmat suit.

Bill shrugged as he pushed a button and the arm to the gate went up. "You tell me. They're too busy to call us and give an update. Read that how you will. I'll radio your crew and let them know you're headed back."

* * *

Broken glass crunched under her boots as Joss stepped over one of the framed diplomas that had fallen off her home office's wall. Grabbing her work go-bag, she brought it out to the kitchen, setting it on the coffee-splattered newspaper she wouldn't get to finish reading.

Powering on the satellite phone, she rifled through the bag's contents—full-body hazmat suit, masks, gloves, rubber boots—until she found the bottle of pills. Shaking one into her hand, she knocked back the radioprotective potassium iodide with some of the still-warm coffee she wouldn't get to finish drinking.

"C'mon…" Joss whispered impatiently as the sat phone booted up. Taking a deep breath, she stared out the kitchen window at the smoke rising in the distance while she waited.

Behind her in the living room, last night's empty Chinese takeout container sat on the unopened moving box she used as an end table. She'd been back for nine months, but so far, her office was the only room in the house that showed it. After throwing a coat on over her worn brown sweater and faded blue jeans, she grabbed her keys from a hook on the wall with a glance down at the set of Thomas the Train picture books covered in Thomas the Train wrapping paper that sat on the counter. It seemed like another lifetime when she'd planned her day to include a post-office run to drop off her nephew's birthday gift, which, she realized now, probably wouldn't get there in time.

The phone in her hand beeped and the screen lit up. Joss looked down as an alert box popped up, confirming that what she'd *assumed* had happened had actually happened.

INCIDENT AT CLOVER HILL NPP
REPORT IMMEDIATELY
POSSIBLE LEVEL 7

Joss tossed the go-bag over a shoulder and hurried out to her car without glancing in a mirror to see if she still had sleep in her green eyes or if her shoulder-length brown hair needed to be brushed. There was no time, and none of it mattered anyway.

When you work in nuclear power, you never fully forget what it is you do. How dangerous it is, how horrific the potential could be. You always, *always* respect the potential.

But you learn to let go of the fear.

Workdays become routine and uneventful in a strictly regulated industry full of regimented protocols enacted with airtight precision by highly trained professionals. Accidents *don't* happen because accidents *can't* happen. So when the unthinkable does occur, when something *does* go wrong, the fear returns, swift and unrelenting — as Joss assumed everyone inside the plant was just finding out.

But her hand was steady, her heart rate low. Because Joss had always known a day like this was not a matter of *if* but *when*. And she knew that when it came, when the rest of the world discovered what she already knew, while they were tearing themselves apart in fear of the horrifying possibilities — she would be steady.

For her, controlling the fear was easy.

Because it never left. Joss was always scared.

CHAPTER THREE

COUNTDOWN TO ZERO HOUR

16 HOURS AND 36 MINUTES

FIVE-YEAR-OLD CONNOR HAYS was belted into his car seat in the middle row of the minivan playing on his iPad. In the far back row, his thirteen-year-old sister, Caity, was glued to her phone, bobbing her head along to whatever music was blaring through her hot-pink headphones. The teenager completely ignored her father.

"Call her phone," Valerie Hays said, looking over at her husband behind the wheel. "We might actually get a conversation with her that way."

Paul shook his head, glancing up at their daughter in the rearview mirror. "She wouldn't pick up." Both parents laughed, knowing it was true. "What about you, bud?" he asked Connor. "You wouldn't send us to voicemail, would you?"

Connor looked up from his iPad. "What's voicemail?" he asked.

"Speaking of electronics," said Valerie. "We need to set limits on screen time for the weekend. We only see your parents a couple times a year and they aren't going to want to just watch them—"

The road beneath the minivan shook with a distant *boom*. Both kids looked up, eyes wide. Valerie reached for her husband as the van momentarily veered. Paul gripped the steering wheel with both hands.

"Dad, what was that?" Caity said.

Valerie spun in her seat, looking out the back. "Paul, we didn't hit something, did we?"

"No..." he muttered, checking the dash.

"Dad, what *was* that?" Caity's voice was pinched with fear.

"I don't know," Paul said, still trying to figure out what was going on. He looked at the Waketa fields and woodlands that surrounded the two-lane country road. They were rounding a bend, headed down the hill toward a bridge. Everything seemed perfectly normal.

"But *Dad*, are we *okay*?"

"We're fine!" Paul snapped. "I don't know what that was!"

Connor started to cry.

"It's okay, buddy," Paul said, turning around to face the kids. "Caity, I'm sorry. We're fine. It was probably just—"

"Paul. *Paul!*"

He spun forward at his wife's screams. Ahead, coming up over the tops of the trees, was an enormous slab of gray metal. It was so large and moved so fast, it was hard to tell if it would sail right over their heads or veer to the side or pound straight into them. By the time he realized it was the wing of an aircraft and that the wing was going to land right in front of them, it was too late. The van was already on the bridge.

The wing smashed into the ground with such force, the trees shook. Birds flew up into the air as the whole family screamed. Valerie threw her hands out in front of her to brace for impact while Paul gripped the wheel tight. He slammed on the brakes, but in the middle of the tight two-lane bridge, swerving wasn't an option. The minivan's brakes locked with a screech as the vehicle nosed down, trying to come to a stop.

Opposite the van, facing them head-on, the wing tore deep divots into the grass as its momentum sent it sliding up onto the bridge. It twisted as it kept moving, blocking the entire roadway until it was on the bridge, coming right at the van with a horrible scrape of metal and concrete. Everything went silent as the family waited for impact.

And then they hit.

The family was thrust forward violently, arms and heads jutting out unnaturally far from the intense force. The front windshield shattered; the airbags exploded in a flash of white. The thick, sturdy metal of the hood and front end of the van crumpled like foil. The front tires blew, pinched in the impact, as the wheel-hubs assembly left a trail of sparks on the ground.

The incoming wing was ten times the van's size and weight. The metal slab rode up effortlessly onto the bumper, hood, and front two wheels, smashing it completely flat in an instant. Pinned underneath, the van was pushed backward.

The family's bodies whiplashed, their heads smacking into seat backs, breaking bones and lacerating internal organs. The steering column rammed into Paul's torso and the crumpling door frame crushed Valerie's skull. The back of the van sustained the least structural damage but got the worst of the whiplashing force. Caity's spinal column absorbed the brunt of it. Connor, in the middle, strapped tightly into his car seat, could do nothing but hold on.

The wing pushed the van backward on the bridge, and the car twisted, its rear bumper bursting through the metal guardrail. With the wing pinning the front end of the van down so it scraped along the asphalt in a blaze of sparking metal, the back end of the vehicle hung out over the edge, dangling off the side of the bridge, with a thirty-foot drop to the icy Mississippi River below.

The wing's momentum began to slow. Riding up, it came to a stop covering the entire bridge. The massive portion of aircraft that only minutes earlier had been miles high in the air traveling hundreds of miles an hour was now battered and beaten, fractured to expose its own internal organs—including the massive tanks where hundreds of thousands of gallons of jet fuel were stored.

It might have been the friction as the metal dragged on the ground; it might have been a spark from the van. The start was unimportant. The end was inevitable. A massive fireball erupted, mushrooming up into the air in a ball of hot orange flames. As the fuel vapors were consumed, the initial blast receded in a thick cloud of dense black smoke, leaving below a steady burn-off of what fuel remained in the tanks.

Everything around them stilled. The birds were gone. The wing was stationary. And the van had come to a stop hanging out over the river. The only things moving were the flames across the wing and the car's spinning rear tires. The only sounds came from the radio playing through the shattered front windows.

Connor looked around, too stunned to cry, too scared to move. His little hands clutched the sides of his car seat, one tiny scrape on his forehead the only visible indication that anything had happened. He waited for someone to help him, someone to come get him, someone to tell him what to do. But no one came; no one said a thing.

"Mommy?" he said quietly.

There was no response.

His chest fluttered up and down as the tears began to well and his heart began to pound.

"Mommy!"

CHAPTER FOUR

COUNTDOWN TO ZERO HOUR
16 HOURS AND 35 MINUTES

ETHAN ROSEN REACHED into the darkness around him, but his hands found only air.

He stood frozen in the pitch-black control room behind the wraparound desk, not wanting to move, afraid to take a step, his pulse pounding in his ears. Ethan knew the second the lights came back on, everyone would look to *him*—because he was it. He was the plant manager, the guy in charge. They would expect him to have answers.

But Ethan had no answers. He only had one question.

And it was the same question everyone in the control room had:

What just happened?

Then, just as quickly as his world went dark, it erupted into light.

Ethan's hazel eyes squinted at the blinking red, orange, and white lights all around the R2 control room. An incessant, high-pitched ringing in his ears muffled the alarms that were blaring at an otherwise deafening level. Ethan struggled to focus as he gazed through the dust swirling in the air that fell from the swaying overhead lights onto his wavy brown hair and navy-blue sweater like an early winter snow. Looking down, he found shards of broken ceramic in a splatter of coffee at his feet, the mug's Clover Hill logo now fractured and unrecognizable.

Dazed and in shock, Ethan felt removed from what was going on, like a movie was playing out before him. Everyone in the room was looking at him, up there on the elevated platform of the Reactor Two monitoring station, and they were nodding, responding to a loud voice that was bellowing over the sirens. With some surprise, Ethan realized it was his own voice.

He was asking them over and over: "Is everyone okay?"

They were all nodding: Yes.

The world around him began to speed up and come back into focus, and Ethan's senses sharpened. Sound returned and he could hear the panic in the voices of his colleagues. Everyone spoke at once; his brain was only able to pick up isolated phrases that leaped out like the visible words in an otherwise redacted text.

"—don't know—"

"—explosion? Attack—"

"—reactor open—"

"—earthquake. If not—"

"—loss of primary—"

It had been a normal day and then, in one violent moment, it wasn't. A bomb? Equipment failure? An earthquake? Was it over or had it just begun? From their position in the windowless control room, they knew nothing. Absolutely *nothing*. And in the face of all the unknowns, they were spinning out.

Ethan punched a few buttons, and the droning alarms shut off. In the shock of the immediate silence, everyone stopped talking and turned to him.

"All right, listen up."

Ethan's voice, though calm, felt like a shout in the now quiet room, but his evenness was a stark reminder of where they were and, more importantly, *what they should be doing*. Panels covered with switches, gauges, readings, figures, flashing lights, and lit-up buttons filled every wall and every counter in the nine-hundred-square-foot room, each at the moment absolutely begging to be read and tended to.

"Stop. Right now. Take a breath," Ethan said, mindful to speak in a slow, even cadence. His coworkers responded in a collective deep inhale. The warning lights kept flashing, the crisis roiled on, but for four seconds, everything stopped as Ethan brought them back to center.

"Our problem is, we don't know what our problem is," he said. "We can handle anything. But we need to know what we're dealing with. Dwight, get me a radio. Vikram, begin mode-switch abnormal-procedures checklist. Maggie, call back."

Dwight ran off, lanyard swinging, and disappeared out the door into the hall. Vikram grabbed a laminated page from a file divider but began the callout without having to look.

"Mode switch is in shutdown," Vikram said, leaning into a panel, reading values. "APRMs are downscale. RPV pressure is nine-five-zero pounds, down slow." Vikram checked the laminated page quickly, shifting to his right to read another gauge. "Gradual water level is minus-four-zero inches, up slow..."

While his staff worked, Ethan took a step back. Turning away, he discreetly grabbed his phone from his pocket. His hands shook as he typed the text:

Nice day for a drive east

Three dots appeared instantly. His wife's response came just as fast.

I love you

Ethan pocketed his phone.

"...Entries on low RPV level and high dry wall pressure," Vikram said.

"Mode switch is in shutdown," Maggie said, standing by Vikram's side, verbally and visually confirming the gauge readings herself. "APRMs are downscale. Reactor pressure nine-five-zero pounds, down slow. RPV level minus-two-five inches, up slow. EOP entry conditions on low RP level and high dry wall pressure," she concluded.

Dwight ran back into the room and, tripping on the step up to the platform, passed the radio to Ethan.

"That's all correct," said Vikram. "All rods are in."

"All rods are in," confirmed Maggie, finishing the checklist.

The reactor had safely shut down, the control rods were in. The plant, at first assessment, was under control. But as everyone in the room took in Dwight's shallow breathing and ghost-white face, they knew it wasn't.

Ethan watched the young man trying to compose himself and realized that in order to get the radio, Dwight would have passed down the long glass corridor of the second-floor hallway that looked out onto the plant's campus.

Dwight was the only one of them who'd seen what was going on out there.

"What happened?" Ethan asked him.

34

Dwight could only shake his head. "It's...I...I can't..."

"Steve," Ethan said urgently into the radio. "Do you copy?"

Steve slipped his arms through the suspenders and hitched up the thick turnout pants before grabbing his bunker coat out of his locker and tossing a helmet on his head. Steve was chief, so his helmet was white, while the rest of the firefighters' helmets were black. Sprinting for the waiting fire truck, he pressed the talk button on the radio and held it close to his mouth.

"We copy."

"Steve, we're having trouble making sense of these readings." Ethan's voice crackled over the speaker as Steve hopped up into the shotgun seat; the door was not even shut before the truck peeled out of the bay. *"What are we looking at? Was this external? A mechanical failure? A fire?"*

Steve pressed the talk button and answered, his stunned tone contrasting with Ethan's panic:

"Yes."

The light bar strobed and the sirens blared as the fire truck made its way through the aircraft debris scattered across the power plant's campus, two wheels jumping the curb to navigate around a row of burning aircraft seats. Looking to his left, Steve was breathless at the sight of the detached nose of a plane. A searing-hot fire engulfed the cockpit, its flames pouring out the shattered windshields, leaving dense black smoke scars on the white exterior paint.

None of it felt real. It was too extreme, too big. Every man in the fire truck was speechless as they all took in the scene, their brains struggling to translate what they were seeing into something that made sense. Steve didn't know how to explain.

"What — what does that mean?" Ethan's voice was sharp, as if he were holding the radio close to his mouth. *"We can't see from in here. What happened?"*

"A plane, Ethan," Steve said flatly. "A plane happened."

Ethan felt the blood drain from his face.

On September 11, 2001, he and his colleagues had watched the second plane hit the South Tower on the break-room TV just up the hall from where he now stood. He remembered distinctly how, in that moment, as they realized it was no accident, everything shifted.

The country was under attack.

His boss had run out of the break room, shoving the door open so hard it smacked against the wall. At the time, Ethan hadn't understood his boss's panic. Later that day, as they received security directives from a dozen government agencies, he did.

Whenever anyone asked Ethan if he had reservations about the safety of nuclear power, his answer was always the same: unequivocally, emphatically no. Yet if he was asked about fearing a 9/11-style attack on a nuclear power plant, he hesitated.

Truthfully, it terrified him. At times, kept him up at night. Because he knew what everyone who worked in nuclear power knew. The "tests" the government had run in the wake of September 11 that allegedly proved that American nuclear reactors were impervious to attacks on nuclear-power-containment structures were at best incomplete and at worst suspect. Officials had needed to reassure Americans that every U.S. nuclear power plant was indeed safe from attack, so they designed tests to deliver those results. Every model used small planes traveling only up to three hundred miles per hour. None of the tests approximated what had actually happened in New York or explored what could occur beyond those parameters.

The point of the tests wasn't to learn the truth. It was to calm a worried public. Because officials knew the truth was too terrifying. No one had a clue what would happen if a large commercial airliner filled with fuel and traveling at hundreds of miles per hour crashed into a nuclear power plant.

"Get Red Top on the phone," Ethan said to Dwight, meaning the Red Top nuclear power plant, 117 miles to the southeast. "Steve, what's the visual on impact damage?"

"We got an extensive debris field," Steve said. "It's not just one area. Or one point of impact. The plane. It's, it went—"

"Everywhere," muttered George, Steve's second-in-command, as he leaned over the truck's steering wheel to look up at the damaged R1 cooling tower. Enormous, ragged-edged chunks of concrete lay all around the base.

"Debris from the plane, the plant. It's all over the place, Ethan," Steve said. "We've called for off-site support, but our comms were spotty. Waketa Township should be first response. Our boards showed automatic fire suppression activation in six buildings. Reactor Two's auxiliaries seemed the most active, so we're headed—whoa!"

Steve braced himself on the dash as George slammed down hard on the truck's brakes.

"Hang on," George said, reversing back around the curve. The road in front of them was impassable—twisted hunks of smoking metal blocked the way.

"Someone needs to run security footage and guide us," Steve

demanded. "Every way we go is blocked by debris. We have no access. We need to know what's clear. Currently, we're on the northeast corner of D block trying to get to R2."

"Copy. Stand by. We're getting video systems back online now," Ethan said.

"That may be more of a challenge than he thinks," George muttered as everyone in the truck gaped at the damaged distribution transformer on the right-hand side. The severed ends of a massive power line sputtered, the surging power audibly sizzling as the downed, ragged line shot out sparks. Now they understood why their communications systems were a mess.

"I'm no electrical engineer," said George, "but having the power line connected to the power plant is important, right?"

Steve pressed the talk button. "Ethan. Primary distribution is severed."

"How damaged? Is it a—"

"No. Not damaged. It's severed."

Everyone in the control room understood the implications of a severed distribution line. But instead of panicked screams, a soft murmur rippled through the room.

Ethan cursed under his breath before pressing the talk button. "That explains the loss of grid power. Okay. What does—"

"Stand by. We're getting to R2 auxiliaries now and—"

The radio cut out for a moment. When Steve came back on, the pitch of his voice was elevated: *"Cask breach. We've got at least one exposure."*

The soft murmur in the control room was replaced by a deafening silence. No one dared move as they waited for more.

"That's one confirmed exposure," Steve said a moment later. *"And we got, ah — Ethan, we got significant structural damage to the south side of the building housing the R2 fuel pool."*

The words hung in the air.

Structural damage. Fuel pool.

"Steve. Confirm," said Ethan as clearly as possible, practically kissing the radio. "Was that structural damage to the Reactor Two spent fuel pool?"

"That's affirmative. And we're wet. We got water leakage — "

"Where?" Ethan asked. "Where's the leakage? How high up?"

"High. Fifty, fifty-five feet."

At that, the staff in the control room sprang into action. Any damage to the plant was bad. But structural damage, no matter how minor, to the spent fuel pool wasn't just bad — it was potentially catastrophic. For the first time since the crisis started, they heard palpable fear in Ethan's voice: "Maggie, get me water levels. Dan, status on the coolant pumps. Vikram, monitor the ambient pressure in the building. Steve, can you gauge how much water we've lost? Steve? Steve, do you copy?"

A clipboard lay a short distance away from the man on the ground, the loose ends of the papers lifting in the breeze. Roused by the fire truck's siren, the man tried to sit up, raising his head from a wide pool of blood on the concrete pad. Behind him lay the toppled remains of a dry cask nuclear-waste storage unit and the burning aircraft engine that had taken it out.

"Masks on," Steve hollered to his crew. With thick fitted gloves covering their hands, the men in the truck pulled the masks of their self-contained breathing apparatus over their heads. As Steve adjusted his mask, he watched the man coming to, looking around, realizing where he was and what had happened.

Steve recognized the guy. He remembered sitting at a table behind him at lunch one day. His name was Vinny. He'd told this story about how his grandma got drunk one Christmas and launched the tree out into the front yard, ornaments and lights and all. He'd had the whole cafeteria in stitches, describing how all the grand-kids had stood there with their jaws on the floor watching drunk Grandma, cigarette dangling from her lip, javelin the tree out of the house.

The dry cask—a seventeen-foot-tall, five-foot-wide oblong pillar of concrete—was on its side, shattered and cracked all the way through the outer cask, the inner cask, and the two inches of concrete between them. Exposed were its contents: a tightly packed bundle of 204 twelve-foot-by-one-foot radioactive fuel rods. Ignoring the still-bleeding gash on his forehead, Vinny stared in horror at the exposed nuclear fuel not two feet from where he lay. Without having to read his mind, Steve knew the crucial questions Vinny was asking himself.

How long have I been lying here? How much exposure did I get? How long until I die?

Steve flashed back to his first week of training at the plant. Their instructor had passed around pictures of the firefighters from Chernobyl. They were the first responders after the reactor blew, clueless as to what they were dealing with and what it would do to them.

Steve had never been able to get those images out of his head.

The Soviet firefighters, stretched out on hospital beds, had bright red burns covering their pale skin. Initially, acute radiation poisoning looks like nothing more serious than the result of an afternoon at the beach without sunscreen. But each picture became progressively harder to stomach as the radiation destroyed their bloating, disfigured bodies from inside and out with increasing speed.

Vomit-covered bedsheets next to swollen limbs, skin peeling away from muscle. The unfathomable pain brought them to tears, but they cried blood, relief coming only once they slipped into comas, after the swelling in their brains had rendered them unconscious. They gasped for air as they drowned in the radiated soup that had been their internal organs. And when death finally came, they weren't surrounded by their loved ones. At that point, medical staff didn't know what they know now. They didn't know it couldn't be passed through contact, so no one was allowed in. The men died alone, begging for death as they were burned alive in their personal living hell.

The sound of the truck doors opening snapped Steve out of his dark trance. To his left, near the back of Reactor Two's auxiliary buildings, was a huge, still burning portion of the aircraft's fuselage. Steve called out names; those men were to put out the burning aircraft. The rest of the men set off with Steve for the dry cask.

As they moved toward Vinny, Steve watched him stand up and stumble as he tried to strip off his clothes. Vinny saw them approaching.

"No!" he screamed. "Stay back!"

Steve kept moving forward. "Sir. You need—"

"Stay *back*!"

Steve stopped in his tracks. A few steps behind, his crew did the same.

Vinny's eyes filled with tears as he looked at the firefighters—the first on-site, the first to help. His voice raw, he said, "It's too late."

Steve watched as Vinny took off his contaminated button-up and khakis and tossed them on top of his employee lanyard next to the broken dry cask. He knew Vinny was hoping this would help.

Maybe if he shed the contaminated clothing, got it off his skin, and moved away from the source, maybe it would be enough.

They both knew it wouldn't. This wasn't a lightly radiated substance he'd briefly encountered. He'd been lying next to exposed fuel rods wearing no protection. He was already dead. The only question was how long until he died.

A utility truck driven by two plant employees in full hazmat gear came around the corner. They stopped a distance away, and Vinny—barefoot, in only his boxer briefs—jogged over to them and climbed into the bed of the truck. The driver backed up and drove off as Vinny gazed around at all the destruction, shivering in the spring air. He looked small and young and scared, like a little boy. And in an instant, before he could stop himself, Steve's mind flashed to Matt.

Was his son scared? Had he seen the plane or heard the crash? Of course he had. Matt was so smart, he had to know something was very wrong. If Steve could get—

No.

Stop.

Steve forced himself to stop thinking about Matt. There was nothing he could do for his son right now. Steve had to do his job. His duty was to the people at the plant; his obligation was to try to limit the damage. Matt's school had accident protocols. His son was with the teachers and they would know what to do. They would protect him. Steve had to trust them. He could not afford to worry about his son right now. He could not do that *and* do his job. He had to compartmentalize. He had to shut thoughts of Matt out.

The truck carrying Vinny disappeared around the corner. Steve turned to his men. "Let's keep going."

As they jogged back to the others, Steve heard a jarring, unfamiliar beep. Looking down, he saw the small digital screen of his dosimeter light up. The detection device measured ambient radiation dosage in real time. The higher the number, the more cancer-causing particulates of radioactive poison were in the air and on the wind.

Never, not once in Steve's eighteen years at the plant, had the small yellow box affixed to the front of his uniform been activated.

But now, as he watched in horror, the numbers were slowly and steadily clicking up.

CHAPTER FIVE

COUNTDOWN TO ZERO HOUR
16 HOURS AND 18 MINUTES

PRESIDENT MICHAEL WADE DAWSON, the youngest person ever to hold that office, sworn in just eighty-eight days ago at the age of thirty-nine, was wholly unprepared for the disaster about to confront him.

Unmarried. No kids. Only the second bachelor president in U.S. history, only the seventh not to have any children. Even if that all changed someday, in a moment like this, those statistics became more relevant.

A throng of White House reporters and photographers surrounded the base of the Truman Balcony, jockeying for position, each eager to get *the* shot of the historic moment. The president stared out at the members of the press awaiting his arrival and thought: *There are images that define an administration's legacy. This will be one of mine.*

Times like this were hard enough. But they were even harder without a partner to hold your hand or a child to experience it with. All Dawson could do was get through it.

"All right," he said quietly under his breath to the man in the bunny costume beside him. "Let's get this over with."

Putting on that sly half grin that had helped him win Pennsylvania, Florida, and Iowa, the president strode forward to greet the children and parents gathered on the South Lawn.

"Good morning," he said cheerfully as the applause died down, his bright blue eyes and thick blond hair shining in the late-morning sun. "It's a beautiful day and it's an honor to officially welcome you all to the White House Easter Egg Roll!"

The crowd cheered and clapped, a fitting pairing to the cloudless, crisp spring morning where the last of the cherry blossoms were drifting by on the breeze. His message was brief and he spoke not of policy or politics but of hope and renewal. His speechwriters had given it to him, he'd punched it up with a few jokes of his own, and he was about halfway through the embarrassing affair when Dawson came to a stark realization.

He was enjoying himself.

Maybe it was all the bright colors and wide smiles, a scene as un-Washington as it got. Maybe it was because his fading native California tan was finally getting a much-needed dose of sunlight after the long winter. Or maybe it was that, for a handful of minutes, he could set the job down. He could stop worrying and stressing and wondering what fresh hell the next moment might bring. For the first time since being sworn in, he was nothing more than a man having a laugh on a beautiful day.

After his speech, the cameras clicked as he challenged the Easter Bunny to an arm-wrestling contest. A battle he happily lost.

"Aw, c'mon," President Dawson said to the bunny, feigning protest. "Tony always lets me win."

The press pool laughed, but White House Chief of Staff Tony Yoshida didn't hear. He was huddled in quiet conversation with an aide.

The band started to play an upbeat Sousa march as the president jogged down the steps for a photo op with the Easter Bunny and some children dressed in their Sunday finest. Dawson crouched beside them as they showed him their eggs, describing how they'd decorated them, explaining why they'd chosen this or that color. He listened in earnest, smiling, enjoying their stories.

"Tony, did you know purple is Eliza here's favorite color?" Dawson asked his chief of staff, who had appeared by his side.

"I did not. Sir, we —"

"And did you know that this guy is stronger than you?" the president said, bringing over the man in the bunny costume.

"Sir, we need to get you inside."

"It's true. This bunny beat me easily in a test of strength." Dawson held out his hand. "What do you say we go best out of three?"

The bunny nodded and the two were beginning to set up for a rematch when Tony turned his back to the press and leaned into the president's side.

"Mr. President, a plane has crashed into a nuclear power facility."

Dawson froze.

The cameras clicked.

When previous presidents met their defining moment, most had had time to absorb it, process it, internalize what it meant and what it would mean. They had privacy and discretion while they took the blow and figured out how to respond. Not him. Dawson's defining moment was playing out in real time next to a giant bunny while everyone watched and the cameras rolled.

With a barely discernible nod to Tony, Dawson shook the Easter Bunny's hand. "You win. Excuse me," he said, and turned toward the White House. He walked briskly, realizing his usual number of Secret Service agents had nearly doubled without him noticing. He wasn't fully through the door before the agents practically lifted him off his feet and rushed him through the hallways.

"What do we know?" he called out to Tony over his shoulder.

"Coastal Airways, a Boeing seven fifty-seven, Minneapolis to Seattle," Tony said, jogging to keep up. Curious White House staffers stood up from their desks or jumped back out of the way.

"Jesus, that's a big plane. Is any terror group claiming it?"

"Not yet. FBI, NSA, and CIA are monitoring. There was no chatter on any channel, foreign or domestic, leading up. FAA, TSA, NTSB, DHS are all up and live. This just happened, Mr. President. We are very limited in what we know. We want to be careful with assumptions and actions."

"Ground them all."

Tony hesitated. "Sir?"

"I want every commercial aircraft on the ground in the next half hour."

"It's a holiday weekend."

"Busy travel time. Sounds perfect for a terrorist."

"We'd be displacing millions of travelers."

"Give them hotel vouchers."

"But Mr. President, we don't *know* anything—"

The president spun, wrenching his arm out of a Secret Service agent's grip. "It's a plane and a nuclear power plant, Tony. You tell me the odds. I'm not losing another plane. This country will not do this again. Until we know this wasn't a terror attack, we treat it like it is. Ground the planes, now."

Tony Yoshida — his closest adviser, his former campaign manager, favorite college professor, beloved mentor, the father figure he'd never had growing up but always needed, the person he trusted more than anyone in the world besides his own mother — looked at Dawson like they'd never met. Which, they were both discovering, was somewhat true. As president, Dawson hadn't been *truly* tested yet and he had always wondered how he'd handle it, what kind of president he'd be. Both men were finding out.

"Yes, sir," Tony said.

The group continued, turning and going down one flight of stairs. "International borders closed," said Dawson as they turned and went down another flight. "I want security at all power plants beefed up. Priority nuclear. Tell the governors to use the National Guard if they have to. Dams, bridges, tunnels, rail. Soft targets: arenas, public transport, national monuments. Anything we even think is at risk needs to be put on alert."

"Yes, Mr. President."

"What is the condition of the plant?"

"Clover Hill nuclear power plant, located fifty-five miles northwest of Minneapolis in the town of Waketa, population approximately nine hundred. Built in 1973 — "

"These are facts," Dawson interrupted. "I want the plant's condition."

"Yes, sir. We're getting that now. The plant is partially decommissioned — "

"It's no longer in service?"

"We're not that lucky. It's in the *process* of being decommissioned, which takes years. The plant has three reactors on-site; only one has completed the decommissioning process and is offline. The other two are fully operational and generating power."

"What is their status?"

"That's what we're getting now."

The group came to a stop at a door where an agent entered a lengthy code into a numerical panel on the wall. As they waited, catching their breath in the sudden lack of movement, the president's voice softened: "The plane," he said. "Is there any chance of survivors?"

"At that speed, at that altitude," Tony said. "No, Mr. President."

Dawson showed no physical reaction.

The panel beeped and the wall slid open, revealing an elevator. The president, the chief of staff, and six agents piled inside. Dawson placed his right hand flat against a screen on the wall and stared into a lens at eye level. A green laser slowly moved up and down his palm and fingers while a thin red laser scanned his retinas. A moment later, another beep, and the elevator started to descend.

The occupants of the cramped elevator were silent. Their ears popped. President Dawson took a deep breath, held it, and slowly exhaled. He knew this was the last moment of stillness before they entered a world where the words *nuclear* and *radioactive* and all the horrors they represented became commonplace—but he had one last question before they did.

"How many were aboard the plane?" Dawson asked.

"Passengers and crew combined, two hundred and ninety-five people, sir."

There was a ding and the elevator doors slid open to a spare, windowless, subterranean bunker located five stories beneath the western side of the North Lawn: the DUCC—Deep Underground Command Center. Ten-foot-thick concrete walls fortified a structure intended to serve as a makeshift housing and command center for the president and staff during an attack, invasion, or nuclear incident. It had its own food and self-contained air supply, so the whole country could be run from these few rooms for months.

The president burst through the first door on the right, and the handful of personnel in the room, mostly military, turned to face the commander in chief. Wall-mounted banks of screens and monitors displaying every aspect of the crisis surrounded a long conference table in the center of the room. Real-time radar screens tracked air traffic, both commercial and military. On one screen was a diagram of the type of nuclear reactor used at Clover Hill. On the next screen were specs, details, and logistics of the plant. There were demographics of the town of Waketa and various maps of the region. Other screens showed stock market charts and indexes, live interstate cams, traffic-flow monitors, CNN, Fox, MSNBC.

"Mr. President, nine minutes ago, at zero-nine-three-four central, Coastal Airways Flight Two-Thirty-Five dropped off radar," said deputy national security adviser Nancy Reid, passing a stack of papers to Tony. "Shortly after, all power in downtown Minneapolis and the surrounding suburbs momentarily turned off. It has since been restored."

"Does that mean the plant itself still has power?" asked the president.

"We're not sure," someone said.

The president turned to the voice, which came from the wall of video-call screens. The boxes constantly adjusted as participants hopped on the call, the labels in the lower right-hand corners displaying their titles or departments: FBI, DEPARTMENT OF HOMELAND SECURITY, SECRETARY OF AGRICULTURE, SECRETARY OF TRANSPORTATION, NUCLEAR REGULATORY COMMISSION. In a moment like this, names didn't matter. The person who'd just spoken was the secretary of energy.

"Power grids are interconnected, multilayered webs," the secretary continued. "If you take out a nuclear power plant, the grid will stay up because the system has redundancies and is set up for contingencies. The plant in question is a relatively minor power provider."

"With all due respect to the people of Minneapolis," said Dawson, "I couldn't care less if their refrigerators are still running. What was the impact damage at the plant? Are we looking at an open reactor spewing radiation into the air or not?"

"Sir, we don't know. It's chaos over there," said the chair of the NRC. "We need to give them time to handle the crisis. Communicating with us isn't their priority, nor should it be. We are mobilizing our resources, but until we hear from them, which will happen as soon as they are able, we're piecing together what we can with what we do know."

"Fine," Dawson said, running a hand down his face. "When will we know if they have power? And what happens if they don't?"

"Hard to say, because we're no longer communicating with its grid."

The president leaned forward on the table. "I don't know what that means," he said through gritted teeth. "So let me be very clear: Speak to me like I'm five. I'm a smart guy, but I'm no nuclear engineer, and neither is the average American, and that's who I'm going to be addressing here soon. I need to understand what I'm telling them. Got it?"

Heads nodded.

"Mr. President, we're still trying to figure out what is and isn't working across the board," said the secretary of energy. "We think the distribution line from the plant was damaged in the crash, which cut them off of grid power. When we lost the plant, the frequency dropped, which made the whole system unstable. The system was overloading. And when it looked like the overload might make the whole grid fail—the grid for the entire Twin Cities region; we're talking power for three, four million people—the system essentially went into self-protective mode and just cut it off. The grid cut them free."

The president blinked at the wall of screens. "To protect itself, the grid severed connection to Clover Hill."

"Yes. The grid basically said, *Don't bring those problems here.*"

"Which is good for the grid. Bad for Clover Hill."

"Exactly. It means they're on their own."

The president crossed his arms, considering. "Can a nuclear plant actually power itself?"

"It can, but it shouldn't, and it's not done for long."

That voice came from an unlabeled box, a person who had just hopped on the call. On-screen was Ethan, arms of his sweater pushed up, a thin coating of dust covering his dark, wavy hair. In the background, emergency communications staffers worked diligently.

"It's called *islanding* or *island mode*," Ethan continued. "It's an automatic emergency stopgap if the power plant disconnects from the grid. It keeps the cooling systems going while the backup generators kick in. We are out of island mode and are running exclusively on EDG power."

"You are—" Tony said.

"Ethan Rosen. I run Clover Hill."

The room stilled in attention.

"You're *at* the plant currently?" asked the president.

"Yes, Mr. President."

"Are any of the reactors open?"

"No."

People in the room and on the screens shifted at that news.

"How certain are you?" the president asked, his expression stoic. "That's with, what, gauges and readings? Or a visual confirmation?"

"Sir, it's a war zone. We're still trying to figure out the extent of the damage. But I *can* confirm the plane did not directly hit any of the reactors. All three containment vessels held. All three reactors are intact."

There was an audible sigh of relief in the room and on the screens. Dawson wasn't convinced.

"You don't seem relieved, Mr. Rosen," said the president.

"I'm not. Look, the plane hit with enough force that it registered as an earthquake. That triggered automatic responses throughout the plant. The reactors themselves scrammed."

"They shut themselves down. That's good, right?"

"Exactly. And, yes, it's a standard protective protocol. It's what should have happened."

"But..."

"But it's not just about the reactors. When the plane crashed, we think it hit the primary distribution line first. And it didn't just damage the line—it snagged and severed it. Which not only cut us off the grid but made the plane twist. Or something. We're trying to get the security feed up to play it back and see. But whatever happened, it made the plane break apart. There wasn't just one point of impact. The plane broke apart, and huge chunks of the aircraft went in every direction. They hit dry casks. Auxiliary buildings. External batteries. The damage is extensive and widespread."

"And that's what you're trying to assess right now. The damage."

"Exactly. What's working and what's not. And we're most worried about—" Ethan paused, then looked directly into the camera. "Mr. President, sir, how much do you know about nuclear power?"

"Let's say nothing."

"Right. Okay. So..." The engineer rubbed his hands together, thinking. "Okay, so the whole situation of a nuclear power plant ultimately comes down to one thing: Heat. Controlled heat is what generates power. Out-of-control heat is what causes a meltdown. Daily operations are nothing but maintaining that balance. At a nuclear plant, you control the heat with two things: Power and water. At the moment, the plant is struggling with both.

"Now, the plant has multiple ways to power itself," Ethan continued, crossing his arms. "The first is through the grid. As we already said, that's a dead end."

"We can't just reconnect the plant to the grid—" Dawson began.

"If the line's severed completely, it's not going to happen," interrupted the secretary of energy. "Even if it were just damaged, it would take weeks to reconnect. But severed—"

"Who knows how long," said Ethan.

"There's not another—"

"Another distribution line?" Ethan said, finishing the president's thought. "That's called a secondary distribution line. And no. This plant is too small to have a secondary distribution line. So since the grid wasn't an option, we moved to redundancies—EDG power. Emergency diesel generators. They are what's running the plant at the moment."

"They're big enough to do that?" asked the president.

"Not forever. Not like the grid. They will eventually, obviously, run out of diesel and need refueling. And EDGs themselves can fail. But in theory, yes. They can run the plant. And they are."

"And if the EDGs fail?"

"Batteries. External battery power. Some may have been damaged, but even if they weren't, backup batteries can't feed power for the whole plant, just critical load."

"Critical load?"

"The equipment most crucial for running the plant safely. Coolant pumps. Other systems that keep the water in the reactors and pools cool. Remember, it's about controlling the heat."

Dawson looked to the man on the monitor labeled FEMA. "Gene, where are we at with getting them fuel and more generators and batteries?"

The FEMA director said, "We've contacted local utilities to request their emergency stock. Minneapolis is the closest big utility. Semitrucks are en route for load and transport."

"Can confirm," Ethan said. "I was on a call with Red Top before I hopped on with you. They're the nearest plant and their teams are organizing their supply as we speak."

"Good. Gene, I want regular status updates," said Dawson. "Mr. Rosen, I want you updating me regularly."

"You don't, actually. You want me focused in the control room. Who you want is Joss. She's our regional NEST rep."

"NEST?"

"Nuclear Emergency Support Team," said Tony, reading from the papers he'd been handed earlier. "The Department of Energy's nuclear-incident first responders. Rapid-response teams of nuclear engineers and scientists. Jocelyn Vance—Joss, apparently—covers the upper Midwest region. Prior to this post, she was in Washington at the NRC working in policy, and before that she was getting a PhD in nuclear engineering from MIT."

"And she's on her way to the plant?" asked the president.

"I'm surprised she's not already here," said Ethan. "She lives in Waketa. She's *from* Waketa."

"Tony, get her direct number," said Dawson. "Mr. Rosen, if the reactors have shut down and are currently not open and not leaking radioactive material, if we shore up the power supply by bringing in more generators and batteries—aren't we good?"

Ethan paused. "As I said earlier, sir, it's not just the reactors."

The president's gut tightened. There was something in the way he'd said it. Something foreboding, something that almost felt like pity—a scientist who knew what they were up against pitying the clueless bureaucrat in charge.

"A nuclear power plant's main function is to generate power," Ethan said. "But it also *stores* nuclear waste. People focus on the reactors being so dangerous because...well, because they are. A reactor is where the active nuclear material, little pellets of enriched uranium, each about the size of a gummy bear, are all stacked together in big, long rods. Using nuclear energy to generate power is, yes, a very dangerous activity if not done properly."

Ethan took a breath before continuing. "But once the uranium is fissioned, once it's burned, the rods are removed from the reactor core and replaced with new rods containing freshly enriched uranium pellets. But the fuel rods become *more* radioactive as they are burned in the reactor."

The engineer paused.

"Meaning, Mr. President, when the fuel rods leave the reactor, they are more dangerous than when they were in it."

"So where do these more dangerous fuel rods go once they're removed from the reactors?"

"Two places. Both are on-site. One is dry cask storage."

Tony slid an image across the table to the president, a picture of rows of large, oblong concrete canisters positioned vertically on outdoor concrete pads. Dawson flipped it around to show the engineer.

"Yes, sir," Ethan said. "Those are dry casks. They're the long-term storage option. Inside each of those pillars are the oldest rods. The ones that have cooled the most. Once the rods are inserted, each cask is filled with inert gas, placed in a steel cylinder that is welded or bolted shut, then surrounded by concrete. But just because they're the oldest and coolest doesn't mean they're not still dangerous. The half-lives of some back-end nuclear by-products are millions of years."

The president glanced up from the image. Ethan nodded, understanding his look.

"Yes. You heard me correctly, sir," he said. "Nuclear waste is toxic for millennia. And I know at least one of our casks has been damaged and ruptured and one plant employee has been exposed."

"Damn it," the president muttered. "How do we contain it?"

Ethan hesitated. "Sir, that one cask may be the least of our problems."

Dawson and Tony shared a look before the chief of staff passed another image to the president.

"The other storage option," Ethan said, "is the spent fuel pool." As he went on to describe the picture the president held in his hands, Dawson sat down slowly.

"Immediately after the fuel rods leave the reactor," Ethan said, "they're put in the pool. It's an enormous aboveground swimming pool filled with regular old water inside a big warehouse. The pool is at least forty feet deep. At the bottom are storage racks that hold the fuel assemblies. The pool is a safe storage location for the rods to cool after their immediate removal *because* of the water. The water is crucial. It acts as a natural shield. Every seven centimeters away from the rods, the radiation is halved. I wouldn't drink it, but you could swim on the surface, no problem."

The president glanced up.

"I'm serious. But the water—and this is the crucial part—it keeps the rods from burning. The pool has cooling pumps that continuously circulate the water, keeping the temperature down."

"And the pumps aren't working," said Dawson.

"No, no. The pumps are working fine. The problem is the pool is leaking."

"Leaking?"

"Yes, sir. Parts of the plane struck the building housing the pool, causing substantial structural damage to the pool itself. Sir, the pool is losing water."

The president held up the picture of the pool and the building it was in. "You're saying nuclear waste is stored in a facility like this? This looks like a Walmart."

"And it's about that fortified."

The president tossed the image aside and leaned back in the chair. "What happens if we can't fix the damage and the pool drains?"

"As the pool drains, the rods will become exposed. When that happens, what water's left will heat up and boil off, releasing radioactive steam and hydrogen into a building not designed to contain it. An explosion will occur if the fire hasn't already destroyed the structure."

"What fire?"

"Well, chances are, before an explosion could happen, the entire thing would go up in a zirconium cladding fire."

"What does that look like?"

"Like Chernobyl was a campfire."

"And how would we put it out?"

"We wouldn't."

"Look," the president said, growing frustrated. "Being alarmist to a degree that—"

"Mr. President, I'm not being alarmist. If a fire starts in the pool, it will set off a chain reaction that will melt down every reactor and every pool at the plant. Remember, there are three reactors. Each has its own pool. This plant has been in operation three hundred sixty-five days a year since 1973. Every ounce of nuclear waste created during that time is stored on-site. A fire of this magnitude, mankind has yet to conceive of a way to put out. It would burn forever."

No one in the room or on the screens moved.

"Mr. Rosen," the president said in an even, flat tone. "I ask again. What does that look like?"

Ethan took a moment before he answered, seeming to consider what he could say that would accurately describe the situation they were up against.

"The fire would create an uncontrollable spread of invisible, toxic, cancer-causing radioactive particulates that would be dispersed in the air and carried by the wind. It would get in the soil. The water. Our food. Insects. Livestock. It would be in everything we touched, ate, drank, and breathed for…for forever."

At that moment, the screen showing CNN went into breaking-news mode.

The rest of the world was about to find out.

President Dawson studied the live radar of current air traffic over a map of the whole country, focusing particularly on Minnesota. The heart of Middle America. In the center, right at the very top. There was nothing attention-grabbing about it. No Hollywood or Times Square. No Rocky Mountains or Grand Canyon. For most, it was just a place that was there. A place you went if you had family.

The president stood and stepped around the table, homing in on the map of Waketa, population nine hundred. Everything he'd heard today about the plant was probably emblematic of the rest of the town too. Considered too small to truly matter, too unimportant to get the attention it needed and deserved. The priority and resources freely given to things considered *too big to fail*, this town, this plant, had never received. And now, because the rest of the country had decided places like Waketa and Clover Hill were small enough to fail, America might learn that the adage "You're only as strong as your weakest link" was true.

"Nuclear power plants are purposely built near water, correct?" President Dawson asked.

"They are, sir," Ethan confirmed. "They need a large water source to draw from. Clover Hill draws from the Mississippi."

The deputy national security adviser typed on her keyboard. A moment later, maps and details of the Mississippi River system came up on a large monitor.

"If a fire started, would the contaminated water flow to the river?" asked Dawson.

"Without question," said Ethan.

The Mississippi River spanned 2,300 miles, making it the fourth-largest river system in the world. President Dawson's eyes traced the river's path from Minnesota on down—Wisconsin, Iowa, Illinois, Missouri, Kentucky, Arkansas, Tennessee, Mississippi, Louisiana. The river passed through ten states total, and that wasn't including any of its sizable tributaries. The river started practically in Canada and ended in the Gulf of Mexico, slicing straight down the center of the country like a spine.

"Arne," said the president.

The head of the EPA said, "Somewhere between twenty to thirty million people rely on the Mississippi and its tributaries for fresh water. Over fifty cities rely on the Mississippi and the Mississippi alone for their *entire* water supply."

"Melissa," said Dawson, turning his attention to the box labeled SECRETARY OF AGRICULTURE.

"The majority of land in the Mississippi basin is used for agriculture, crops mainly for export. Ninety-two percent of the nation's *total* agricultural exports come from this region alone. Seventy-eight percent of the world's *total* imports of soy and feed grain come from crops grown in the Mississippi River basin. I cannot impress upon you enough how catastrophic the ripple effects on food security would be and the massive global implications, particularly in regions of the world already affected by climate-change-induced droughts, famines, and mass migration."

"Jorge."

"To that point," said the secretary of state. "The Bureau of Population, Refugees, and Migration will have more accurate figures than I can give you right now, but if the entire center of the country becomes unlivable for generations to come, we're looking at a mass migration to the east and west with displacement figures somewhere in the sixty- to seventy-million range—and that's just for the Midwest. We're talking about primarily rural populations moving to large coastal cities where there's a higher cost of living after they have lost all earning potential and whatever land equity they might have had. And these coastal cities are already facing their own real estate scarcities and affordable-housing crises along with an untenable population of unhoused that they have no idea what to do about."

"So a refugee crisis of Americans on American soil," Dawson said. "Diane."

"We'd lose over a million full-time jobs in agriculture alone," said the secretary of labor.

"Jerry."

The Fed chair looked squarely into the camera. "Total financial collapse."

The president sat in stunned silence. The implications of what this meant, what this could mean, were staggering—and these were just the broad strokes. Finally, he looked to the chair of the Nuclear Regulatory Commission.

"Dave," said the president.

The head of the NRC, a man who had been in quiet contemplation this whole time, leaned forward. He was soft-spoken, which only made his words carry more weight.

"The International Nuclear Event Scale has seven levels. Level seven is a major accident, meaning a significant release of radioactive material with long-term, widespread environmental and health ramifications. There have only been two INES level sevens: Fukushima and Chernobyl. The situation we're faced with today has major global implications. It far exceeds our current scale." He paused. "Mr. President, this could be our first level eight."

"What would a level eight mean?"

"It would be an extinction-level event, sir."

CHAPTER SIX

COUNTDOWN TO ZERO HOUR
16 HOURS AND 09 MINUTES

DANI ALLEN HAD never doubted that she and her crew could handle any fire.

Until today.

"Power is out." Chief Loftus's voice boomed over the intercom through the Waketa Township fire station. *"Phones are down, 911 is down. Cell service is down."*

Lights along the hallway ceiling, over the doors, and out in the bay flashed red. At regular intervals, high-pitched tones filled the firehouse as the company hurried into their turnout gear.

"There is no switchboard," Chief Loftus continued. *"There are no calls for help. Our entire community is in a virtual blackout."*

"Jesus Christ," Levon Miller muttered, pulling the thick, flame-resistant bunker pants up over his long underwear. Zipping up, he grabbed his bunker coat out of his locker with one last glance at the picture taped inside: a selfie of himself and Carla, taken in the cab of the fire engine as they were driven from the church to the reception hall. She looked beautiful. Her jet-black hair, dark brown eyes, and dark tan skin against a strapless cream-colored wedding dress. His dirty-blond mop and pasty-white skin looking even pastier in that rented tuxedo. Both smiling a just-won-the-lottery grin. It was his favorite picture. He'd never been happier.

Levon glanced up at the clock on the wall. Carla should be outside monitoring recess right now. He wondered if she'd seen or heard the plane crash; he wondered if she was okay.

Of course she was. Carla was one of the smartest, most resourceful people he knew. She was fine. She was with her students, and she was fine.

She had to be.

Levon kissed his fingers, touched the photo, then banged his locker shut.

"Today will be a day of tough choices," Chief Loftus continued. *"We will be needed everywhere. We cannot be everywhere. Let me repeat myself: Today will be a day of tough choices. But we will not stop until the job is done."*

Dani shook a pant leg down over her insulated, steel-toed rubber boots while trying to block out the thoughts of her six-year-old daughter, Brianna. Dani had never had a problem compartmentalizing work and home. But work didn't usually involve home. Today it did.

Looping her arms through the elastic suspenders, Dani glanced down at the bench, to Bri's kindergarten school picture tucked inside her helmet. She could have been looking at her own picture at that age; mother and daughter were practically identical: Same toothy grin. Same dark brown skin, hair, and eyes. Same tightly coiled curls. Mother and daughter shared a love of guacamole, and neither liked pickles. Both paid attention to detail and were resistant to change. Dani always wondered if, as Bri aged, she too would have great taste in friends. And, later on, if, like her mom, she too would have terrible taste in men.

"Here's what we know," Chief Loftus said as Dani and Levon hustled, fully suited, into the bay where the chief was addressing the rest of the company. "The plant has been hit. The plant has been compromised. I don't know how badly — *they* don't know how badly. We go and we do what they say. They got shit burning we don't even know about. So today, your egos don't exist. The only words I want to hear you say are *How can I help?* Because the difference between what they know and you don't is the difference between living and dying. No one's a hero today. Today, we just do the job."

"The priority is Clover Hill," Chief Loftus continued. "That's the first domino. But the plane created a debris field several miles in diameter with damage to residential and commercial structures. There are injuries. We must assume fatalities. We've got a seventeen-car pileup that has shut I-35 to all traffic in both directions at Appamatok—"

"*Seventeen?*"

"Fucking hell."

They all started talking over one another. That one call alone would have been the biggest thing they'd ever faced.

"Chief, hold on. Thirty-five is the main way—"

"Yes. The main way in and out of town," Loftus said, finishing Boggs's thought.

"But we need backup," said Levon. "How are they getting here if not up thirty-five?"

"They're gonna, what, come up Schnebly Hill?" said Frankie, the truck engineer.

"With no thirty-five, we won't have backup for hours," said another firefighter.

"One engine and one ladder." Frankie shook his head. "That's what we got. That's it. That's nothing. This is a huge crisis. A goddamn national crisis. We can't do this alone. We need—"

"We need—Frankie, what day in this job have we ever had all we need?"

The bay went quiet. Loftus didn't usually raise his voice.

"We are a small rural firehouse facing maybe the largest crisis this country has ever seen, and until we know otherwise, we're facing it alone. Help will come. State. Federal. It will come—but not yet. For now, it is up to us and we are on our own, which we know all too goddamn well is no different than any other day."

"Same as it ever was," Dani said.

Firefighters repeated her words, nodding as they bumped fists.

Chief Loftus nodded too. "We run the day like we run every day. Making it work because there is no other choice."

Moments later, the ladder truck company, Ladder 42, rolled out of the station and turned left to approach the power plant campus from the north. Levon and Dani's engine company, Engine 42, followed, turning right to approach from the south. As they went, Dani looked over to the firehouse and, not for the first time, considered that word.

It *was* a house, in the literal sense. There were beds, showers, a kitchen. They were on duty for days at a time, so they lived there, together, in that house. But what people who didn't work with fire didn't appreciate was that it wasn't just a house — it was a home.

A home where brothers and sisters spent holidays and weekends together and fought over whose turn it was to do the dishes. Brothers and sisters who knew everything about one another. Their ups, their downs, their fears, their vulnerabilities. Brothers and sisters who were always there to give you shit and never let you forget an embarrassing moment. Brothers and sisters who were there to help shoulder the burden or offer a hand up.

They were a pack. A pack of wolves, running toward the chaos as one. They never knew exactly what they would face. No two calls were the same. But they always knew the wolves out in front and by their sides had their backs, because they knew they had theirs. A firefighter understood that any day on the line could be the last. That kind of relationship with death was uncommon, but that's what made them not common people. And when, day after day, call after call, you stand shoulder to shoulder and put your life on the line together, you are no longer just firefighters.

You're family.

CHAPTER SEVEN

COUNTDOWN TO ZERO HOUR

15 HOURS AND 57 MINUTES

AS THE COUNTRY was facing the worst nuclear disaster any nation had faced since Fukushima, Joss was staring down the barrel of a gun.

She tapped her finger on the steering wheel, alternating glances between the white smoke rising from the plant and the potbellied man in the security shed studying her credentials. The gangly young man standing next to him was the one pointing the gun into the car, and as she waited, she imagined the firearm's recoil knocking him off his skinny little feet.

Joss was the kind of woman people described with words like *strongheaded, clever, fiery, determined*. Adjectives that were up for interpretation, depending on whether Joss was working for or against you. Safe to say, the men in the security shed wouldn't mean them as compliments. But ask anyone in Waketa, questionable bedside manner aside, they'd say they'd consider themselves damn lucky to have Joss Vance in their corner.

Joss ran her hands through her hair with a pointed sigh. She'd tried all the standard approaches: Asking nicely, politely correcting, firmly demanding, although not necessarily in that order. But nothing had gotten her past security, so now Joss was attempting her least favorite tactic: Shutting the fuck up while they worked it out on their own only to come to the exact same conclusion she'd told them at the start.

"Ma'am," the older guard said, hitching up his pants. "I've never heard of this NEST."

"Yes, sir. A lot of people haven't," Joss said, smiling as sweetly as she could manage. "But I assure you, it's real. You can see there, I have clearance."

"You have research clearance. Not operational clearance."

"That should be enough for that bar to go up and my car to go through."

"Not today, it's not."

Joss bit the inside of her cheek to keep from saying what she wanted to say. Instead, she said, "Sir, I deeply respect what you do, and I am grateful for the thoroughness with which you're doing it. You and I, we both know *nothing* is more important than maintaining a secure facility."

"Yes, ma'am."

"The wrong person gets through? We're talking big potentials for big problems."

"I'm glad you understand, ma'am," he said.

Joss pointed across the way, and both security guards turned to look at the felled tree and the shredded chunk of metal lying next to it that displayed the bright blue *C* of the Coastal Airways logo.

"Pretty sure the big problems already got through," she said.

"Well—"

"Look, I realize that every five minutes you're getting some new security mandate and protocol and lockdown procedure you didn't even know existed. And I get that you want to exercise caution. You don't care who I am or what I do; you just want to do your job right. And any other day, that's exactly what should be happening."

Her voice was rising, despite her best efforts, but Joss knew every second wasted out here was a second closer to the worst case scenario.

"But today?" she said. "You really should care who I am and what I do because I know why you've got a metallic taste in your mouth. And I know why that little device up there is clicking every so often," she said, pointing at the wall-mounted pressurized ionization chamber inside the booth measuring ambient radiation levels. "I too just want to do my job right, but I can't if you won't let me. And my job is to know what the fuck is going on and figure out what the fuck to do about it. So either lift the gate or get Ethan Rosen on the fucking phone and tell him Joss Vance stopped by just to let him know that Reactor fucking Two is venting white fucking smoke!"

The man stared. "And I suppose, ma'am, you know why it is?"

"Well, either we got a new pope or the building's about to blow."

A beat passed before the guards exchanged a look. Finally, the older man nodded toward the panel. The kid with the gun pushed a button, and the security gate rose.

Joss reached into her go-bag in the passenger seat, grabbed a bottle, shook several pills into her hand, and held them out to the men.

"These are potassium iodide pills. They'll keep your thyroid from absorbing radioactive iodine. Take one now, take another in twenty-four hours until they're gone."

The men hesitated, then took the pills.

"By the way, that gun can't protect you now," Joss said. She glanced into the security booth. "But *that* can."

As she drove off, in the rearview, she saw the men gaze into the booth at the pile of protective hazmat gear.

The radio beeped.

"Understood," Ethan said to Steve through the radio. "Let us know when you're set up." Leaning on the desk, he turned to Vikram. "Once they get in, we're—"

The door to the control room burst open.

"Are you aware you're releasing white smoke?" Joss said.

Ethan straightened with an already exhausted sigh. "Hello, Jocelyn."

"Is it burn-off steam?"

"We don't know."

"Hydrogen buildup?"

"We don't know."

"Fuck, Ethan! Then what are your pool levels? If the temperature—"

"No shit!" Ethan hollered.

The other controllers in the room watched the two like it was a tennis match. Ethan never raised his voice. Or swore. This was new.

Vikram leaned over to Maggie and Dwight. "I can't tell if they want to kill each other or fuck each other," he whispered.

"Both," they replied in unison.

"But if the reactor—" Joss started.

"Joss, we know it's not the reactor," Ethan said, cutting her off. "It's the pool."

Joss's face went white.

"Building power is limited to critical load," Steve reported into the radio, breathing heavily, as he and his crew turned the corner and started up the next flight of stairs.

The interior stairwell was dark, lit only with the ghostly fluorescent glow of emergency lighting. The only sounds beyond the clomping of their heavy boots on the concrete stairs were the occasional beeps from the dosimeters fixed to their turnout jackets. Steve glanced at the large placard next to the door as they passed.

"Fourth floor," he said.

"Okay, fifth floor is your entry point," Ethan said over the radio.

Joss stepped up onto the platform to check the levels and gauges as Ethan went to grab a readout from the printer. The two bumped into each other and both immediately stepped back, avoiding eye contact. Ethan felt his face flush. It was the closest they'd been in fifteen years; at the handful of regional meetings they'd both attended over the past nine months, she'd always positioned herself on the opposite side of the room from him.

"But you're not in station blackout," Joss said, noting the zeros in every digital value. "Why are you dark?"

"When we lost grid power, all values went into question," Ethan said. "We had no clue if the numbers we were getting were live or frozen from the point of impact. Without accurate numbers, we weren't confident making any decisions. The security cameras went out when we lost power too, so there went any chance for visual confirmation. We had no choice. We recorded what the panels said, then did a hard system reboot."

"Which is why you didn't have any information when I came in," Joss said. "You're in the middle of the five-minute reboot."

"It's also why we sent the fire brigade to get a visual on the pool," he said. "We need to know if we can trust the numbers." He looked over at her. "Congratulations. You're caught up. And no, no need to apologize."

She ignored him. "And the reboot is over in—"

"Back online in ten," Dwight said.

"In ten seconds," Ethan said.

"Fifth floor." Steve's voice crackled over the speaker. *"Stand by."*

Steve paused at the door to make sure his crew was ready.

"Look for anyone injured. Look for damage. Get in, get out," he said.

He opened the door, and they started to pile into the spent fuel pool containment room. As they passed him, Steve heard the cadence of the clicking dosimeters pick up.

The cavernous warehouse had flat concrete walls, thirty feet from floor to ceiling. Everything in the space was industrial and utilitarian: Pipes. Concrete. Metal. Raised platforms and catwalks. A huge, adjustable crane. But no one who ever set foot in the room mentioned that stuff.

The only thing they talked about was the pool.

Crystal clear, sparkling blue water. The kind you'd kill to get into on a hot afternoon. But appearances could be deceiving, and Steve knew that lying at the bottom of the rippling oasis was something sinister.

Steve was the last one in, following his crew as they did a sweep of the area. He planned to head straight for the hose attachments to ensure they were still viable for refilling the pool if needed, but the second he got a good look at the room, he stopped in his tracks.

"We're up," said Vikram, wheeling his chair to the console as the displays blinked to life.

"Cross-check everything with the initial figures," Ethan called out as the control room's personnel sprang into action. They wrote down figures, calculated differences, referred to checklists. Joss looked over their shoulders as they worked, occasionally reading a figure aloud or passing papers between staff.

Dwight tapped a keyboard. "Hang on, I think we might..." he muttered. "Hey, guys. Guys! We got feed."

He made a few more keystrokes, and a monitor at the front of the room brought up security feeds of the plant. The screen was sectioned into four boxes, each showing a live shot of a different angle of the campus. Everyone in the room stopped. Maggie gasped. Ethan interlaced his fingers over the top of his head. Joss watched their reactions, realizing that none of them had been outside the windowless room since the accident. This was the first time any of them had seen what it looked like out there.

It was carnage.

Each monitor quadrant displayed crumbled concrete, deformed rebar, and shredded metal. One showed a burning section of aircraft fuselage. The carcass of a crushed truck filled another. The quadrant next to that had firefighters battling a blaze in what little remained of some building they could no longer identify. Only hours ago, they had entered a peaceful campus, coffee cups in hand, carrying bagged lunches. And now, a good portion of that campus had been laid to waste.

"Run it back to the crash," Joss said.

Dwight tapped on the keyboard. The images on the screen froze, then rewound. The flames danced at four times normal speed. A fire truck zoomed in and out of frame. The dry cask was broken on the ground. And then, without a hint of what was about to happen, the screens showed the indecipherable chaos as the cameras captured the plane's exact moment of impact — and then it was calm. The cask was upright and whole, the smoke had disappeared, the flames had gone. There was nothing above but the quiet blue sky of a beautiful spring day.

"There! Stop," Joss said.

Dwight cued it up and pressed Play. They all watched the silent video of tree branches moving gently in a breeze as Vinny bent over to check a gauge — and then out of nowhere, a flaming aircraft engine hurtled into the cask, toppling it onto its side.

In another screen quadrant, chunks of concrete rained down. In the adjacent quadrant, the windshield of a utility truck shattered as jagged slabs crushed it from above.

"Go back," Ethan said. "Change the angle. I want to see impact at the main transformer station."

Dwight punched buttons; the tape rewound, the carnage went away, and the angle changed to a heavily wooded area beyond a tall, razor wire fence. Inside the perimeter, the transformer box had stacked coils piled high enough to reach the thick transmission cables stretching out of the frame. The sky was blue; there was nothing there.

Then the plane appeared.

Flying relatively level at first, the gargantuan aircraft suddenly banked left, then nosed down and plummeted. The left wing snagged the distribution line, slicing through it with ease. As the line snapped, sparks shot off in every direction as the remnants of attached cable danced with electricity. The jet cartwheeled, plowing into the ground nose first as the tail shot up, flipping it end over end. Tons of jet fuel sprayed the area, atomizing instantly. An explosion was inevitable: *Bang*. A fireball and a cloud of flames and black smoke rose into the sky.

"The pool—"

"Show the impact at the pool—"

Joss and Ethan spoke over each other, but Dwight was already typing. He rewound and changed angles, and the image of the building that housed the R2 spent fuel pool appeared, still intact. Suddenly, the image on the screen began to shake, a result of the plane's impact on the other side of the campus.

"It's...it's bad," Steve said over the radio, his voice startling them.

He was talking to them live from the very building they were watching the taped footage of. On the screen, the first parts of the aircraft began falling from the sky like meteors dropping into the atmosphere. Debris of all sizes pounded the ground, the sidewalk, the roof...and the side of the spent fuel pool building.

"Confirmed," Steve reported. "We have major structural damage to the pool itself."

He stood at the edge, looking down into the water. Undulating beams of sunlight streaked in through cracks, fissures, and holes caused by the plane's impact. Chunks of concrete rubble lay in heaps atop the fuel assemblies at the bottom of the pool as little bubbles rose to the surface from the chemical reactions. Against the pool's wall, under the damage, shredded sections of the stainless-steel liner clung to the sides like loose teeth.

Steve looked at the sunlight cutting through the water, knowing that where the light was coming in, the water was going out. The pool *was* leaking.

"The water we saw outside," Steve said. "It's from the pool."

Just as he finished his assessment, his dosimeter let out a loud, steady alert.

"Is that your reader?" Ethan asked, hearing the alarm. "Get out. Get out now."

"All right, every—" Steve's voice cut out as he gathered his men.

Joss was scribbling furiously on a piece of paper. "Clover Hill uses high-density closed-cell racks, correct?" she asked.

"Correct," said Ethan.

"When was your latest load discharged from the reactor into the pool?"

"Five weeks ago."

Joss cursed under her breath. That recently. "What was the loading pattern? Please, God, say one-by-eight." She looked up when Ethan didn't respond. "One-by-four?"

"Adjacent."

"Jesus, Ethan."

"You think I don't know that? With what secondary storage am I doing one-by-eight? The casks are full. There's no budget for more. We're out of room. This isn't news. You know that better than anyone."

"Okay, okay," Joss said, continuing to write. A few moments later, she stood up straight. "Check my math," she said, turning the paper toward Vikram and Maggie.

As they worked, scribbling figures on their own papers, Joss frowned at the sheet, her mouth moving silently as she reran the math in her head, calculating how long they had before the spent fuel heated to ignition temperatures, starting a catastrophic and uncontrollable fire that would create an environmental disaster the likes of which had never been seen. In the background, the footage of the plane's impact played on a loop.

Maggie finished first, setting her pencil down and looking from Joss to Ethan. She nodded. Moments later, Vikram leaned back in his chair and said, "That's what I got too."

Ethan knew Joss loved to be right. But the dread on her face told him that today, she wished she hadn't been.

"How many days do we have?" Ethan asked.

"With rods that fresh, packed that tight," Joss said. "If we keep losing water at the current rate, we've got less than sixteen hours."

CHAPTER EIGHT

COUNTDOWN TO ZERO HOUR
15 HOURS AND 44 MINUTES

THE FIRST-GRADERS STOOD at the classroom window, their eyes glued to the billowing columns of smoke rising up in the distance from the direction of Clover Hill.

Behind them, their teacher, Miss Carla, wasn't looking at the radioactive smoke. She was looking at the tiny six-year-olds and thinking of how their young, developing bodies were at greater risk of getting cancer from radiation than adult bodies exposed to the same doses. Of how alarming the rates of pediatric leukemia and thyroid cancer were after Chernobyl. Carla knew all the statistics, but her students did not, and if she had anything to say about how the rest of this day went, they'd never find out the hard way.

Pulling her desk away from the wall, she unplugged the power cord connected to her computer and hot-pink lava lamp. The lamp was a class favorite. Not that it was on. Nothing was on in the small, two-story schoolhouse except the neon emergency lights at the front and rear exits.

Outside her classroom, she heard a few teachers speaking in hushed tones in the hallway.

"—calls go through?"

"No. No calls. No texts. I don't even have internet."

"Me neither. Guys, I'm going to freak out. What if it is Clover Hill? Seriously. What if?"

"If there was a problem at the plant, the sirens would have gone off. They haven't."

Carla poked her head outside her classroom. "Did you guys unplug everything?"

"Why? Is the power back on?" Mr. Baker, a sixth-grade teacher, asked.

"No. But when it does come back, we don't want to overload the system."

The sound of footsteps running up the stairs made the teachers turn.

"Nichole?" Carla said to the frazzled woman appearing at the top of the stairs.

Nichole hurried down the hall clutching her purse as her work lanyard swung from side to side. "Miss Carla," she said breathlessly. "Hi. I'm just...is he—" Before Carla could reply, Nichole stuck her head into the classroom. "David," she said sharply to her son, beckoning him over with a wave of her hand. "Get your stuff."

Mr. Baker whispered to the other teachers, "Doesn't David's mom work at Clover Hill?"

"Nichole, we saw the plane and heard the crash," Carla said, keeping her voice low. "Everything all right at the plant?"

Before she could reply, David appeared at the door.

"Mommy, what's wrong?" he said, giving voice to what they were all thinking.

Nichole looked from her son to the teachers as everyone waited for her answer. "Nothing, sweetheart," she said, not even attempting a smile. Putting her hands on his shoulders, she spun him toward the stairs. As they hurried down the hall, David looked back with a wave to his teacher. Carla returned the wave, suddenly aware of how hard her heart was pounding.

"How many kids are left in your classes?" Carla said once David was out of earshot. "I now only have five."

In a town of less than a thousand people, the school was small to start with. That day, attendance was particularly light because some families had left town for Easter weekend. And many of the students' parents, like Nichole, had already come in and grabbed their kids. Carla thought this might be the one thing working in the teachers' favor.

"I've got seven."

"Four."

"Just two."

"Good," said Principal Gazdecki, coming around the corner, walkie-talkie in hand. He'd been running the school for twenty-seven years and knew the name of every student and parent and sometimes even their pets.

"Get a head count," he said, walking backward down the hall. "I bet we can all fit in one bus. Let's start loading up."

Most of the other teachers stared.

"For relocation," Carla said, reading their confused expressions. "We're in the ten-mile emergency planning zone. If they issue a relocation order, we're paired with McMinn County. We relocate to Harriman High."

All of this, it seemed, was news to the teachers. One of them was new to the area, but most of them had grown up in the shadow of the plant. Yes, the school's nuclear incident preparedness training was only one thirty-minute unit done annually at the start of the school year. *But still,* Carla thought, *they should know these things. Shouldn't they?*

"Just keep the kids calm," Carla said. "Nothing's confirmed yet. There's been no siren. We're just being cautious."

They looked about as convinced as she felt.

"All right, my weasels," Carla said with forced enthusiasm when she reentered her classroom. "We got an unplanned field trip! Grab your backpacks and line up at the door."

The kids turned from the second-story window. Over their heads, Miss Carla could still see all the thick, black funnels of smoke that dotted the valley—the largest of which rose up from the plant. The kids looked confused and scared. Carla couldn't blame them. But mainly, they looked small, so small. Plastering a big first-grade-teacher smile on her face, Miss Carla clapped her hands. "C'mon, adventure awaits."

A handful of minutes later as the line of students made their way down the stairs, Leo, the sharpest kid in her class, asked Carla if the plant had blown up.

"I don't think so," she said. "If it had, they would have used the siren by now."

"But how would they turn the siren on if they blew up?"

Carla drew a blank. Before she could make up an answer, Benjamin saved her.

"Miss Carla, am I going to grow a tail?" he asked, breathless as he hustled to keep up with the group.

Carla glanced over her shoulder. "A what?"

Benjamin was the smallest of the first-graders, the runt of the class, his thick glasses making his wide eyes look even larger. "Ronnie Darrow said we're going to grow tails because of the nuclear plant."

"Just because Ronnie Darrow is a sixth-grader doesn't mean he knows everything. None of you are growing anything."

"Miss Carla, is Mr. Levon at the plant?"

Carla's stomach knotted at Sophie's question. Just last week, Levon had come into class wearing all his fire gear to teach them stop-drop-and-roll and how to crawl under smoke to reach a door. But the highlight for the kids was getting to sit in the fire truck. Later that night, at home, Levon had beamed with pride at the news that most of the class now planned on being firefighters when they grew up.

Carla glanced over at Brianna, assuming the little girl was as worried as she was, since her mom was a firefighter too. Sure enough, Brianna's dark brown eyes looked up at Carla for reassurance. Carla could envision Bri's mom, Dani, braiding her baby girl's ponytail that morning.

Brianna and Dani lived just up the road from Levon and Carla; Levon and Dani carpooled to the station, and Carla drove herself and Bri to and from school. Granddaddy Marion lived with Brianna and Dani, and since he was now retired, most days he cooked big meals for both families to eat together. They weren't just neighbors, they weren't just friends, they weren't just colleagues, and they weren't just teacher and student — they were as good a family as any of them had.

"He might be at the plant," Carla said, answering Sophie but looking at Bri. "I don't know. But wherever he is, he's with his crew and they know what to do and how to help. Okay?"

Bri nodded.

"All right, stay together and sit as a class," Carla said, counting heads as her students piled onto the bus. Just as the last went in, Carla saw a flash of red in the shape of a '95 Dodge Ram pickup tearing up the road.

She had never seen Marion drive that fast. He never did anything fast. Brianna's granddaddy was a man of few words, slow and methodical in everything he did. But moments later, after he parked and got out of the truck, Marion actually set off in a jog toward the bus.

Marion had been one of Clover Hill's first employees. He'd spent the entirety of his forty-seven-year career there, retiring only three years ago. He'd helped build that plant; he knew it backward. So when he jogged up to Carla, pulled her aside, and looked her dead in the eye, a chill went up her spine.

"Get Brianna. Let's go."

"Well, but..." Carla noticed Bri watching them from a window in the bus. Carla waved for her to come out. "Okay," she said. "But I need to stay."

"You're coming with us." Marion was firm.

"I can't. My students. I—"

"Noah, Eric," barked Principal Gazdecki to two sixth-graders getting on the bus. "Check every window. Make sure they're shut. *Tight*. Got it?" He turned. "Marion." They shook hands. "No siren from Clover Hill yet," he said. "You don't think I'm overreacting?"

Just then, Bri appeared at her granddaddy's side. She took his hand and looked up at the adults. Marion cleared his throat noncommittally.

"I think you got the right idea, Mr. Gazdecki. Now, Miss Carla," he said, waving at her to come along as he walked to the pickup with Bri.

"Marion. My kids. I can't..."

Mr. Gazdecki turned to Carla. "Where's he want you to go?"

"With him."

"But where?"

Carla could only shake her head and shrug.

Mr. Gazdecki watched Marion and Bri get in the pickup. "Go."

"But my students—" Carla protested.

"There are fifty-seven students total with thirteen teachers, four administrators, and one lunch lady. That's a three-to-one kid-to-adult ratio. We got this. And parents are going to keep coming for their kids all day. Because families need to be together. And *that's* your family. You should be together. Go."

As Carla hurried across the parking lot to the idling pickup, she zipped up her jacket. The guilt eating at her only got worse when she hopped up into the cab and saw the pile of gear Marion had secured in the bed of the truck. Zip-up full-body hazmat suits. Full-face breathing masks. Thick rubber boots. Long rubber gloves.

If Marion was that worried, she was terrified.

"Staying won't fix anything," Marion said, reading her expression.

"Doesn't feel that way."

"What's wrong?" Brianna asked, sitting between them.

Marion put a gentle hand on her head and stroked her thick, black hair by way of an answer as the truck wound down the hill past the soccer field, past the oak tree, toward the main road. Suddenly, Carla sat up straight.

"Stop...stop!"

He did, and Carla jumped out, shut the door behind her, jogged back up the road, and peered down into the thicket of trees that lined the river. "Hey. *Hey!*"

The pack of sixth-grade boys clearly up to no good spun on their heels. Matt Tostig, the only fifth-grader among them, hastily zipped up the backpack they'd all been peering into and slung it over his shoulder.

"Absolutely not," said Carla. "Get out of there. Go back to the school."

"But Miss Carla—"

"*Now.*"

As they scrambled back up the embankment, a few protested. She'd have none of it. "A bus is about to leave, and you need to be on it. Not another word, Aaron," Carla said, using a tone of voice she rarely used. "And Ronnie, stop scaring the little kids. No one's growing a tail."

The boys weren't happy, but they didn't argue.

Except Matt.

"But Miss Carla," he said, "we were going—"

"Matt, I don't care where you were going or what you were going to do."

"But we were just—"

"*No.* Get up there. Now!"

"God, you're being such a bitch."

Everyone froze. Matt looked over at his buddies, gauging if he had gained any cred, but calling a teacher the B-word was a step too far, even for a sixth-grader.

Carla's heart broke. Matt was one of the sweetest kids she'd ever had in class. His mom, fourth-grade teacher Mrs. Tostig, had died a year and a half ago after a lengthy battle with lung cancer, and now his dad, Steve, the fire chief at the plant, was raising their only child on his own. Everyone knew it was proving difficult for both father and son. The alchemy of their grief and Matt's preteen angst had the boy acting out rebelliously lately. Carla knew the last place he needed to be in this terrifying moment was alone.

"Your dad just called, actually," Carla lied. "He said you needed to come with us. First-responder families are staying together."

Matt eyed her skeptically. "He did not."

"Yes, he did. Come on. Get in the truck."

"He wouldn't—"

But before Matt could say another word, the sirens went off.

Everyone flinched. The other boys scrambled up the road, gravel sliding out from under their sneakers, and took off in a sprint for the school. Matt climbed in the truck, taking Brianna's place on the bench seat, putting his backpack at his feet. Carla set Bri on her lap.

With all four in the truck's front cab, they sped off, the truck's speed steadily increasing. No one spoke; no one asked where they were going. They trusted that Marion had a plan.

But after a few minutes, the guilt in the pit of Carla's stomach turned to confusion...and then fear.

The truck was headed toward the plant.

CHAPTER NINE

COUNTDOWN TO ZERO HOUR

15 HOURS AND 39 MINUTES

THE PROBLEM WITH being a fireman in a small community was that you knew almost every victim and their families by name. So as Engine 42 made its way to the south entrance of Clover Hill with siren blaring and lights blazing, the dark pillars of smoke, large and small, that popped up along the horizon all around them felt personal.

One might be a house fire; it looked awfully close to the Vasquezes' place. Another—a car crash? That was near the spot where Roosevelt Road took a sharp turn at the bottom of Fred Clarke's land. But they had no idea. No one could call in for help.

"How are we going to get to them all?" asked Boggs, the rookie. None of the firefighters answered. They didn't want to say it aloud.

We're not.

Dani and Levon clocked the elementary school across the field, thinking the same thing. The most important person in each one's world was inside that building. Her daughter. His wife. Did they have any idea how much danger they were in, how bad the situation could get? Were they scared? Probably. But not nearly enough.

Dani thought of Brianna, already without a father—what if she was without a mother too? Who would take care of her? Marion, of course. But Daddy was getting older and he wasn't in the best of health. What would happen to her baby girl if something happened to both Dani *and* Marion?

That was Dani's worst fear as a firefighter. Not her own death— orphaning her child.

Clover Hill's footprint was enormous. Land in Waketa was cheap, and the plan, way back when the plant was built, was for rapid expansion. But growth never came, and every effort to sell the land failed, seeing as no farmer could get land *that* close to a nuclear plant insured. So the space went untouched for decades, creating, ironically, countless acres of pristine nature preserves.

As they passed the wide swaths of rich Minnesota soil and rugged woodlands along the winding Mississippi River, Dani couldn't help but think of "the Zone." The thousand-square-mile exclusion zone surrounding Chernobyl—forbidden to humans, reclaimed by nature—an area so many families had called home before the accident, now desolate and uninhabited.

Pripyat before the accident could have been Waketa's sister city; it was the town where the employees of the Chernobyl nuclear power plant worked and raised their families—families who were forced out of their homes with only what they could carry, forced to leave their animals in the pastures and their fields to grow over. Pripyat was the center of the Zone. No longer a quaint hamlet in the countryside, the town was now nothing more than a creepy time capsule of a frozen moment in history: Abandoned apartments with clothes still in the washing machine, food left to rot in the fridge. Rusted cars lining weed-covered streets, gas still in their tanks. Empty classrooms; pencils on desks; textbooks open; April 26, 1986, still written on the blackboard. The Zone was a geographical freak, cast out from the rest of society, left to rot in its own mistakes.

It was unthinkable that something like that could happen here, Dani thought. But surely that's what the people of Pripyat had thought too.

As the road sloped down toward the river, the fire engine rounded a curve, then suddenly braked hard. The firefighters whiplashed as the rig came to an abrupt stop.

"Oh my God," Frankie muttered.

Piling out of the truck, they jogged down to the two-lane bridge, struggling to make sense of what they were looking at. The bridge was completely impassable. Because lying across it was the wing of an aircraft. A gargantuan, shredded metal slab of machinery…

…that burned.

The air reeked of jet fuel. With each step closer they took, the heat became more intense. The firefighters stared in awe at the bright orange flames leaping off the wing's flat surface and reaching high into the air. Thirty feet below, the Mississippi River raged.

The wing was wedged into the bridge like a cork in a bottle, and the firefighters knew they did not have the time, manpower, or equipment to remove it. Which was fine; they would simply turn around and find another way to the plant, viewing this as nothing more than an impassable road they would deal with later.

If not for what they saw as they got closer.

A minivan had met the wing head-on. Its bumper, hood, and front two wheels were smashed completely flat and pinned underneath the wing. The vehicle must have twisted as it was dragged along under the wing, because the van now hung out over the river like a plank off the side of a ship. The bulk of the van—the passenger interior all the way to the back bumper—remained intact, albeit beat up. But the van now dangled out over the water in the middle of the bridge, its rear wheels still spinning, U2's "Beautiful Day" blaring out of the van's speakers.

While the wing was burning, the van was not...yet. The most intense section of fire was at the front of the wing, closer to the firefighters than to the van—but the position of the wing, wedged like it was, made it impossible for the firefighters to reach the vehicle because of the flames. They tried to see inside the van, but even from that distance, they had to shield their eyes from the blaze. Dani shifted to the side for a better angle. She was the first to see inside clearly.

Blood-covered deflated airbags in the front. Behind the wheel, a middle-aged man stirred. Next to him in the passenger seat was a middle-aged woman, blood oozing from a severe head wound. Her motionless body made it clear she was gone. In the far back row of the van, sitting all by herself, was a teenage girl. Maybe thirteen? She wore hot-pink headphones, her head resting at an unnatural angle. Like her mother, she was utterly motionless.

Dani called out to the other firefighters, "Adult female, front-seat passenger. Teenage female, back row, driver side. Both likely deceased. Driver is middle-aged male, alive. Badly injured—"

Dani stopped cold. She'd just gotten a good look at the middle of the van.

"Middle row. Bucket seat, passenger side," Dani said, her voice shaky. "Young child. Male." The little boy was too far away for Dani to hear him, but she knew what a four- or five-year-old's cries sounded like. "Alive."

Dani and the team sprinted for the truck.

Frankie was the first to the engine. He hopped into the driver's seat, put the truck in gear, and began positioning the rig as close to the bridge as he could. Dani and Boggs didn't wait for the engine to stop moving before they hoisted themselves up, grabbed their helmets, and started unloading the hose. Levon ran down the edge of the embankment toward the water to get as close as he could to the van, but he was still over twenty feet away.

"Sir!" he yelled to the man in the driver's seat, cupping his hands around his mouth. "Sir, can you hear me?"

The man behind the wheel looked up. Confused. Probably concussed. But his eyebrows raised slightly in acknowledgment, although Levon wondered if he was merely registering noises and lights around him.

"Sir, can you turn off the car?"

"Engine Forty-Two requesting foam trailer at the bridge off Route Seven near Carver Valley Elementary," Dani said into the radio at her shoulder as she hoisted a tightly folded hose onto her other arm. "Class B fire. Jet fuel and auto. Two victims, one adult, one child. Two survivors, one adult, one child."

"Sir! Can you—" Levon paused, taking the megaphone Boggs handed him. "Sir," he repeated, his voice projecting loudly across the river to the van. "Can you turn off the car?"

The man blinked at Levon a few times, then looked ahead as if it had just dawned on him that he was in a car. He reached forward, and a moment later the van's back wheels stopped spinning and Bono's voice stopped blaring out of the shattered driver's-side window. With that, the sound of the river rushing grew louder.

"That's great," Levon said. "Great. What's your name?"

The man thought for a second, then said something.

"Paul?" Levon tried, reading his lips. The man nodded. "Paul, we're gonna get you out of there. What do you—no. No, look at me, Paul. Stay with me, man. Paul, what do you do?"

"I...I'm..." Paul said, his voice faint and far away. Levon could barely hear him. "ER," Paul continued. "A doctor."

"Fantastic. Look, here's what we're going to do, Doc—no, look at me. Stay with me."

But Paul had seen her. He stared at his wife's lifeless body, dumbfounded. Levon watched as the gamut of emotions played out on Paul's face: disbelief, panic, grief, anger, more. He reached up for the rearview mirror, grimacing in pain, and angled it to the back. The horror of discovery played itself out all over again at the sight of his daughter.

Paul next tried to turn to check on his son, but the pain and the way he was pinned in made it difficult. Through wide, tear-filled eyes, the little boy watched his dad struggle. Levon could see Paul talking to his son, and the son seemed to be answering his dad, but Levon could barely hear what they were saying. After a moment, Paul stopped straining to see his son and faced forward, bowed his head, and cried.

At the rig, Frankie initiated the aqueous-film-forming foam pump. The faded yellow tube jerked to life and, seconds later, a dense white foam shot out of the hose in Dani's hands, raining down with precision on the base of the fire. Levon glanced at the other members of the crew. There was no need to talk. They all understood the situation. Until that fire was out, there was no conceivable way to reach Paul and his son.

Movement inside the van brought Levon back; looking over, he saw Paul's focus turn from his son to himself as he started to examine his own situation more closely.

"No, don't, Paul," Levon said. "Don't look down there. We'll get you out, then we'll handle it. Look at me. Stay with me, Doc."

Paul ignored Levon's pleas, checking out his legs before he explored the injuries on his torso. His hands worked with a doctor's precision across his abdomen and when he held them up a moment later, Levon could see the thick layer of dark red blood coating his fingers.

Levon raised the bullhorn to talk to Paul, but the doctor slowly shook his head. Paul was dying and he knew it. Now so did Levon.

Dani, still working the foam hose, witnessed this silent exchange between the two men and the back of her neck went numb.

She was about to watch this man live out her worst fear.

"Paul," Levon said. "Paul, listen, we're—"

But the man ignored Levon, the firefighters, the burning wing, and the river below and focused on the only thing that mattered anymore: his son. From his car seat, the boy cried, mouthing one word clearly over and over.

Mommy.

"Mommy's sleeping," Paul said to his son, his voice breaking. "It's okay, buddy. It's going to be okay."

Paul winced in agony, pressing his hands to his abdomen, trying to stanch the bleeding.

"Connor," Paul said to his son through clenched teeth. "Connor, this is important. You need to listen to the firemen. They're going to help you, but you need to listen. You need to do what they say. Can you do that? Can...can you..."

His tears slowing, Connor nodded, his mop of blond hair going up and down.

"I love you, buddy. I love you so much," Paul said to his son as his head began to droop. He slumped forward, rested his head on the wheel. "I'm...I'm going to sleep for a little bit too."

And with that, his eyes closed forever.

As the firefighters stared at the van, there was no longer a burning wing. There wasn't a plane crash. There was no seventeen-car pileup. No national catastrophe. There was no ticking clock counting down to an uncontrollable nuclear crisis.

There was only Connor.

There was only that one little boy.

CHAPTER TEN

COUNTDOWN TO ZERO HOUR

15 HOURS AND 27 MINUTES

"ASSUME EVERYTHING HERE can kill you," said Steve.

The Waketa Township ladder truck had finally arrived at the plant and the local firefighters were hanging on every word of Steve's briefing.

When someone says, *If you don't want to die, listen to me,* you typically listen.

"Don't sit. Don't lean. Don't touch," he continued. "There's no time to test what pieces of the rubble are radioactive and what's safe, so it's guilty till proven innocent today. No bare-skin contact. Masks on at all times. You're firefighters. You fight smoke and fire. Today's enemy is invisible. You can't see it or smell it. You have no idea where it is. Because of this, you might be tempted to think it's not that bad and you're not in danger. Let me be clear: It is, and you are. You might not regret it today. But if you let down your guard, I promise you that in a year or two when the doctor tells you it's cancer and there's nothing they can do, you'll regret it then."

The local firefighters were scared shitless and they looked it.

They should be, Steve thought as the image of Vinny in the truck bed flashed in his mind.

Steve shouted out assignments and directions; it was one of his men for every two of theirs. As they headed out, Chief Loftus's radio beeped.

"Engine Forty-Two calling in a second request for the foam trailer at the bridge off Route Seven near Carver Valley Elementary."

"Request denied, Forty-Two," Loftus said into the comms. "Our sole trailer is at the plant. Where you should be. Get here now."

"Sir, we have a situation."

"So do we, Dani," said Loftus. "A nuclear meltdown. Unless you can top that, you are needed here. I cannot authorize those resources for anything less. I told you today would be about tough choices. I'll make this choice for you. Get your engine to the plant, now."

Dani slammed the radio back into the holder.

They would be out of foam in minutes and the fire was nowhere close to extinguished. Water wasn't an option; it would only make the fuel-based fire spread. Foam was the only way to put it out—and every bit of foam in the county was going to the plant.

"Loftus denied the trailer request and ordered us to the plant," Dani said as she jogged back down to the crew.

The other firefighters stared in disbelief. That denial was a death sentence for the boy.

"He wants us to just leave the kid?" Levon said.

"He wants us to help stop a nuclear meltdown," said Frankie.

"Yeah, by abandoning a little kid who needs us."

"Lee, c'mon. Waketa's only got one truck, one ladder, one trailer. And one nuclear disaster."

"But federal help will come for them," Dani said. "The plant will get what it needs. Connor will get nothing. No one's coming for him. We leave now, we know exactly what happens to the boy."

"And if we stay, then what?" Frankie shot back. "You know we can't do shit with that fire burning, and we have no way to put it out. A plane's fuel tanks are in the wings. You know that, right? That was a big plane. Needs a lot of fuel. That wing seems to have plenty left to burn. And the other wing, by the way—where is it? Burning up a nuclear power plant? Fuck me, Chief. Keep the foam trailer there, we're on our way. How is it anything besides that?"

"I'm not leaving Connor," Dani said.

"That's not your call!"

"I'm not going either," Levon said.

Frankie couldn't believe what he was hearing. "Forget the fact that you're disobeying a direct order. You're saying that one life, one kid, is as important as everyone else's combined. 'Cause you get it, right? You do get the stakes? Nuclear meltdown?"

"Take the truck, then," Levon said. "If you want to walk away, take the truck."

"It's not about what I want to do! It's about what we have to do! We go, I will never sleep at night. I know this. I will watch his dad die over and over again while I hear the boy call out for his mom, and I will rot inside like the spineless piece of shit I am. But a nuclear power plant is burning. We have no choice."

Infighting was unusual for them. They all looked at one another, not sure where to go from here. Especially because none of them was wrong.

"Boggs. What's your call?" Dani asked the rookie. "We go, we know what happens here. We stay, we *still* may not be able to get to him, and it probably means our jobs."

"And to be fair, it could mean the fate of the whole country too," Levon added, extending a hand to Frankie, who nodded.

Boggs listened, never turning his attention from the wing. "I'll do whatever you decide," he said as the foam began to sputter out of the hose. "But I became a firefighter to help people. If a single life isn't enough to qualify, this isn't the job I signed up for."

The other three looked at one another.

Frankie swore under his breath. "All right. Let's get the kid out."

Steve stood under a stream of hot water watching his skin turn pink as he scrubbed the bar of soap against his arm. Body scoured, he quickly lathered shampoo into his hair and leaned his head back. He closed his eyes and mouth as whatever poisons he might've come in contact with slid down the drain. There was no conditioner in the decontamination zone. Conditioner made radioactive material stick to your hair.

The wet, clear plastic walls of the temporary shower blurred what was happening on the other side, but he could still make out the plant workers in full head-to-toe hazmat suits hosing down his turnout gear just outside the improvised emergency station. Ninety percent of radioactive material could be eliminated just by removing your outer layer of clothing and washing your skin.

The other ten percent wasn't as easy to shed.

Survivability of an event like this came down to several factors: the length of time one was exposed to radiation, one's proximity to said radiation, and the potency of the radiation. The strategy was to avoid exposure if you could, protect yourself when you couldn't, and then clean it off quickly after the fact.

Whatever happened beyond that was out of your control.

As he shut off the water, a soft-toned *ding* rang out, followed by the sound of a throat clearing.

"All right, everyone." Ethan's voice came over the PA through every speaker at the plant. *"We've got our bearings. We know a baseline. Time to act. Here's what we have working for us: It was an isolated event. It wasn't an earthquake with aftershocks. There's no tsunami coming. We don't know for sure, but we're assuming there're no more planes crashing."*

"Because they'd be shot down before they ever got the chance," Steve said to no one, toweling off.

"The incident is over. These are our conditions. Whatever's working is working. We have stabilized the plant."

Steve pulled a clean, plant-issued sweatsuit off the stack as Ethan continued. The men didn't know each other well, didn't interact much. Steve stayed in the firehouse; Ethan stayed in the control room. They came together at quarterly meetings or the occasional training session, but that was it. He wondered how it would go between them the rest of the day.

"Any nonessential personnel still on-site are to evacuate the plant immediately. Essential personnel, if you are at an undamaged portion of the plant, leave a skeleton crew of minimum viable operators to ensure things continue running smoothly, but beyond that, every engineer, technician, operator—every spare brain in this plant—is to report to R2 control to work the problems we are facing."

Steve pulled the sweatshirt on over his head and stepped into some disposable sandal slides. He was heading for the door when

Ethan concluded, *"We're going to figure this out. We're going to get through this. For our plant, our community, and for our families."*

Steve stopped in his tracks.

Damn it.

He'd been doing so well. He'd shut it out, *all of it*. It wasn't that Matt and Claire hadn't come to mind. He'd been thinking of his son and his wife constantly. But every time they did, he immediately compartmentalized—and they slipped away. He made himself busy, replacing his grief and worry with some task, some protocol, some procedure. He'd become a master at compartmentalization. He'd had to. It was the only way he'd been able to survive the past sixteen months since Claire died.

Steve thought about Matt, wondered where he was. Was he okay? Was he scared? Steve shut his eyes. *Don't. Focus. The school has protocols. They have emergency-preparedness plans. Trust it. Let it go. They got him. He's fine.* That was his new mantra: *Trust it. Trust it. Trust it.*

But as he stood there in the quiet hall outside the decontamination zone, without a crew to protect or a fire to fight, the thought of his only child was too potent to shut out.

Since his mom had passed, Matt hadn't been able to compartmentalize like his dad. Matt was eleven, and although the boy liked to think that was full-grown, he was just a child. A child in pain. Matt didn't need protocols. He needed tenderness, love, vulnerability, attention—everything Claire had given him. On his best days, Steve was hardly capable of accessing those things for himself. How was he supposed to share them with his boy?

Since Claire's death, Steve felt constantly in over his head. He had no idea how to be a single father, how to be both mom and dad. He had no idea how to process his own grief or understand his own feelings. How in the world was he supposed to help Matt do it?

Every day, Steve just wanted to hit pause on everything and scream as loud as he could, *I don't know!* It was all moving too fast; if he could just pause it all, he could figure it out. But that wasn't possible. So, instead, he compartmentalized and just kept going.

Steve knew it wouldn't work in the long term. Matt's acting out was the first warning that the ways they were getting by were unsustainable. But Steve also knew that in order to make his way through this grief, this pain, he would have to ask for help. And while Steve was great at many things, asking for help was not one of them.

Steve hustled to the R2 control room, but when he turned a corner, he stopped in his tracks. Members of the plant's emergency response team in charge of on-site medical had set up rooms for the injured. Steve and his crews had assisted many of the people who had been transported there—people who were hit with debris or injured in the impact. But so far, only one person Steve knew of needed to be treated for radiation exposure.

Steve peered through the glass pane in the door at Vinny, alone, stretched out on a bed, eyes swollen shut. If someone had told Steve how quickly the radiation would take hold, he wouldn't have believed it. The bright red skin. The oozing blisters. The moaning in pain. It was the pictures from training brought to life *that* fast. It was only when Steve heard footsteps approaching that he turned away.

Steve headed down the hall and thought again of Claire. Of her lying in the hospital bed, tubes twisting in and out of her body, as the staff did everything they could to fight the cancer. Compared to Vinny's suffering, her death seemed almost merciful.

Almost.

"—then. Let's focus."

Ethan was organizing the troops as Steve walked into the control room. The two men acknowledged each other.

"We got two major issues we need to solve," Ethan said. "One:

How do we fix the structural leaks in the spent fuel pool? Two: Do we vent the accumulating hydrogen in the pool's containment building? We do not have time to work these problems individually. They will be worked simultaneously. Every person in this room is smart enough to figure this out. Every person in this room is trained and qualified to be here. Every person in this room *will* contribute. Got it?"

Heads nodded.

Ethan split the room into two groups. "Steve, you're with pool damage. You guys are Red Team. Me and Joss are on venting; we're Blue Team. Red Team, head to the training classroom on the first floor. Blue Team, stay here."

And with that, they all went to their groups, focused and motivated.

"All right," Ethan said to the Blue Team while the Red Team filed out. "The white smoke and whether or not we vent is the biggest problem. Because if we get that wrong, the pool damage won't matter. We will have already lost the whole plant and the town."

CHAPTER ELEVEN

COUNTDOWN TO ZERO HOUR

15 HOURS AND 19 MINUTES

CARLA COULDN'T BELIEVE she was leading two children into a nuclear power plant while it was melting down.

She and the kids sat quietly in the cab as they watched Marion cross through the tall weeds and overgrown grass to an abandoned security shed. "Stay here," Marion had said moments earlier before slipping a breathing mask over his head and getting out of the truck. Now Carla watched as he tried the shed's door handle, then put his hands up to the glass to peer inside.

"Where are we?" Brianna asked, her voice sounding bigger in the small space of the cab.

Carla shook her head. Obviously, they were at Clover Hill, but this was a way she'd never been and didn't even know existed. The better question was *why* were they here?

She watched Marion try to lift the security gate's lowered arm, but it barely budged. Taking a Leatherman from his pocket, he crouched in front of the post where the arm connected and forced open a pressure-fit plate. Sticking the end of one of the tools inside, he jiggled and twisted. Eventually, the arm dropped a couple inches as the restraining gear released. Standing, Marion tried the gate again. This time, it began to lift with ease.

"Scoot," Carla said, lifting Brianna off her lap to switch sides with Matt so she could get behind the wheel. She shifted the truck into drive as Marion lifted the gate up over his head. But as she inched the vehicle forward, it was obvious Marion alone wouldn't be able to lift it high enough to clear the truck. Carla backed up. Marion lowered the arm and put his hands on his hips, thinking.

"Matt," Carla said, reading Marion's gaze into the cab. "Do you know how to drive?"

A few minutes later, Carla was outside in a mask and rubber gloves and Matt was behind the wheel looking entirely too pleased with himself. Brianna stood with her hands on the dash, talking a mile a minute, probably reciting the rules Carla made Matt swear to before she got out.

"Marion, *what* are we doing here?" Carla hissed, joining Marion at the gate, the first chance they'd had to speak alone.

"It's the safest place—"

"*Here?*" she said, the frustration and incredulity making her voice rise. "*At* the plant?"

"Will you trust me?"

"But we've got the kids! We've got *Brianna,* Marion! You've taken us *to* the problem. In what way could that possibly—"

"Trust me!" Marion's voice boomed, even with the mask muffling his words.

Carla glanced over her shoulder and saw both kids staring wordlessly, watching the adults argue. She turned her back to them and lowered her voice. "Marion, we need to evacuate. We need to get them away from here."

"To where? To sit in traffic? With the truck running out of gas when we can't get more? I *am* protecting my granddaughter. I am protecting my family," Marion said, pointing at Carla. "You *know* that. Now trust it."

The two adults stared at each other for a moment before Carla ended the conversation by joining Marion's side.

Adjusting her grip on the gate's arm, she gave a nod, at which point Marion counted down, then they both lifted the barrier together, slowly working their leverage down the arm until it was raised all the way up. Holding the gate's arm high above their heads, the adults nodded to Matt, and the Dodge slowly rolled forward. Once it cleared, Carla and Marion lowered the arm back down and hustled over to the truck. Carla went to open the passenger side, but the door was locked.

"Matt, c'mon," she said, her voice muffled by the mask. Matt grinned mischievously and the truck began rolling forward. "Matt!" she said again as Brianna jumped up and down. After the Dodge made a few more stops and starts, Marion's glare finally convinced Matt to put the truck in park. As the adults piled back in, Carla scolded Matt, but not half as hard as Brianna did. Marion, though, was hiding a smile.

As they drove down the plant's back forty, the looming pillars of black smoke got closer.

"Is Mommy here?" Brianna asked. "Is that where we're going? To see her?"

Neither of the adults answered right away. They had no idea where Dani and Levon were, but the child didn't understand that no answer *was* the answer.

"You know, I don't know where your mom is," Carla said in a faux-casual tone. Were they here? Were Dani and Levon at the plant too, in the thick of it, being exposed to who knew what?

"I hope not," said Bri. "Granddaddy, you always said if she was called to the plant, it was because something bad happened."

Marion didn't say anything.

"If something bad happened, then why are we here?" Matt asked.

Carla honestly didn't know, so she didn't say anything—but it struck a nerve. Matt's question echoed what she said to Levon whenever they discussed raising a family in Waketa:

If it's possible that something could happen at the plant, why would we raise our children here? How could we knowingly put them in that kind of danger?

The answer was complicated. This was where they were from. Where they knew people, where their roots were. They were happy here. This was home.

Beyond that, *they* had been raised here. And nothing bad *had* ever happened at the plant; who's to say it ever would? Sure, it was a risk—but what were the odds?

Plus, if they did leave, where would they go? They'd have to start all over. Who would they know in this new place? What kind of community would be there, what kind of support would they have?

The conversation always went round and round, both sides being valid, with neither Carla nor Levon willing to take a firm stand either way. But if they were honest, they knew their discussions were more hypothetical than anything. Because the truth was, a move to a city bigger than Waketa would cost money. Money they didn't have.

Carla knew if she got pregnant—*when* she got pregnant, she

corrected herself—they'd simply have to live with the doubt, fear, and guilt of staying because the bottom line was clear.

They couldn't afford to leave even if they wanted to.

After a few more moments of driving along the trees, Marion cleared his throat.

"We designed this place during the Cold War. And Japan, the Cuban missile thing, they weren't so long before." He paused to glance over at the kids, seeming to understand they had no idea what any of that meant. "Well, at the time, it didn't feel too long before. Anyway. We designed an underground system, a network of bunkers."

Marion turned left. Up ahead, Carla noticed a rusty door in the middle of a concrete structure built into the natural contours of a hill in a wooded area. To anyone not looking closely, it was just another foliage-covered hill.

"The idea was short-term protection," he said. "Somewhere to go, just for a bit, while everything settled down. Somewhere *safe*, not caught up in the panic of evacuation traffic. Somewhere to be while officials figured out what had happened and what to do about it." He paused and glanced over at Carla. She gave a barely discernible nod. "But," Marion continued, "time went on. No attacks came. Public fear eased. And so Clover Hill decided the budget for the bunkers didn't make sense."

He parked the truck in front of the door, turned it off, and glanced around the area, the engine clicking as it cooled.

"We got only one of them built. Never used it either," Marion said, looking through his janitor-style ring of keys. "I'd be willing to bet most of the people working at the plant nowadays don't even know this place exists. Which is why"—Marion held up a key—"they never asked for the key back when I turned in my badge."

* * *

"Why are we discussing this as if there's a choice?" Joss said, her frustration starting to show. "We don't have options. We do everything we can to make sure that pool doesn't ignite. *That* is our option. Public perception, panic, a few people who may or may not get cancer down the line — it doesn't matter. Not when you consider the alternative."

"It matters to the people who work at this plant. The ones who are at highest risk," Ethan said, the calm in his voice trying to counter the rising anxiety in hers.

It had taken all of three minutes for the Blue Team's measured conversation to turn combative.

"I agree with Joss," said Vikram.

"You're fine with releasing a radioactive plume into the atmosphere?" said Maggie.

"Of course not," he said. "But I am when I consider the alternative."

"Exactly," said Joss.

"But we don't even know that enough hydrogen would collect to create an explosion," countered Ethan.

"And you're willing to take that chance?"

"Let's say we do vent," Maggie said. "We issue an official evacuation order. Panic ensues. We go from a controlled incident to an actual accident. And *that* is a whole different scenario for the public. Plus, we officially have radioactive exposure, with all the downwind effects. When, maybe, if we don't vent, the hydrogen levels stay manageable, and there's no panic, no radioactivity, no explosion at all. It's all fine."

"Or," Vikram countered, "the levels *do* become unmanageable, the building blows, and then we sure as fuck are releasing radioactive material. Except now, it's an uncontrolled release."

"Without having an evacuation already started," Joss said.

"Exactly."

"So it's risk management," Maggie said. "Do nothing, it might be okay. Do something, we for sure vent radiation into the atmosphere, but we limit the damage and fallout."

"Again, the risks don't matter," said Joss. "The pool is the priority. It *is* the whole ball game."

"There's a bigger picture, Joss," Ethan said.

"Ethan. The bigger picture doesn't exist if we get this wrong. You know this."

As Joss and Ethan stared at each other, she wondered how they could possibly be having this argument. She was used to people not getting it. She'd spent fifteen years in Washington being on the losing end of the "low-probability, high-consequence" debate with bureaucrats and businessmen who were more concerned with re-election or the bottom line than public safety. She was used to being dismissed as an alarmist. She was accustomed to the perverse mentality that big risks were fine, a nuclear meltdown be damned. Because the counterargument was always *What are the odds such an unlikely scenario will ever happen?* Well, it was happening right before their eyes.

She'd accepted that some people — many people — wouldn't get it. But she'd never imagined Ethan would be one of them.

How many nights as undergrads had they spent howling at the moon? In their particularly nerdy, ideologically pure, long-winded railings, they'd ranted against a system that refused to address its own vulnerabilities. They had been idealists, kids of a nuclear community, born in the shadow of Clover Hill. They'd been raised in awe of the potential for good in nuclear power. A limitless source of clean energy that protected the environment while lifting their community, the country, the world. A way out of the country's reliance on foreign oil. An alternative to carbon-emitting fossil fuels. Nuclear wasn't the problem; it was the solution.

They weren't idiots. Of course they knew nuclear came with risks. They were fifth-graders when Chernobyl happened. They understood exactly what could happen if something went wrong. So the answer—at least according to the voices of influence they heard around their respective dinner tables and in the drugstore checkout line and from the teachers talking in the hallway at school—was not to be like the Soviets. They would do it right. The answer was to respect the risks and address them from the start. Regulate appropriately so Clover Hill would never become a Chernobyl.

For most people, Three Mile Island and Chernobyl introduced fear. For Joss and Ethan, the incidents merely added another layer of respect to an industry, an idea, they had already been taught to revere. The problem wasn't nuclear. The problem was the system. The people in charge who weren't willing to pay what it cost to ensure the worst never came to pass. A small price to pay, Joss and Ethan assumed, if you considered the alternative. With the right people convinced, the future would be secure.

They had been naive. She saw that now. She'd had no idea how impossible it would be for common sense to outweigh profits. They'd been *hopelessly* naive.

But they weren't wrong.

There was a difference.

And despite the diverging paths their lives had taken, Joss had always assumed Ethan knew that.

"Joss," Ethan said. "You don't get to decide what is small enough to sacrifice for the greater good."

"Then who does?" she snapped. The question hung unanswered.

"No, I'm asking, Ethan. What other room has people sitting around making these calls? It *is* up to us."

"Then we make the decision together—"

"*What* decision? Ethan. It's as—"

"Damn it, Joss!" Ethan smacked the table. "You may be the smartest person in the room, but you are not the only smart person in the room."

The door opened and a woman from the emergency response communications team stuck her head in. She held out a satellite phone to Joss, the palm of her hand covering the mouthpiece.

"Dr. Vance? You're needed to do a briefing."

"Like fuck you want me talking to the press."

"It's the president. You'll be briefing the president."

President Dawson along with everyone else in the bunker Situation Room watched the screens in silence. The images spoke for themselves.

"*It's Coastal…we…please help. He's dead. The captain's dead. He had a medical, I think a heart attack. The FO's in the lav. He's not here. He's…the pilots are gone!*"

There was so much fear in the flight attendant's voice as it came over the PA and through the cabin in the now-viral videos the passengers of Flight 235 had posted and live-streamed on their social media accounts as the plane went down. One heartbreaking moment after another played out in surreal real time, the entire crash captured for the whole world to see.

The destruction in the cabin. The parts of the aircraft as they broke off, flying past windows. The beverage cart careening down the aisle. The first officer pounding on the cockpit door. The door opening. The captain's body. The ground getting closer...and closer...and closer. And all the while in the background, the passengers were doing the only things they could do: scream, pray, beg, profess, atone, forgive.

"We're going down. Please help us!"

President Dawson turned his attention to the plant's security-camera feed, which was no less harrowing: The wing clipping the power line. The plane cartwheeling. The resulting damage. The debris field. There was no doubt in his mind that the first officer had tried to pilot the plane away from the plant.

No terror group had claimed responsibility. None of the intelligence agencies had found any indication that the crash was anything but an accident. Every plane in the domestic airspace had been accounted for. And the footage from the plane was the final convincing piece. This was a human tragedy, but it was *not* a terrorist attack.

"Mr. President?" said the deputy national security adviser. "Homeland Security and the FAA are advising we pull the nationwide ground stop."

"Agreed," said Dawson, clearing his throat as he turned from the images. "Tony. I want to see the statement."

The chief of staff looked up from his call with the speechwriters and gave a thumbs-up.

"Mr. President?" said another staffer. "I have the NEST contact at the plant for you. Line three."

Joss waited in the empty hallway, listening to the silence on the other end of the line and thinking about the cup of coffee, half drunk, still sitting on her kitchen table next to the morning paper, half read.

That morning when she'd heard the distant *boom*, she'd been worried. In her gut, she knew it was bad. But she'd had no idea it would be waiting-to-talk-to-the-president bad.

"Ms. Vance."

The deep baritone was instantly recognizable. "Mr. President," Joss replied.

"Where are we at?"

Joss gave him the rundown from their angle, assuming she wouldn't need to explain things people had no doubt already briefed him on. His silence affirmed that; he listened intently, seeming to absorb the information on the plant damage, the spent fuel pool, and the ramifications of the damage. He only interrupted once she began discussing the debate on what to do about the white smoke coming from the spent fuel pool building.

"What happens if you don't vent?" he asked.

"Potentially nothing," she replied.

"Or potentially…"

"You know the *Hindenburg*?"

"Yes."

"That."

"Plus radioactive material."

"That too."

The president was quiet. Then he said: "Ms. Vance, do you have children?"

"Ah…sir?" she said, not expecting that. "No. No, I don't."

"Me neither."

"I know. That's why I voted for you."

When he didn't laugh, Joss immediately regretted her comment. Before she could backtrack, Ethan poked his head out of the control room.

"We're venting" was all he said before disappearing back into the room.

"Did you—" Joss started.

"I heard," said Dawson. "What are the next steps?"

"We issue a formal evacuation declaration for the plume zone."

"How large is that?"

"Based on anticipated radiation levels and wind patterns, we're calling it fifteen miles."

"Make it twenty."

Joss was stopped cold. Never, not once in her twenty-year career, had she encountered a politician who wanted to *exceed* a recommended health and safety guideline. "Yes, sir."

"I understand I-35 is completely shut down in both directions."

Joss shrugged. "I'm here. You know more than me."

"Are there suitable alternates for evacuation routes?"

"Does your staff know how to use Google?"

She could tell in the silence that followed that President Michael Dawson wasn't used to being talked to like that. Now, whether that was good or bad, *that* she couldn't tell.

"Fair point" was all he said. "What kind of time frame are we looking at?"

"They're probably issuing the evacuation order as we speak. We'll need to do minor preparations, then we go. I imagine we'll vent in approximately twenty minutes."

"I'm making an address in five. Have your comms team send my chief of staff details and talking points, and I'll reinforce the evacuation order. After that, I'll find an intern for all my googleable questions. And, Ms. Vance, I want regular updates from here on out."

"Yes, sir."

"Ms. Vance?"

"Yes, sir?"

"Do you have a favorite president?"

She paused. "This feels like a trap."

"Mine's Kennedy. Seventh-grade social studies, we all had to choose a president to do a project on. I chose JFK, and that was it. My whole life decided right there in Mrs. Knapp's third period. I was blown away. His vision. His boldness. What he accomplished. The leader he was. How he went after hard policies, no matter how unpopular they were, no matter the cost. He was my superhero. He was *exactly* what I wanted to be when I grew up. Even his assassination—I mean, I was an amped-up seventh-grade boy. I thought, *Well, not everyone will like what you're doing. Sometimes, progress and change come at a price.*"

Joss glanced at the clock on the wall, wondering where this was going. Any other day she would have loved a casual retrospective therapy session with the leader of the free world—especially after that whole *Make it twenty* executive flex. But right now, she should be elsewhere doing more important things. Namely, preventing a nuclear meltdown.

"I remember being in the library when I found the picture of John-John saluting the casket," he continued. "Caroline, she was right there too. Everyone in the picture wore black. But the kids were in those red shoes and those matching powder-blue jackets. And I thought—how silly. That they dressed them like that. As if people didn't already get that they were just innocent little kids. I'm the oldest of five, and when I found that picture, my younger brother and sister were the exact same ages as Caroline and John were in '63. And I thought of the idea of them, my brother and sister there, like that. And I just remember thinking...*Why'd he do that to them?*"

Kennedy, Joss thought. *Not Oswald. He means their father.*

"I've read your file, Ms. Vance. I know the work you were trying to do here in Washington. Something tells me we're more similar than you might think."

"As I said, Mr. President," Joss said, "it's why I voted for you."

She sensed the president nodding in agreement. He said, "I've got four years to do some good. Eight if I'm lucky. After that, I want kids. I want a great big family, just like the one I grew up in."

Now Joss was nodding. "Yes, Mr. President. And I will do everything possible to make sure we have a world you'd want to bring them into."

Carla sneezed as she folded up another dusty white cloth. This one had been covering a small couch next to a midcentury-modern parquet coffee table. It was the last dustcover, and looking around the space, she couldn't help but marvel at how much the bunker was like stepping back in time.

There were two bedrooms with four bunk beds in each. A small bathroom with a tub shower, pedestal sink, and toilet. Two large pantries. One had medicine, toiletries, and first-aid supplies—including potassium iodide, which they'd all immediately taken. The other was stocked with shelf-stable food that had expired twenty years ago. A small gas stove was the only appliance in a tidy kitchenette besides a large water-filtration system. And on the opposite side of the modest living room was a built-in desk that ran the entire length of the wall. The shelves were full of various devices and electronics, and as Marion fiddled with them, one would occasionally beep or light up.

Matt stuck his finger in and out of the VCR, pushing the little plastic flap up and down. In one of the bedrooms, Brianna sat down on a lower bunk as though considering what a night's sleep there would be like. Carla knew the novelty would wear off quickly for the kids and she looked around for anything they might enjoy—books or crayons or toys, anything—but idle young hands clearly weren't considered in the bunker's design. Before she could figure out what to do about this, though, the room crackled with static.

"Hot dog," Marion said to himself.

"What is that?" Brianna asked.

"This," Marion said, fiddling with dials as the static went in and out, "is the plant's old communications system. If I can find the right wavelength, there's a radio-based plant-wide emergency line that connects all the different zones, put in place in case the phone lines ever went down. This was before cell towers, when landlines were the only phones."

"So it's like a CB party line?" said Matt.

Marion and Carla turned, surprised, although they shouldn't have been. Matt was a tech-obsessed kid who'd grown up in farm country, where old-school gadgetry like ham radios and citizens band radios were still commonly used.

"Yes, it works like a CB party line. Very good," Marion said.

They all stood there expectantly while Marion continued to fiddle with dials and knobs. The most use Marion would get out of a smartphone would be as a coaster. But this? Marion was in his element.

"Does anyone copy?" he asked, holding down the button on a handheld microphone. But no one answered, not even after multiple attempts. The excitement wore off quickly. After a while, Matt flopped down on the couch with a bored sigh.

"Miss Carla," said Brianna, "I'm hungry."

"All right, let's see what we got..." Carla crossed to the large pantry with the little girl and began checking it out. "Expired in 2002, expired in 2006, expired—"

A thumping noise made them both spin, but it was just Matt absently picking up the leg of the coffee table and letting it drop.

"Hey, now!" Carla said, turning back to the pantry. "This one's still good. How does meat loaf sound?"

The little girl stared blankly at the nearly twenty-year-old card board box in Carla's hand. Matt let the table drop down again with a thump.

"I agree," Carla said, putting the meat loaf box back on a shelf and digging deeper into the pantry. "There's got to be peanut butter or something…"

"Does anyone read?" Marion asked into the radio.

Thump. Matt again.

Marion pressed the mic's button again. "This is the emergency bunker. Does anyone—"

Thump.

"Matt, please!"

"Knock it off!"

Both adults snapped at Matt at the same time. He stared up at the ceiling—but he didn't drop the table again. Carla kept looking for food. Marion continued twisting dials. Suddenly, crackly voices came over the speaker.

"*—within minutes.*"

"*So if we don't do that, when the vent starts—*"

"Dad!" Matt said, jumping up off the couch. "That's my dad!"

Marion shushed him as they all circled around to listen to the radio. Matt's dad and the other voices were discussing the next steps of whatever they were about to attempt; who was going to do what, how, and when. Carla tried to follow.

"So," she said, "they're going to vent the built-up gases to avoid a potential explosion, but when they do, what they vent into the air will be radioactive?"

Marion nodded. "Correct."

"So how are they telling everyone to evacuate?" she said.

Carla and the kids looked at Marion, but he had no answer.

"They won't know," she said. "There's no power, no TV. There's barely any cell service. There may be none now. How are people going to know about the radioactive cloud?" Carla thought of the school bus filled with students and her colleagues. She thought of the businesses on Main Street. All the families and homes around the community. The voices continued to talk over the radio, but she was no longer listening.

Then it clicked. She pointed at the radio.

"Is there a radio like this one at the plant, one that can reach the community?"

Marion considered, quickly catching up to where she was going. He wheeled the desk chair down to another stack of equipment and turned a few dials; red and green lights lit up next to digital read-outs. "Yes," he said. "CB. Like Matt said. We can talk to any farmers listening—"

"School buses have CB too—" Carla said.

"We get them to spread the word to tune in to that channel—"

"Then we feed them regular updates from here, from what we hear over the plant's radio. They spread it via word of mouth and any text messages they can get through. This is it, Marion!" Carla said, pulling up a chair next to his. "This is how we help."

"Okay," said Marion. "Then we need to figure out how to—"

"Where's Matt?" Bri asked, facing the room, her back to the adults.

Carla and Marion spun around.

Matt wasn't there.

"Matt," Carla said, her voice rising as she went from room to room. "Matt, c'mon." Back in the big room, she found Marion closing a closet. He shook his head.

"His backpack's gone," said Brianna from the entryway. They

both hurried to the door leading up to the surface and found the little girl looking up the stairs at where they'd left their hazmat gear. Carla pulled Bri away so she could see. There, at the top of the stairs where their masks were hanging, was an empty spot.

Matt's mask was gone.

CHAPTER TWELVE

COUNTDOWN TO ZERO HOUR

14 HOURS AND 52 MINUTES

PRESIDENT DAWSON NEEDED to project strength to three hundred million Americans when, in truth, he was terrified.

"My fellow Americans, good evening."

He'd gotten used to delivering speeches before large crowds in grand rooms with ornate decor. Now the room was empty but for his chief of staff and an aide. The room was small—one camera, no teleprompter. The presidential seal hung on the wall behind him, but beyond that, there was nothing but the chair he sat in; not even a desk to lean forward on. There were no reporters to ask follow-up questions; he had no way to gauge reactions. It was a moment stripped down to its very essence: One man talking to a nation.

"Today, the unthinkable happened," he began. "We lost two hundred and ninety-five souls in a tragic plane crash, and my heart goes out to their families and friends who know all too well what beauty and joy was taken from this world in their passing. By now, you've likely seen the videos and messages circulating online and in the media from some who were on the flight. It's hard to watch. I cannot imagine the fear and pain those aboard must have felt. I am sorry their loved ones have had to see it. But it was ultimately a gift to us all and I am grateful to them. By bearing witness, they showed us *exactly* what happened on that plane and why it went down, removing all speculation and second-guessing."

President Dawson paused.

"Flight Two-Three-Five's captain suffered a medical emergency at thirty-five thousand feet and became incapacitated immediately. Control of the aircraft was lost at that time. The rest of the crew was not able to regain control. As a result, the plane crashed. It is that simple, that tragic. That is what happened."

He leaned forward, placing his elbows on his knees, interlocking his fingers.

"This was not an act of terrorism. Firsthand accounts we've all seen from those on the flight confirm this, as does all intelligence from the CIA, the FBI, the NSA, Homeland Security, and initial reporting from the NTSB. This was *not* an attack on our nation. This was an isolated event. This was an accident.

"We did not know that in the beginning. At that time, we knew nothing. And with what little we *did* know, I made the decision to ground all commercial aircraft nationwide. I do not regret it, even if in hindsight it might seem extreme. I do not and will never take any of your lives for granted. But considering what we *do* now know,

I am lifting the nationwide ground stop on all air traffic. It is safe to fly."

He paused again, letting that sink in.

"The tragedy of the crash should be enough pain and trauma for a nation for one day," he continued, sitting upright, placing the palms of his hands on his knees. "But unfortunately, my fellow Americans, we are being tested further.

"Coastal Airways Flight Two-Thirty-Five crashed about fifty miles north of Minneapolis, Minnesota, in the small town of Waketa. The debris field and damage done to that community is extensive—but the brunt of the plane's impact was delivered to the Clover Hill nuclear power plant. Let me be clear: There has *not* been a reactor breach. I repeat, none of the reactors are open. The air quality in the surrounding areas is currently within EPA standards. But significant damage to the facilities *has* occurred, and on-site at Clover Hill, there *is* atmospheric radioactivity that exceeds EPA standards.

"In order to maintain control of the situation, the staff at Clover Hill are taking important preemptive steps. Listen closely. In the next twenty minutes"—Dawson pulled up his sleeve and checked his watch—"that's...approximately two p.m. eastern, one p.m. central, eleven a.m. Pacific—Clover Hill will be venting built-up hydrogen gas from one of its auxiliary buildings. This is a necessary preventive step to ensure continued safe plant operation. But as a result, the level of atmospheric radioactivity for Waketa *will* exceed EPA standards. Earlier, Governor Koerner declared a state of emergency for Minnesota. I am now declaring a national state of emergency and am issuing a mandatory evacuation order for all citizens of Waketa and anyone within a twenty-mile radius of the plant.

"As you are planning your route, be advised," he continued, taking a note from his pocket, "a seventeen-car pileup has closed I-35 at Appamatok to all traffic in both directions. Avoid this area—you *will* get stuck in traffic. Instead, to go east, take Bugle Road to Hubbard into Big Falls. To go west, Medena Line Road to State Route Nine into Maple Grove."

Dawson folded the note. "Now, let me be clear," he continued. "If you are outside of the evacuation zone, there is no need to leave. Please stay where you are and do not clog the roads. Out of an abundance of caution, shelter in place with your windows closed. But please keep the roads clear so those in the evacuation zone can get out."

His mind flashed to the snapshot details of this town that had been on the monitors in the bunker Situation Room. Small town, Main Street people. Their whole lives turned upside down. They didn't ask for this. This was so unfair.

"If you *are* inside the twenty-mile radius, please, do not panic. Simply gather your loved ones and evacuate. This is mandatory. This is for your own safety. And your safety will remain paramount for all of us today. We are with you. You are not alone."

The people of Waketa were on their own.

A small group of neighbors gathered in the street comparing notes, floating theories, wondering what would come next. They were in a blackout. The only thing everyone knew for sure was that there had been a loud *boom* and everything shook, then the power went out, and then, a little bit later, the sirens came on. Any other details were sketchy.

There were rumors about a plane crash; some said they'd seen the plane. And supposedly there was a huge pileup on I-35, and something was wrong at the plant. But those bits were all unconfirmed hearsay, blanks filled in by word of mouth.

Because in reality, no one knew what had happened. No one

knew they were in imminent danger. And no one knew they were supposed to evacuate.

"Where's Rand?" asked Rand's next-door neighbor.

Rand's wife, with their ten-month-old on her hip, pointed west. "Took the truck to see if anyone needed help. He swears what he heard was a jet engine."

"But that big? That'd be a *big* plane."

"Well, did he find anyone? Was it a plane?" asked another neighbor.

Rand's wife shrugged. "You got a phone that works? He hasn't come back, so..." She shrugged again.

"Ginny, I found it!"

Everyone turned. Across the street, LeRoy came down his front-porch steps, leafing through the wall calendar Clover Hill sent out each January to every Waketa household. In the back of the calendar were several pages of important information on what to do in the event of a plant accident.

"Well, what's it say?" Ginny asked her husband.

"Says...it says the PNS, prompt notification system, should tell us—"

"That's that text thing they send out," said Rand's wife. "We can't get texts."

"It says here, 'If you hear the sirens, it could only be a test. The first Wednesday of every month'...no, that's not it," LeRoy muttered, skimming for anything that would be actually useful.

"Well, if we do have to evacuate," Ginny said, "our car's low on gas."

Rand's wife shifted the baby to her other hip. "Oh, and there's no power—"

"Mm-hmm," Ginny said, nodding. "No power, no pumps. We wouldn't make it halfway to Big Falls."

"Okay. Okay, here," LeRoy said, holding the calendar up. "Says 'Hearing a siren does not mean you should evacuate. It means turn on your television and listen for instructions.'"

"But we don't have TV. Here, give me that."

Ginny took the calendar from her husband, and the neighbors read it over her shoulder, trying to make sense of what to do. Suddenly, up the street, Rand's truck came flying around the corner, practically on two wheels. They watched him tear up the street and come to a screeching stop in the middle of the road; a cloud of dust followed a second later.

"What happened?" his wife asked, frightened by the expression on Rand's face as he rolled down the window, waving for everyone to come close. He put his finger across his lips for them to keep quiet and turned up the volume, and a deep, calm voice with a slow, methodical drawl came out of the truck's CB radio.

"...*medications. Government-issued IDs. Anything your family may need and can't get elsewhere. Turn off all lights, appliances, and water. As you leave, tie a white towel or cloth on your front door. Emergency workers will see this and know everyone in your house has left. The order is for twenty miles in all directions...*"

Wide-eyed and slack-jawed, everyone listened to the instructions Marion laid out. Instructions that confirmed their worst fears. The neighbors immediately scattered to their homes to get ready to evacuate, but just as they were jogging up front porches and over front yards, they heard a noise and stopped.

Looking up, they saw three military helicopters headed their way. All three dangled massive payloads. All three were moving fast.

"C'mon. We gotta go," Rand said, ushering his wife and baby inside. "You know that help ain't for us."

* * *

The control room at Clover Hill was abuzz with activity, and a constant low murmur filled the room as everyone prepared for venting. Engineers and operators called out meter and gauge readings, checking and double-checking the figures as they moved from panel to panel with purpose. Most ignored the communications staffer who ran in with a sat phone.

Breathless, the comms guy said, "Ethan, the batteries sent from Red Top are here."

"Great," Ethan replied, too busy to look up from his calculations.

The comms guy held out the phone. "They want to talk to you. They want to know where to put them."

"Put them—what? Where are they now?"

"They're airlifting them in. By helicopter. There's three."

"There's three helicopters with batteries currently over Clover Hill?" The comms guy nodded. Ethan shrugged. "Okay. Well, just have them put them on the grounds somewhere out of the way. We don't need them now and I can't deal with it."

Everybody kept working and the comms guy was almost out the door when Joss and Ethan both suddenly looked up, clearly thinking the same thing.

"Wait!" they yelled in unison.

The comms guy turned.

"Get me on a radio with one of their pilots," said Ethan.

CHAPTER THIRTEEN

COUNTDOWN TO ZERO HOUR
14 HOURS AND 43 MINUTES

CONNOR AND THE FIREFIGHTERS at the bridge were not only downwind of Clover Hill, they had no clue that a risky venting procedure was about to happen there. A procedure that, if it went wrong, would expel untold quantities of lethal radioactive material directly at them.

But even if the firefighters had known, it wouldn't have changed anything.

Until Connor was safe, they'd stay exactly where they were.

"All right," Levon said to the firefighters, grabbing the megaphone. "Let's try one more time. Hey, bud!" His voice boomed across the water. "What do you say we try to open the door again?"

But the boy just sat there glued to his seat like every other time they'd tried to get him to do it.

Frankie said, "Maybe he can't hear us?"

"He can. He looks up every time we talk to him," said Boggs. "Maybe he doesn't speak English."

"His dad spoke to him in English," Levon said.

"Is he like, I don't know, learning disabled or something? Maybe he doesn't understand what we want him to do."

"Wait, can kids that age talk?" Frankie said.

Everyone turned.

"Are you serious?" said Boggs.

"For God's sake, Frankie," said Levon. "The kid's, like, five."

Frankie held his hands out. "The kid's five? I don't know. I don't have kids. I don't know what that means."

Dani had stopped listening to them. She focused on Connor instead.

It was hard to see him clearly through the window's glare and the far distance—but she had an idea. She asked Levon for the megaphone and stepped forward.

"Connor, sweetheart," she said, her voice as soft and comforting as she could make it through a bullhorn. "Are you in your car seat?"

The boy nodded yes.

"Can you unbuckle your car seat?"

Connor shook his head no.

The radio in Joss's hand squawked: *We're set up. Ready for venting when you are.*

The transmission came from a National Guardsman in one of the twin-engine Bell 412 helicopters that were currently hovering over the Clover Hill campus. The chopper had been outfitted with radiation-sensing devices, and the plan was for it to conduct low-altitude flights over the building and surrounding areas to measure background radiation. This would give accurate, real-time figures that would not only inform the evacuation needs, but also provide immediate feedback on the success of the venting.

Joss pushed the talk button. "Roger that. Affirmative. Stand by for venting."

"We're ready when you are," Maggie said from the panel across the room.

Joss and Ethan shared a look, their expressions identical: *Last chance. We're sure, right?*

This was the last moment to call it off.

"Go" was all Ethan said.

Maggie and Vikram turned to the board. "Venting in three, two…"

Leaves crunched under Matt's feet as he crossed the open field on the far side of the Clover Hill campus. Inside the mask, his warm breath left moisture around his mouth, a contrast to the cold, dry air outside. He looked up at the trail of white smoke in the distance and the helicopter hovering near it. *That's perfect,* Matt thought.

The plant was eerily still and quiet. Not a person in sight. No utility trucks driving by. It was nothing like he remembered. Whenever he visited his dad at work, the place was always rushing with noise and activity. Today it was a ghost town. In the nearly empty parking lot, he stopped to look at a silver four-door sedan surrounded by broken glass and buckled plastic parts. A huge aircraft tire lay on top, having flattened the car's roof.

Matt slipped his backpack to one shoulder and continued on. If only the sixth-graders could see him now. They'd definitely think this was cool: Sneaking out. Being where he wasn't supposed to be, alone, because everyone else was too scared. He was being dangerous and awesome and he could imagine everyone surrounding his table at lunch, listening to him tell the story. Everyone would think he was so badass. Matt wondered if this might even get him a seat in the back row of the bus.

Walking out into an open area between buildings, he unzipped his backpack and carefully pulled out the drone the sixth-graders had been so eager to see. Miss Carla wasn't here to stop him now. Unfolding its four arms, he set it down on a flat patch of grass, took the remote control from his bag, and tossed the bag off to the side before pressing the power buttons on both the remote and the drone.

Blue LED lights flashed on the bottom of all four propellers as Matt went through the stabilization and calibration sequences: connecting the drone to the remote, connecting the device to GPS, waiting the forty-five seconds for the GPS to acquire a signal. Matt then connected the app on his phone to the drone via Bluetooth, and a moment later, video feed from the drone's camera began playing on the screen. Leaning his phone up against a rock, Matt could now see everything the drone saw.

He pressed the geomagnetic correction button on the left side of the control, and red lights on the front and rear of the drone flashed. He picked it up and rotated the drone counterclockwise horizontally until the red lights turned from flashing to steady, indicating the internal gyroscope was attuned and the calibration process was complete.

Matt set down the drone and took a few steps back. Taking the remote in both hands, he began manipulating the joysticks with his thumbs—and the drone lifted off the ground. It took a moment for Matt to stabilize it, but once he had it flying level, he went for the top of the remote to adjust its speed.

Matt pressed a button and the drone headed straight for the column of smoke.

At the bridge, there was finally some progress. Dani and Connor were now working together.

"Is there a big red button on the harness?" Dani asked.

Connor nodded.

"I bet you already tried, but it's tough to push down, huh?"

Again, the boy nodded.

"That's okay. It might be a little stuck. Let's try again," said Dani. "I'll count down, and when I say *go*, push really, really hard! Okay? Okay, here we go. Three. Two. One—go!"

The firemen all cheered him on, clapping and calling out his name, yelling all sorts of variations of *You got this, bud*. But the boy stayed still in the chair.

"Explain to him that we need that door open," Frankie said. "Because that wing and bridge and van will never be more stable than they are right now. We need to gain access while it's still okay to be moving it around."

"I'm honest-to-God serious, Frankie," said Levon, "have you ever met a child?"

"I just think if he understood—"

"It's not a conceptual issue. It's a strong-opposable-thumb issue."

"Connor, do you like superheroes?" Dani asked.

Connor nodded—with a smile. The first that they'd seen.

"Me too," Dani said, returning the smile. "Who's your favorite?"

He was too far away for them to hear perfectly, but the firefighters mumbled to one another, confirming what they'd interpreted his moving lips as saying.

"Batman?" Dani said. Connor nodded. "He's my favorite too. Know why?" Connor shook his head. "'Cause he's just a guy. He's just a person like you and me who worked really hard and became Batman. Bruce Wayne is just a person who made himself into a superhero. He was just a kid like you, you know? I bet he started his training when he was about your age."

She omitted the fact that Bruce Wayne was only a little older than Connor when his parents were killed, which was what set him on his path to becoming a superhero. Like Bruce Wayne, Connor was now an orphan.

"You want to start your training right now?" Dani asked. At his head nod, she said, "Okay, let's begin with your strength. If you want to be a superhero, you need to be superstrong. So, try this: Go ahead and close your eyes. Are they closed? Okay, now focus on putting all your power, every single muscle in your body, focus it all through your thumbs and into that red button—and then push."

He was trying. The firefighters could see he was trying so hard. They cheered him on, but it was clear he wasn't getting it.

"It's okay!" Dani said. "Bruce Wayne failed over and over and over again—but he kept trying over and over and over and over again too. Keep trying, Connor. You've got this."

The little boy's face scrunched up in effort. The firefighters cheered while they watched the boy—when his face suddenly lit up. The firefighters whistled and hooted as Connor slid out of the harness and climbed down out of the car seat.

* * *

The ticking clock on the wall in the control room was the only sound in the space. Everyone focused on the gauges, watching the numbers, not yet daring to come to a conclusion.

"Hydrogen accumulation is at three-point-three percent," Maggie said.

That was lower than her callout thirty seconds earlier.

Another thirty seconds passed.

"Three-point-one percent."

*Tick...tick...tick...*It felt like the clock was mocking them.

"Two-point-eight."

Joss looked at Ethan. It'd been six minutes since they'd started the vent. They had enough data to call it. Wordlessly, they agreed.

Ethan put a hand on Vikram's shoulder and squeezed. Dwight sat in a chair and finally let himself exhale. Joss ran a hand down her face with a sigh.

"Hydrogen accumulation one-point-four," Maggie said.

Joss held down the trigger on the radio. "How are your numbers looking up there? We're looking good down here."

A voice came over the radio, just audible above the thwacking of the chopper's rotor: *"Radiation is increasing, but at a rate near what you anticipated."*

"Is it under EPA standard?"

"No. We're well over EPA. The evacuation was necessary. We'll expand our test radius and—left! Left!"

All focus in the room snapped to the radio in Joss's hand.

"It's...there! Left side. No, rise. Rise!"

The radio cut out and it was dead silent for a split second before the room sprang to life.

"Someone get the live security footage—"

"On it."

"Maggie, monitor the—"

"You can't do that!"

Joss was taken aback by the white-hot rage in the pilot's voice. "I don't—do what?" she stammered. "What's happening?"

"You can't put a surveillance drone in our airspace and not tell us."

Joss looked at Ethan. He shook his head. "That's not us," Joss said.

"That thing in our propeller, we're down—"

"It's not us! We don't know what you're talking about."

Matt couldn't believe the footage he was getting. This was so cool: The firefighters running around. The burning plane parts. The white smoke. The helicopter—although that was bad. Way bad. He got too close there, he knew he did. But he pulled back! It was fine. Nothing happened.

But his hands were now shaking. He wondered what his mom would say if she knew what he was doing. His face flashed hot with shame. He knew what she would say. It's what she'd say about a lot of the things he was doing now that she was gone.

Oh, Matty. I'm so disappointed in you.

Shame flashed over to anger.

Then she should have stayed.

Matt flinched, startled by a door bursting open as two men in hazmat suits ran out of a building. He froze, trying to make out what they were screaming at him. Seconds later, he was grabbed by the arms and hauled back to the building.

He didn't fight them, but he didn't exactly comply, and somewhere along the way, the remote was knocked out of his hand. Right as they got to the building, Matt looked over his shoulder to see the drone hit the ground.

* * *

Connor's little face was pressed up against the minivan window. Even from a distance, his bright blue eyes shone. The Renaissance painters' cherubic angel babies looked like variations of Connor.

Levon had the megaphone now. "All right, my man. Is there a button to make the door slide open?"

Connor looked down to the right, then nodded.

"Excellent. Here's what you should do. I want you to push the button, then step back. Waaaay back. Okay? Push the button, step back, the door will slide open, and we can come get you. Okay?"

Connor nodded again and reached over for the button.

There was a click. Connor hurried back against the other side. The door popped out of its seal and slid open.

As air entered through the open door, it created a draft with the shattered front windshield. The whoosh of fresh air breathed new life into the flames.

The back draft that consumed the van was instantaneous.

CHAPTER FOURTEEN

COUNTDOWN TO ZERO HOUR

14 HOURS AND 21 MINUTES

THE HOT, ROILING fire billowed in a rush through the van and out the open door as the flames engulfed everything—and everyone—in its path. The firefighters stumbled backward in the fire flash, hands instinctively raised to protect themselves—but Dani rushed forward.

"Connor!" she screamed, not needing the megaphone. The flames receded as quickly as they'd come. The smoke mushrooming up from around the van cleared. She prayed the flash was over fast enough not to burn him, like snuffing out a candle with your fingers, when from somewhere in there, she could hear Connor coughing and crying.

The wind shifted and as the smoke blew out of the van, they saw the little boy sitting on the floor with his knees to his chest, his back against the far side of the van, his body shielded by the seat and car seat. He wailed but appeared to be physically unharmed. Dani called his name, telling him it was going to be okay, that the fire was gone. But the child was inconsolable.

By now he knew better. The fire wasn't gone. And they didn't know if he would be okay.

"Look," Levon said. "We need to get creative, fast—"

But just then, a loud noise downriver got their attention. They turned, and coming upstream was a Waketa Police Department patrol boat.

Carla pulled the hazmat suit out of the bag with a shake, slipped one foot in, then the next, careful not to rip the plastic material. Marion watched her, arms crossed.

"I'm sure he'll—"

"Well, I'm not sure," Carla shot back, cutting Marion off. "We went through this. I'm not sure Matt will do anything reasonable."

"It's not safe out there."

Carla stopped zipping up to stare at Marion. "Why do you think I'm going after him?"

"Then I'll go," Marion said, reaching for his own suit.

"Don't be ridiculous, Marion. Marion, stop—" She grabbed his suit. "C'mon," Carla said, her voice low enough that only he could hear. "We both know someone's got to go after Matt. And we both know it should be me."

Marion shook his head. "It's too dangerous."

"Exactly," Carla said. "We don't know where Dani and Levon

are. We don't know if they're okay. So tell me: What happens to *her* if something happens to you too?"

Marion glanced at the bathroom, hearing Brianna flush the toilet inside.

"Well, what if something happens to *you*?" he said.

"Then it's tragic. But it's just me. No one's counting on us. It's just Levon and me."

Her voice cracked as she said it, and by the look on his face, she knew Marion heard. Carla looked away quickly. Marion went to say something, but before he could, the bathroom door opened, and Brianna came out to stand beside her granddaddy. Carla could smell the Irish Spring soap on her freshly washed hands.

Carla finally looked back to Marion, and Brianna watched the adults stare at each other. Finally, Marion laid his hazmat suit to the side and helped Carla into her gear. While Marion tightened the straps around her wrists and then her ankles, Brianna stood next to him watching Carla finish tucking her hair into the hood. Miss Carla looked down at the little girl and winked. Brianna tried to wink back, but it came out more like a blink. Carla chuckled.

All that was left was her mask at the top of the stairs, so Carla took a deep breath and turned to go—but Marion pulled her back and, taking her face in both hands, kissed her lightly on the top of the head.

Carla swallowed the lump in her throat, remembering the last time he'd done that. It was after her mother's funeral, at the reception in the church's basement. She'd been holding a paper plate full of small scoops of untouched potluck casseroles when she suddenly realized: This was it. Both her parents were dead. Her siblings had moved away. Levon was all she had left.

Marion had been watching her from across the basement and he came over, placed his rough, weathered hands on either side of her face, gently tipped her head forward, and kissed the top of her head with soft, warm lips.

Both times, then and now, it didn't make the pain or fear go away. But it did make her aware of some inkling deep inside her, some quiet voice that was trying to get her to understand: *You're not alone. It's going to be okay.*

Carla took the steps two at a time. At the top, she reached for her mask—when a voice that wasn't Marion's or Brianna's suddenly filled the bunker. Carla froze, trying to make out what the voice was saying, when Marion called out, "Carla! Wait!"

Steve stood alone in the hallway outside the decontamination zone stewing silently, more furious with his son than he'd ever been. What was Matt thinking? Hearing footsteps down the hall, he looked over as Ethan came around the corner.

"He's in?" Ethan asked, pointing at the decontamination zone. Steve nodded. "Good. For what it's worth," Ethan continued, "we found the comms line to the bunker, and Matt was right. They're there. And apparently, they've been trying to talk to us the whole time."

Steve didn't say anything, just grunted an acknowledgment. The tension was so palpable that Ethan felt bad for the kid, knowing the wrath he was—albeit deservingly—about to face. They stood there awkwardly for a bit, stuck together in the kind of moment even your best friend or brother might not know how to handle, let alone a coworker you barely knew. Finally, Ethan just walked away, but before he got to the corner, he turned.

"My grandpa tells this story of how one spring during planting, when he was a little boy, he was out in the field with his older brother, Roy. My grandpa was real young at the time. Six? Maybe not even that? And they'd stopped to adjust something with the seed drill—and somehow, Roy's hand got caught in the seed drive. Blood is everywhere. My grandpa is crying. His big brother's hurt bad and it's a real nasty, real scary scene. So Roy tells his little brother to run back to the barn to get the tool they need to disassemble the part where his hand is stuck. So my grandpa says okay. Takes off for the barn. He's running across the field, fast as he can, and he's thinking about Roy. He's thinking about his big brother and all that blood, and he's scared. So halfway to the barn, he gets so worried—that he turns around and runs back to check on Roy and see if he's okay."

Steve couldn't help himself and smiled. "Did they get his hand out?"

"Minus a few fingers, yes. He got in big trouble for that. My grandpa got in big, big trouble." Ethan waited a few beats. "Kids make bad choices when they're scared."

"A few fingers aren't the same as a nuclear meltdown."

"Might not feel that way to him."

The door opened and Matt came out, hair wet, wearing a Clover Hill sweatsuit that was way too big for him. Ethan left for the control room, his footsteps fading as he got farther away. Steve stared down at his son, who stared down at the floor. Steve waited to hear the control-room door close before he spoke.

"Look at me."

Matt looked up reluctantly, withering under his father's glare.

"What were you thinking, being out there?"

"Dad, I—"

"Look at me!"

Matt looked back up, and that stubbornness he got from his mother flashed in his eyes, and just for a second, it was like she was there. Keeping her husband in line, reminding him, *Babe, he's just a kid.* And in that split second, Steve wasn't mad about the bullshit stunt Matt had pulled. Because she was back.

But as fast as she came, she was gone.

Steve turned away and made for the other end of the hallway. Matt followed, trying to keep up with his dad's long strides.

"You know how dangerous the plant is. You know this isn't a place for messing around. And you come here *today* with your drone. You leave the people trying to keep you safe."

"I'm sorry."

Steve didn't even turn around. "You are? *Now* you are? Well. You're going to have to do better than that. Not here, not today. But you *will* do better than that. Do you understand?"

When Matt didn't respond, Steve turned. Matt was halfway back down the hall, standing on tiptoes, peering through the glass panel in a door.

Steve knew what he was looking at, but he didn't need to go down the hall to see for himself how much worse Vinny's burns were. He could read the horror on his son's face.

Watching his boy stand on tiptoes in adult clothes that were way too big, Steve thought Matt seemed once again like the kid he knew and not the preteen he barely understood. It broke his heart to witness more of his son's innocence and joy ripped away by yet another trauma. He was a child. He wasn't supposed to know suffering and pain and death as intimately as he did. It was so unfair.

If Claire were still alive, Matt wouldn't be here, exposed to radiation and seeing things no one should have to see. Claire would have him safe with her. And she'd still be alive if she hadn't gotten cancer. And she wouldn't have gotten lung cancer if she hadn't smoked — a habit *he* had gotten her into when they first started dating. A habit he was able to kick but she never was. Steve would always blame himself for her death, and now he was putting their only child in harm's way too.

He didn't know which was worse, the guilt or the grief, and most of the time they were indistinguishable from each other, just a daily, ever-present sensation that he was suffocating.

"Hey, bud," Steve said, his voice a little gentler. "C'mon."

The break room was empty when they went in. Steve set Matt up with a soda, a snack, the remote for the TV. Told him to stay there.

"Can I help?" Matt asked as his dad made for the door. "I want to do something."

"Absolutely not," Steve said. "Unless I come get you or a voice over the PA says to do something, you stay in this room and you do not leave. Do you understand me?"

Matt was back to staring at the floor. That had been colder than Steve wanted it to be, but he didn't know how to express all the things he actually wanted to say. It came out hard because it was easy to be hard.

"I'll check on you later," Steve mumbled as he left, knowing he should go to the boy, be with him, be the comforting parent he needed. But with Matt, there was what Steve wanted to do and what he actually did. And every day, it felt like the space between those things was only growing wider.

The boat had seemed like a good idea at the time.

The firefighters knew they couldn't reach Connor from the ground, and a helicopter rescue was still a ways out, if at all, so that left only one way to get to the boy: from the river. But as they stared down at the small-town police boat, they didn't know what they had been thinking.

The fast-moving river tossed the small patrol boat around, its single outboard motor fighting a losing battle against the current. As soon as the vessel arrived, it was obvious that keeping the boat stationary would be nearly impossible. And what good would it do if they could?

"We bring a ladder down to the boat, extend it up, lean it against the van, pull him out," Boggs said.

"With an unstable base? Nothing to anchor to on top?" Frankie shook his head. "No."

"How deep is the river right there?" asked Boggs.

"Too deep for anchor," Dani said.

"So we tie mooring lines to the bridge. Anchor the boat that way, then stick a ladder—"

"And anchor the ladder to *what*?" said Levon. "We already know the van is unstable. All of it is. We don't want to put any more stress on it. We mess with it too much, I'm worried the whole thing might collapse."

"The van?" asked Boggs.

"No," said Dani. "The bridge."

Down on the water, the three policemen in the boat seemed to be having a similar conversation. Lots of pointing: the van, the bridge, the fire truck. Lots of heads shaking: *No, that won't work.* A bright orange life vest similar to the one everyone in the boat was wearing dangled from one of the cop's arms.

"What if the kid jumps?"

The firefighters turned to Frankie.

"There's no way we could get him to jump," Levon said. "And even if we did, then what? Freezing water. Fast current. Seriously, then what?"

"The boat goes after him. Gets him out. Gets him dry."

Boggs was skeptical. "What happens if they can't get him in time?"

"They will," said Frankie.

"Say they don't. Say he goes under. Doesn't come up. With that current?"

"They *will*."

"And if they *don't*," said Boggs, "we're saying he's got to choose between drowning and burning to death?"

"Can the kid even swim?" asked Levon.

The firefighters didn't have an answer. Levon grabbed the megaphone.

"Hey, Connor. Can you swim?"

Connor looked up but didn't reply. He'd stopped crying, but he still sat on the floor hugging his knees to his chest. Dani took the megaphone.

"Batman," she said. "Are you a swimmer yet?"

The little boy shook his head no.

With that, they knew there was only one option.

Helicopter pararescue.

Engine 42's initial call to dispatch requesting a chopper rescue had been met with *We'll work on it*. There had been no update since. If help did come, it would be federal, likely the National Guard. But Engine 42 had no way to contact them, and anyone who did was busy at the plant or the I-35 pileup. Essentially, it was exactly as the firefighters had feared: There was too much happening too fast with too high stakes elsewhere. Connor would be a last priority.

They were on their own.

The patrol boat motored over to shore, where the firefighters met them.

"I'm sorry," one of the officers called out once they were within earshot. "This is a no-go. You need pararescue."

"We tried," Levon said.

"'We'll work on it,'" Frankie said, making air quotes. "The priority is the plant."

"They won't even spare one of the choppers that just left?"

The firefighters stared at the officer.

"The *what*?" said Dani.

Engine 42 had been at the bridge all day. They had no idea what was going on at the plant.

"The three National Guard helicopters that just left Clover Hill."

Levon, Frankie, Boggs, and Dani all looked at one another, and for the first time since they'd spotted Connor sitting in the van all alone and crying, they felt hope.

CHAPTER FIFTEEN

COUNTDOWN TO ZERO HOUR
14 HOURS AND 06 MINUTES

AT THE PLANT, they'd survived problem one. Now they had to figure out how to survive problem two.

These idiots are going to get us killed, thought Renee, the shy and unassuming fluid-dynamics engineer sitting at the back of the control room, biting the inside of her cheek in frustration. She'd tried, many times, to say her piece but hadn't been able to get a word in.

"We get a crane and lift—"

"Again, tell me where we're getting this crane from? R1's is permanently fixed. R3's was damaged in—"

"Guys, " Renee said, but still no one was listening to her.

"We use the fire truck's ladder—"

"It's not tall enough! Nothing is."

Renee bit down hard enough that she could taste blood. "Damn it, *listen!*"

The whole room turned.

"It wouldn't matter even if we did have a crane or a ladder that was tall enough," she said. "The outward water flow is too strong. There's nothing to push against it. We have to fix it from the inside."

Her manager, Larry, the main reason she could never get a word in, scoffed. "I told you. That's not happening."

Before Renee could respond, the deafening bleat of the pool-water alert went off, making everyone flinch. Ethan shut it off with the side of his fist.

Every second they spent debating the problem, the water level was dropping. Every second they wasted bickering was a second closer to an uncontrollable fire they could never put out. Every second was one second closer to radiation in the air, the water, the soil. Every second was that much closer to the point of no return.

Ethan glared at Larry. "You've established what doesn't work," he said with an unsettling calm to his voice. "I need what does. If she's got a solution, I want to hear it." He turned to Renee. "Please. Continue."

Renee cleared her throat. "We fix it from the inside."

Larry, who looked like steam was about to come out of his ears, and half the people in the room shook their heads. The other half were dead serious.

"From inside the pool?" Ethan said. "You mean in the water?"

"Yes. We use what we have," Renee said. "We use the fixed overhead gantry crane inside the pool building and position it over the biggest hole. We take a portion of the stainless-steel lining that was blown off and slip it down over the damage on the side of the pool."

"Slide it down like a sluice gate?" Joss asked.

"Yes. Exactly. Like a sluice gate closing. The sheet will stay—"

"Unless," interrupted one of the other Red Team engineers, "the damage to the building changes or there's a disturbance in the water flow. It could slip out of position; it could go out the hole. It could make the damage worse."

"Which is why," Renee countered, "we would need to secure the sheet."

"Secure it?" asked Ethan. "How?"

"We weld it into place."

Silence.

"Underwater?" Ethan said, not understanding.

"Yes. The pool is concrete lined in stainless steel. So we have underwater welders weld a sheet of it to the pool's own stainless-steel lining. Once they're done, the outward water flow stops. *Then* we can reinforce it from the outside once we get the right equipment here. But in the meantime, the leak is sealed. And we can refill the pool. It's a patch. A patch over a hole."

Joss and Ethan shared a look. It was a long shot, but theoretically, it could work.

"Where do we get an underwater welder?" Ethan asked.

"That's the problem," said Dwight. "We talked to FEMA, who talked to the National Guard. Within our time frame, they said they can get us dive gear and divers. What they can't get us is any underwater welding gear."

"And the gear is—"

"Highly specific. Specific helmets, comms, tools designed for that and only that. They're sourcing as we speak—"

"Won't happen," Joss said, cutting in. "We need this done in the next hour and a half, tops. It'll be a month before putting a Navy diver in radioactive water for a risky, untested maneuver gets approved, to say nothing of getting them here with the gear to do it. Either we get someone local, or we do something else."

"*R.J. Brown.*"

When the speaker crackled, everyone in the room turned.

"*Ray Jay Brown,*" said Carla from the line to the bunker. "*We went to high school together. He used to do repairs on ships that ported on the Mississippi. Former Marine. Once he got out, he started a boat-repair company, but when Clover Hill announced it was decommissioning, business started moving downriver, and work dried up. His company went belly-up eventually. I heard he's now a trucker. Heavy-duty towing or something. Although I think he was fired from that. He's had some trouble with alcohol. But, look, he knows how to do it and he's local.*"

Any other day, even the thought of something like this being a viable alternative would have been ludicrous. But today, Ethan only said: "You got his number?"

"Phones are down," Joss said.

"Right. You know where he lives?"

"*I do. And I can drive.*"

"That's generous. But with all due respect," said Joss, "I think we can handle it."

"*All due respect to you too, ma'am, but you show up at R.J.'s in a Clover Hill truck waving a badge, he'll shoot you just 'cause.*"

"Right. You drive," Ethan said before Joss could argue.

Dwight held up a hand. "Am I the only one hesitating here? We're really putting the entire fate of this planet into the hands of an alcoholic out-of-work trucker?"

Before anyone could speak, the low-water-level alarm rang again. The next threshold of caution had been reached. Ethan shut it off and said, "That's exactly what we're going to do."

CHAPTER SIXTEEN

COUNTDOWN TO ZERO HOUR

13 HOURS AND 57 MINUTES

EVERYTHING IN TOWN was burning, destroyed, or completely untouched. It looked like the aftermath of a tornado that took the barn but missed the house.

"Were you a Mustang?" Carla asked, glancing over at the high school's marquee as the red Dodge Ram tore past it at a speed far exceeding the school-zone limit. It was the first thing either one had said since they left the plant.

The area around the school was desolate, as was most of the town they'd driven through. Neither of them had commented on it, but they were both thinking it: *Where is everybody?* Had they already evacuated? Were they locked up inside, sheltering in place? Occasionally they'd see a car barreling down a road, seemingly headed out of town. But then a little farther down, they'd pass a man rocking on his front porch.

"Class of '94," said Joss. "You?"

"Class of 2011."

"Of—wait, *what?* How old were you on September eleventh?"

"Second grade. So eight."

"I was in grad school. Fuck, I'm old."

What Carla remembered most about September 11 was how Mr. Evans kept wiping his eyes while he was telling the class that something bad had happened. It was the first time she'd seen a grown man cry, and the way he seemed so determined not to let a single tear fall only made her feel more scared and more confused. It was a weird day to be that age. Old enough to know something big had happened but too young to understand what. The adults had tried to explain it in a way that wasn't scary, which was hard to do when it inherently was. All day, she just remembered an overwhelming sensation of *I don't understand.*

That was her generation's *where were you when* moment, like the Kennedy assassination or Pearl Harbor was for generations before. For Carla's students, their moment would be today—and they were first-graders, almost the same age as she had been in 2001. Carla wished she had made that connection earlier today, as it was happening, but you typically realize the whole world has changed only after it has. Not that she would have done anything differently. But maybe.

How many of her students would include Miss Carla in their own stories of today, just as she did with Mr. Evans? Was she a part of Mr. Evans's memory of 9/11, just like she knew she would always include little Benjamin asking if he was going to grow a tail in her memory of today?

The football field was empty—the pale, dormant grass not yet showing signs of spring's arrival. But the stands looked the same, Joss thought, remembering how cold her butt used to get sitting on those metal bleachers during the fall football games. Carla must have seen her looking because she asked if Joss had been a cheerleader.

"Good God, no." Joss laughed. "I was a nerd back when that meant something. Like, stuffed-in-your-locker vintage of nerdom."

"You just looked nostalgic," Carla said.

"Oh, well. Yeah. I was in the marching band. We'd play at halftime."

"Flute?"

"Sousaphone. It's like a small tuba," she added, seeing Carla's expression. "I told you. Nerd."

Carla was right about one thing, though. Joss was feeling nostalgic. She loved those Friday-night games. Afterward, the football players and cheerleaders would go to parties and get drunk while the marching band would go to Bermuda Bliss for Hawaiian shaved ice, still wearing their uniforms. Only a few of the kids had cars, and they'd pack themselves in like sardines, sitting on each other's laps, squished up against the windows, laughing at stupid inside jokes as they sang along to show tunes while doing their best attempts at flirtation.

The first time she'd ever held a boy's hand was on one of those Friday nights in the back seat of Jamie Gilbert's blue Ford Probe. He was the drum major and she'd had a huge crush on him all year but wasn't sure if he felt the same. When his pinkie brushed against hers, she'd frozen, unsure if it was accidental or on purpose, but when he laced his fingers through hers, she figured it out. By the end of the night, they were boyfriend-girlfriend and they'd stayed that way for many, many wonderful years after that.

The boy was Ethan.

The truck passed endless soybean and cornfields and the turnoff for Joss's house. They went past the rich neighborhood with the one house that gave out full-size candy bars on Halloween. They passed the section of the Mississippi where teens still broke curfew while making out in their parked cars. And as they tore down a deserted Main Street, it struck Joss how little had changed.

Most places evolved over time. Grew. Modernized. Not here. Waketa moved ahead so slowly, it was practically in reverse. Before Clover Hill, farming was the only industry around these parts. But when the plant was built, it attracted a new population, eager to get in on the ground floor of all the promise a nuclear town brought.

Problem was, that promise had never been fulfilled.

Growth became stagnation; stagnation became decline. The announcement that the plant was to be decommissioned was the final nail in the coffin. No one wanted to invest in a place that had no future. Some stayed. Most left. Sure, it was still lovely, full of quaint Norman Rockwell charm. A simple, quiet town where you could raise a family. But it wasn't a great place if you had ambition. Which was why Joss left.

Fifteen years in DC going up against red-tape political bullshit had worn her out, though. Beyond getting her idealistic sheen worn off, she was sick of the way big cities viewed pockets of the country like Waketa: Expendable. Too bumpkin to be important. She'd lost count of how many meetings she had been forced to sit in quietly while towns with populations like Waketa's were discussed with clinical impartiality. She'd learned quickly that anything that wasn't located in a swing-state county of importance wouldn't even make it to a briefing sheet. And she'd learned even faster that pointing that out was a surefire way not to get the funding her research needed. It was an exercise in futility, and she'd finally decided she no longer wanted to be a part of the political theater. So she'd come back home.

But as they say: "You can't go home again." Once she *was* back, she became nearly as frustrated with the local people and the provincial mindsets that made them stand in the way of their own progress as she'd been with the bureaucrats and politicians.

She'd always felt stuck in the middle, never fully fitting into either side while seeing and understanding both—and being considered an outsider by each. Somewhere along the way, she'd resigned herself to accepting that the feeling of isolation, whether perceived or actual, was just how it would be.

But she was disappointed. Disappointed for them all. She knew what each side stood to gain but never would because both were blind to what the other had to offer.

Carla turned the truck onto an unpaved road. Hay-colored soybean fields, flattened and awaiting spring, surrounded the private drive, making the modest 1960s farmhouse and barn sitting at the end of the road stand out.

"R.J. won't take well to new people," Carla said. "Especially if you say you're with Clover Hill. I should probably do most of the talking."

"Agreed," Joss said, reading a sun-faded sign nailed to the side of the barn as they passed: NO TRESPASSING—I'M TIRED OF HIDING THE BODIES.

They parked next to a massive heavy-duty tow truck whose maroon paint was barely visible under an inch of dirt. Walking to the house, Carla noticed that some kid had finger-scribbled *Wash me* on the back window. On closer inspection, she saw it actually said *Eat me.* She was thinking it was probably R.J.'s own handiwork when the warning shot hit the ground at her feet.

"Jesus!" she yelled as both women jumped back.

On the back porch, Ray Jay Brown grabbed the rifle's bolt handle, and with a lift and a click and a pull-back, the shell was ejected. Weight shifted to one side, an unbuttoned flannel covering a ribbed white tank, a patchy, dirty-blond beard, R.J. jutted his chin at Carla as he aimed the firearm back at her feet.

"You got my CDs?"

Carla was dumbstruck. "You can't be serious."

"I told her I didn't want to see none of you until I got them back."

"R.J. That was, like, over a decade ago."

"Did Stephanie send you? What'd she say?"

Carla put her hands on her hips. "Are you nuts? That was sophomore year. You dated for, like, two months."

"Three months. What's she doing now?"

"I don't know, R.J.! She moved literally fifteen years ago."

"And took my CDs with her. *All* my CDs."

"Oh my God. Put the gun down—"

"Metallica. Alan Jackson. Blink-182."

"Listen. We need to talk to—"

"Eminem. AC/DC."

"This is serious—"

"Mariah Carey's Christmas album—"

"Listen, jackass. I'll buy you every fucking CD your hillbilly heart desires if you put the gun down, shut the fuck up, and listen to what we have to say," Joss yelled.

Carla and R.J. both turned. Joss couldn't tell if he was impressed or just trying to figure out where in her body to put the first bullet. When he spun and walked into the house, she took it as a good sign.

The inside of the house was surprisingly clean. Spare and utilitarian, but with a tidy sense of calm and a faded smell of this morning's bacon. On the mantel, a framed picture of R.J. in his Marine dress blues, probably taken five years and ten pounds ago, sat beside a framed triangle-folded American flag. On the other side was a picture of a Marine in what looked to be Vietnam. Next to it, a black-and-white photo of a Marine standing under a German street sign. The family resemblance was undeniable.

R.J. plopped down in a La-Z-Boy. The women sat on the couch. Joss got right to it.

In frank, uncomplicated terms she explained what had happened and what the state of the plant was. She told him about the pool, about the damage it had sustained, the repairs that it needed. She described what would happen if they didn't get it fixed—to the community, to the country, to the world. Finally, she got to why they were there. They needed his gear, and they needed his help.

R.J. listened silently all the while with a beer in one hand and the rifle in the other, resting against his knee. When Joss finished, he looked at Carla.

"It's all true," Carla said. "We just came from the plant. I saw the plane. I saw the damage with my own eyes."

"We wouldn't be here if we had other options," Joss added.

"Then I'm the kid picked last for the team?" he said.

"That's not what I meant. Sorry," Joss said. "I meant that I know we're asking a lot. Look, you don't know me. I show up at your house asking for your gear. Your expertise. Your help. Asking you to risk your life for a company that, frankly, betrayed you and betrayed this town. But if you don't, R.J., it's all over for Waketa. It's…" She paused, looking around the living room, trying to figure out where to go next. "It's Kline's frozen custard. It's cruising Main on a Saturday night. It's picking apples at Shady Acres every fall. It's the church's lawn parties in the summer. It's Tuesday-night trivia and dollar-fifty drafts at Minder Binders. All of it's over. Is it fair that it's coming down to you? No. But we're used to not fair around here. So…so, yeah. That's it. We need you. We need your help."

The antique grandfather clock across the room ticked loudly as the pendulum swung back and forth. R.J. took a sip of his beer and stared at the floor while he considered. Finally, he looked up.

"No."

Carla and Joss shared a look. "*No* as in—"

"*No* as in Clover Hill can fuck off, the government can fuck off, you *all* can fuck off. After everything I've done, after everything my family has given, you come here to ask for *more?*"

Joss leaned forward, elbows on knees. "R.J. You understand that if we fail—"

"Oh, I get it. I just think it's real interesting that I get a knock on my door now when someone else needs something. Where was the door for me to knock on when I needed something? There wasn't one. 'Cause it's my fault if I need help. I can't control any of it, it's all bigger than me—but it's *my* fault. I gotta figure it out. Just bootstrap it, son." R.J. clucked his teeth with a shake of his head. "We're left to rot out here—until they need something. *Then* it comes. Then the knock comes. But it only goes one way."

Joss stood up abruptly, surprising them both. She knew a dead end when she saw it and they didn't have time to waste. "Right," she said, taking a vial of pills out of her pocket. Shaking a few into her hand, she laid them on the coffee table. "One now, one every twenty-four hours until they're gone," she said. "Take them. Don't. Whatever. But you and I both know getting cancer treatment covered by Uncle Sam will be a losing battle, so I'd take them."

Carla followed Joss to the door, and they were almost gone when R.J. called after them, "You can have the gear."

They turned. He shrugged and took another sip of beer.

"What's left of it, anyway. It's just collecting dust in the barn. Sold some, but most of it's still there. You can have the gear. But I'm not doing it."

The women loaded the gear into the truck by themselves, but

they could see R.J. watching occasionally from the kitchen window. As they were about to leave, he came out to the back porch.

"If you got a CB, turn it to channel seven," Carla said. "We're broadcasting updates from the plant. Any changes, any directives, you'll hear it there first. Spread that to anyone you talk to. Please."

"All right," he muttered in an uninterested way. "Tell Stephanie I want my CDs back."

Carla shook her head as she closed the tailgate. She got behind the wheel, but before she shut the door, she paused.

"You know what, R.J.," she said, looking out at the barren field, "I get it. I do. I'm pissed too. This life out here? The deck is stacked against us. And that's not just the way it feels, it's the way it is. You don't want to be the guy risking it all for people who don't give a shit about you. That's fine. But you seem real proud of yourself. You seem to think you're putting one over on us by saying no. Whoever that *us* is, anyway—the company, the government. Whoever you've always blamed for keeping you down, keeping you where you are. I get that anger, R.J. I get it, I swear I do.

"But we come to you today, hat in hand, asking for help. You got what we need and you're the only one who has it." Carla stuck a thumb back at Joss. "She's got the president on speed dial and she's saying, 'R.J., you're our only hope.' You want to talk about knocking? Well, we're knocking on your door with the goddamn winning lottery ticket." Carla pointed to the gear in the bed of the truck. "And I'm just strolling out of here with everything I need while you stay here. The story will go on and you won't be a part of it because you couldn't see what you had. It's called leverage, R.J. It's called opportunity. For once in your life, you had the winning hand, but you didn't see it. And *that* is on you."

CHAPTER SEVENTEEN

COUNTDOWN TO ZERO HOUR

13 HOURS AND 42 MINUTES

AS THE CHOPPER raced up the Mississippi, snaking its way along the river toward the bridge, none of the National Guardsmen inside spoke. All they could do was glance back at the smoke rising from the nuclear power plant and feel both guilt and relief that they had been called away from Clover Hill for a single-person bridge rescue.

They'd just left the danger. *This* call should be easy.

* * *

"ETA four minutes."

Dani heard the chopper's status come over the radio, but she was focused on Connor. The boy was staring despondently out the van's open door, and all Dani could think was how badly she wished she knew him better. Knew what kind of little boy he was, how his brain worked. Was he an old soul who understood exactly what had happened? Was he a youngest child who was used to having his days spoon-fed to him instead of having to figure it out? How independent was he? How stubborn? Without knowing these things, she didn't know how to get in there.

"Where was your family going?" Dani asked, the megaphone making her voice sound somewhat tinny. His voice came back as a whisper. "Your grandma's house?" she guessed.

He nodded.

"Grandma's for Easter." Dani was smiling. "I see, I see. I imagine you would have a big Easter lunch. Maybe a ham, and mac and cheese? Some fluffy dinner rolls?"

Connor nodded.

"Let me guess, your favorite is…green beans. You're a green-bean man."

Connor scrunched up his nose.

"No? Then how about…oh, I know. Brussels sprouts!"

Connor smiled weakly and shook his head.

"Carrots, then. Gotta be. Easter Bunny loves them—no? Not carrots? Well, what else is there—what's that?"

Connor's little mouth moved distinctly.

"Pie? *Broccoli* pie? Ew! What in the world kind—oh, *cherry*! Cherry pie."

Connor giggled as he nodded up and down.

"I see. We got a cherry-pie man. Okay," Dani said approvingly. "You know, my daddy makes a very good cherry pie, but on Easter he makes his specialty: banana pudding." Dani whistled. "Yes, sir, that banana pudding is something. It's Brianna's—Bri, that's my daughter, she's about your age—it's her favorite dessert of all time. It's got Nilla wafers and real bananas in it, and he uses Jell-O pudding and real whipped cream. He's adamant about that—it's gotta be *real* whipped cream you whip yourself, not the stuff out of the tub. Bri would eat nothing but that if I'd let her. No ham, no green beans, no mac and cheese. Just banana pudding. I bet she'd share some with you, though. She'd put a big scoop of it on your plate and probably even tell you the secret spice he uses, even though her granddaddy made her swear not to tell anyone. But I think she'd tell you."

Dani thought of the groceries that were on the kitchen counter waiting for tonight, when Bri and Daddy would make the pudding. Bri would pull over that little step stool. Marion would help her measure the ingredients, then she'd dump them in. He'd help her hold the beater as it whipped the cream, and once her arm got tired, he'd take over to finish the job. Dani's shift at the station was done in the morning, and she'd been looking forward to coming home to dye Easter eggs and help with the rest of the meal. The house would be warm and smell like baking bread.

For a moment, Dani was there, and she could see Connor was with her. Maybe in his mind, he was sitting at the kids' table with Bri. It was Easter and they were warm and safe and grateful. There was nothing to do but eat banana pudding and cherry pie. And just as Connor began to smile, they heard the rotor of an incoming chopper.

"Affirmative, we see you," Levon said into the radio as he made his way down to Dani. "The vehicle's door is open. Connor's waiting."

The UH-72 Lakota followed the path of the river north, the pulsing rhythm of the rotating blades becoming louder and more intense as it approached.

"We're getting you out!" Dani told Connor. "It's going to be all right!"

But her screams into the megaphone were lost to the noise that, even to Dani, was intimidating. Connor looked terrified. As the firefighters watched the helicopter position itself high above the van, Dani could feel the vibrations of the thwacking rotor blades in her chest. She could only imagine what it must feel like inside the unstable van—especially to a traumatized little boy who was all alone and couldn't see the chopper and didn't know what was happening.

The helicopter's door slid open. A National Guardsman in a bright red rescue harness positioned himself at the opening. Leaning back, he hung off the side, ready to drop.

"Listen to the man in the helmet! Do what he says! It's going to be all right!"

Dani knew Connor couldn't hear her, but she yelled anyway, smiling broadly, giving him a thumbs-up. It was to calm herself as much as him.

The rescuer dropped down out of the helicopter, the length of cable extending as he went. The chopper moved down with him, descending slowly toward the van.

Suddenly, the trees and grass started to move and sway.

The firefighters held on to their helmets as the rotating blades' powerful downwash blew everything around them—including the fire. The helicopter acted as a bellows, feeding the blaze with fresh infusions of oxygen. Hot orange flames billowed high into the air, encroaching on the van and playing at the feet of the man who dangled from the chopper.

"Up! Lift up!" Levon screamed into the radio, but the chopper was already rising. The guardsman in the harness hung on as the cable swung like a pendulum. As the chopper moved up, the flames went down.

The helicopter went high, much higher than before, creating as much distance from the flames as possible. This time when the line extended and the rescuer dropped down, the chopper held its position, hovering far above the van where its downwash wouldn't be an issue.

"Give him more line," Frankie muttered a few moments after the guardsman had stopped dropping. As though someone in the chopper had heard him, a voice came over the radio:

"That's it. That's full cable extension."

With that, the helicopter began a second rescue attempt.

Everyone held their breath as the chopper slowly lowered the guardsman closer to the van. Dani glanced from the flames to the trees to the man to Connor, over and over. The man was getting closer, and so far, the downwash wasn't bad. The flames were holding steady. The helicopter kept descending, very, very slowly.

"Eyes on me," Dani yelled, pointing two fingers at Connor, then turning them on herself. The child didn't blink. His big blue eyes locked on her. "Stay with me. It's going to be okay."

As soon as the words were out of her mouth, the wind started to whip.

The downwash was still too fierce. It was a game of chicken — the chopper would drop down, the flames would rise up; the helicopter would lift, the flames would recede. The pilot went up and dropped down several more times — until the last attempt, which was a touch too close. The flames lashed out angrily and suddenly the guardsman's suit went up in a blaze.

Frantically, he swatted at his legs, but the awkward angle and swinging motion made the flames spread quicker, and soon they were covering his whole body. The chopper peeled off, flying downriver, away from the bridge. When it was far enough, the chopper dove, dunking the man in the river. A waft of brown smoke rose from the water.

Two guardsmen leaned out the side of the chopper, yelling down to their friend and directing the pilot as well. Moments later, the cable started to rise, taking the burned rescuer with it. As he spun slowly, dangling in the air, the anguish on his face was clear. When his body reached the door, his fellow guardsmen loaded him in carefully, moving with swift, coordinated precision. They were trained to do exactly this—just typically not for one of their own.

Dani watched the chopper with a bad feeling. She knew what was about to happen. "Don't," she muttered. "Don't you fucking dare."

But sure enough, a moment later, the chopper rose. The voice on the radio was final.

"Put the fire out or get a different plan. With that wing burning, this isn't possible."

"No," she cried as Levon pulled her back by the arm.

Helicopter rescue had been their last idea. There was no other way. It *had* to work. Pushing toward the helicopter as it moved farther away, becoming smaller and smaller, Dani screamed into the void, her voice echoing through the woods:

"Come back!"

CHAPTER EIGHTEEN

COUNTDOWN TO ZERO HOUR

13 HOURS AND 34 MINUTES

"CAUTION — APPROACHING THRESHOLD!"

A loud robotic voice had joined the bleating alarm in the control room on the other end of the line. Joss and Carla listened as Ethan shut the warnings off and returned to the call with a loud sigh.

"What do you mean, it 'sorta' worked?" he asked, not even trying to mask his frustration.

Carla took her eyes off the road to shrug at Joss. Neither was quite sure how to explain R.J., so Joss held the sat phone closer and said, "It means we got the gear and we're heading back. But you need to figure out who's going swimming."

After hanging up with Ethan, the women drove in silence for a few minutes while Joss, unable to help herself, smirked.

All this time she had never been able to put her finger on it—until this moment.

She'd dated smart men and funny men. Men who were interesting, and men who were driven. Some were like her, while others had been an exploration of opposites attracting. Most had been fine. Two had been truly great. And a few had been spectacularly unredeemable wastes of her time. But not even one had made her curious about a life together for the long haul.

Why? She wanted that kind of relationship, and most of them had been great guys. So why, *why*, did her gut always declare that *this* wasn't it?

Her friends thought she was too picky. Her mother said she was too selfish. Her therapist had some other rationale that Joss had written off and frankly couldn't even remember—but just now, hearing Ethan's voice on the phone, something had unlocked.

Joss knew *exactly* who she was. Top to bottom, inside and out—she knew what she was about, she knew what she was made of, she knew what she wanted. Ethan was the only man she'd ever dated who knew himself in the same way. *That's* what had been missing. Her first relationship had been with someone as effortlessly at home in his own skin as she was in hers, and Joss had believed that was how most people were and how most relationships would be. She'd been doomed from the start! She'd thought they were the rule, but they were the exception.

It was why their relationship had worked. It was also why it hadn't worked. But Joss finally realized that *that* was what she'd been looking for, what all the other men had been missing. Personal authenticity—and an acceptance of hers. For the first time, and with pride, Joss understood why she'd refused to settle.

After watching the fields go by for a couple minutes longer, Joss cleared her throat. "So how's this going to go?"

"Sorry?" Carla asked.

"Am I dropping you off and then taking the truck back?" Joss said. "Or are you bringing me to Clover Hill and then coming back to town?"

Carla glanced over.

"Did you think I wouldn't notice the potassium iodide and masks in the back of the truck?" Joss said.

"I was thinking I'd get out on Main and let you take the truck back."

"You'll be without a ride."

"Not planning on going anywhere," said Carla. "Look, people don't know where to go, what to do. They don't have iodide. They're not protected, and they don't know how to protect themselves. I can't leave them. I can't just go back to a safe bunker and hope they figure something out. Okay?"

Joss raised her hands in surrender. "Just wondered about the logistics. I wasn't going to talk you out of anything. I'd do the same thing."

The women drove on in silence. Carla made a left and headed toward Main, driving the opposite way they'd come in. As they rounded the corner, Perrow Hill came into view. At its top sat United Grace Church.

Both women leaned in, trying to make sense of what they were looking at:

The church parking lot was packed, every single spot filled, with overflow cars all over the yard.

Carla pulled up parallel to the church at the bottom of the hill, stopping in the middle of the road. There, amid all the cars, was the Carver Valley Elementary School bus. Carla put the truck in park.

"I think I'll get out here."

* * *

"It was my idea, I'll do it," said Renee, the fluid-dynamics engineer.

"But you don't know how to weld," said Ethan.

"Do you? Do any of us?" Renee asked as she and Ethan looked around at all the engineers and controllers and firefighters assembled in the control room. No one raised a hand. "See? I *am* scuba-certified, though. And that's fifty percent of the knowledge that's needed."

"Is anyone else scuba-certified?" Ethan asked the room.

Only Steve raised his hand.

Renee crossed her arms. "Well—"

Steve waved her off. "All of you engineers and brainy types are highly specialized tools. I'm a blunt object. None of you are going because you're not replaceable. And no offense, but you're not exactly cut out for this kind of thing."

Dwight and Vikram in their tucked-in polo shirts, khakis, and tennis shoes exchanged a glance. No one argued.

The firefighters then started saying *they* were going to be the one to do it. One by one, they all volunteered in a real *I am Spartacus* moment that they seemed quite pleased with, but Steve would have none of.

"Billy, Dana, Emily," Steve said with a sigh to one of his men. The firefighter blinked a few times quickly; he hadn't expected to hear his children's names in that moment. Steve turned to the firefighter next to him. "Kayden and Khloe." That firefighter also seemed taken aback. "Your wife, Elizabeth," Steve said, turning to George. "She's due, what is it, next week?"

George cleared this throat. "Week after next," he said.

Steve nodded and looked around at them. "Right. Well, if something goes wrong, I'm not looking a single one of your kids in the eye to explain to them why I let you get in the water. I'm not going to do it."

Like the engineers, they didn't argue. Not because they agreed with him. But because they knew their chief, and they knew that when his mind was made up, his mind was made up.

"So what am I supposed to tell Matt?" said Ethan.

Steve turned. It was as though the temperature in the room had dropped a few degrees.

"We need you here to lead," Ethan continued.

"My men are fully capable of doing their jobs in my absence." Steve's voice was unflinching. "If not, I'm no leader."

"You have experience that—"

"*No one* has experience in what we're facing today."

"In the event that we—"

"Then tell me which of my men you deem worthless enough to sacrifice?"

You could have heard a pin drop.

"Tell me. Which of my men are you going to turn to and say, 'You are the sacrificial lamb because Steve here is more important than you.' Because that's exactly what you're saying."

No one knew where to look, so they all looked at the ground—except Steve and Ethan, who stared each other down.

"Someone has to go in the water," Steve said. "At least I have the decency to look my people in the eye and say, 'I got this.'"

Carla stood at the church's entrance with a box under each arm staring at a scene she could hardly believe.

"Ope, behind you."

Carla stepped out of the way of a man carrying a flat of water bottles. He nodded as he passed, headed for two folding tables in the corner where women were making sandwiches, cutting each one in half and stacking them all up for anyone to grab. Another woman poured water into the church kitchen's coffee maker for a fresh pot. Sleeves of cookies sat beside open bags of chips, and two-liter bottles of soda were next to stacks of plastic cups. A pile of apples, a few bananas. Carrot sticks and cubes of cheese.

On the opposite side of the room, people organized medical supplies: boxes of Band-Aids, half-full bottles of hydrogen peroxide, rolls of gauze, bottles of aspirin. Like the kitchen pantries, medicine cabinets all over town had been raided, and people brought in whatever they had. Nearby, a woman sat on the floor with an ice pack on one of her knees while a nurse in scrubs cleaned the nasty cuts on the other. A golden retriever lay beside them both, his head resting on his owner's lap.

The church was packed with people. With supplies. They were a makeshift army of volunteers simply looking to help. Carla wanted to cry. *This is what community is. It's not a place, it's not a people—it's the acts of love done in a place by those people.*

Up on the altar, the pulpit had been moved out of the way for a table holding a CB radio hooked to a portable generator. Reverend Michaels listened with pen in hand, jotting down notes.

"All right, everyone, we got another," he called out, and the room went quiet. "The Farnsworths out on Kerns Road. Crash damage tore their drive up; they can't get out. Mr. Farnsworth apparently cut himself up pretty bad too."

"My truck can make it," Rand said, his hand raised.

"I'll go with," said the town's vet, making for the medical supply table. "I sewed up his dog's leg last year. I can make their stitches match."

Everyone chuckled. Rand and the vet left. Reverend Michaels went back to listening to the radio. The room went back to work.

"Carla!" Principal Gazdecki called out, jogging over to take one of the boxes from her arms. "Thank God you left."

"Left?"

"Left and went with Marion."

Carla didn't follow.

"Carla. *All* of this"—he waved an arm around the room—"is because of Marion's dispatches from the plant. No one knew what was happening. No one knew where to go, what to do. We knew *nothing*. Until he started giving updates."

Carla was dumbfounded. "And...and so then..."

"So then word spread. Rev made United Grace the official muster point. And we've been triaging here ever since."

As if on cue, Reverend Michaels stood and whistled loudly as he turned up the volume on the radio. The room went silent immediately and Marion's voice suddenly filled the room.

"*...welding gear has just arrived at Clover Hill. They're going to get things set up. Then the mission will start. I'll update when I know anything new. The evacuation order is still in effect. There are no other changes at this time.*"

The room murmured an understanding and a few people clapped. Then they went back to work. Carla was in disbelief. Mr. Gazdecki squeezed her arm.

"See?"

"But...but...where are the kids?" she asked, still trying to catch up.

"Most are out," Gazdecki said with a proud smile. "The bus got stuck in traffic—that pileup on thirty-five made the roads in and out of town literally impassable. Literally. We were locked in. Couldn't go anywhere. I was starting to get really worried. Feeling trapped. I mean, we were like sitting ducks—and that's when the bus driver picked up Marion's transmissions. So once we knew what was going on, we turned around—"

"It was awesome, Miss Carla," said a fifth-grader running by with a cookie from the food table. "We drove through a field!"

"We did," Mr. Gazdecki said with a laugh. "We drove through a cornfield to get off the road and out of traffic. The kids loved it. But we got to the church, and then we got organized, made a plan, and started shuttling the kids out."

"Out? In what? The bus?"

"No. Flatbed tractors. Like a hayride." He laughed again.

"But…to where?"

"The *docks*. You believe that? No one's getting out on any roads, so we've been sending everyone out by boat. There's a whole fleet—fishing boats, motorboats, small private things—from the people up in Bloomfield who are coming down, grabbing our folks, and bringing them back upriver."

"No."

"Swear to God," he said before looking around sheepishly. "Probably shouldn't say that in here." He chuckled. His whole vibe was a wild combination of adrenaline, pride, and love. He radiated purpose, just as the whole room did.

"We got kindergarten through fourth out so far," Gazdecki said, "along with a lot of mothers and their babies. The fifth- and sixth-graders are down in the basement. They're the next group. Once all the kids are out, we'll start evacuating ourselves. Until then, we're here. Helping in whatever way we can."

Carla didn't know what to say. She shook her head in wonder, looking around at the neighbors, friends, and strangers that filled the church—just as the sun shifted to the west side of the building. As sunlight began to pour through the stained-glass windows, the whole scene became bathed in rich jewel tones. Carla's eyes welled with tears. Mr. Gazdecki put a hand on her arm and squeezed.

"I know," he said, his own eyes glassy. "I know."

The two stood there for a moment awash with love before Carla wiped her face, took a deep breath, and joined the work.

It had felt right when they'd been arguing in the control room; it had felt like the only option. It *still* felt that way. But as Steve explained to Matt what he had to go do, the emotional side of the logical choice took over as he fully realized the position he was putting his son in.

Matt listened, picking at the corner of the table with his nail. "It sounds dangerous," he said without looking up.

"It is," said Steve. "What, you think you get those ideas to do all the dumb dangerous stuff you do from your mother?"

Matt cracked a smile before remembering himself and returning to a scowl.

The break-room TV was playing CNN, the volume low and background. Steve watched the rotating images of pandemonium. Barren supermarket shelves in Iowa. Bumper-to-bumper traffic on the interstates. Shoulder-to-shoulder crowds at airports. In-studio panels of experts giving their two cents. Replay of President Dawson addressing the nation. Families in N95 masks filling their cars with their belongings. Plunging stock market indexes. Dairy farmers dumping vats of milk down the drain. It struck him how hysterical it all seemed on TV, and yet here, on-site, in the eye of the storm, it was calm. It was simply people doing their jobs. No panic, no chaos. Just the work.

Unsure what else to say, Steve pointed at the vending machine and asked, "You hungry?"

Matt shook his head.

"You need anything?"

Matt shook his head.

Steve watched his son pick at the table for a while longer, then got up. He stalled a bit. Pushed in his chair. Put an empty chip bag in the trash. Blew his nose. The kinds of benign things you do to fill the silence when what needs to be said won't come.

"I'll, ah, I'll check on you when I'm done."

Matt didn't respond so Steve went to leave. At the door, he stopped.

"It's going to be different," Steve said. "After today, it'll be different, you and me. We're going to make changes. At home."

Matt glanced up. He was skeptical. But he actually looked at his dad, feeling him out, seeing if he was serious. Dropping his head, he mumbled something.

"What's that?" Steve asked.

"You already said that. You said that that time with my fishing pole."

As he looked at his son, the beloved only child of Steve and his now deceased wife, he saw the undeniable pain and betrayal brimming in the boy's eyes and realized that…he had absolutely no idea what Matt was talking about.

"The last time we went fishing. Mom was still home, she wasn't in the hospital yet. My pole. The line…" Matt prompted, waiting. "You told me we would fix it, remember? You said you'd teach me. But you didn't."

Fishing had always been their thing. Steve was a fisherman; his dad had taught him, and he loved teaching Matt. They were always at the river. It was their time to bond, their time to be men. But once Claire got really sick, they couldn't go. Or, more truthfully, they didn't go. Steve hadn't even realized until that moment that they never went anymore. That's how distant, how unpresent, he'd been for his son. For himself. But this experience that clearly meant so much to his son—Steve had absolutely no memory of. He'd never felt like more of a fraud.

Steve walked back into the room and sat down across from his son.

"We'll fix your pole. I'll teach you how. I promise."

Matt held his gaze. He believed him. Or at least, Steve saw, he wanted to believe him.

Right then, Steve saw a flicker of something in Matt he hadn't seen in a long time: his son. Who he *truly* was. The person that grief and loss had tried so hard to destroy. He was still in there! Steve saw the boy who was naturally joyful and curious, an optimist who loved to have fun. Relief washed over him as Steve fought the urge to take his son's face in his hands and say, *There you are! I see you. Please stay with me.*

He prayed his son saw something similar in him. Maybe he saw the dad he once knew, the one who used to laugh, who used to make pancakes on Sunday mornings. A man who would do anything to protect the people he loved, no matter what it cost him. Maybe Matt felt the same relief Steve did. That if his old dad was still in there, maybe his old self was too.

Steve made a decision. They were going to make their way back to each other.

They were going to survive.

CHAPTER NINETEEN

COUNTDOWN TO ZERO HOUR

13 HOURS AND 06 MINUTES

AMERICANS WERE GOING to die today. The only question for President Dawson and his administration was how many.

Surreal images played out on the screens in front of him: Gridlocked evacuation traffic as far away as Ohio. The Canadian and Mexican borders were now closed and not letting Americans in. There were preppers in gas masks in Georgia. Rental cars, everywhere, were unavailable. Toilet paper, everywhere, was gone. Financial institutions were limiting withdrawals to avoid a run on the banks. And that goddamn looped footage playing over and over on Fox of the exact moment Tony had told him the news. The image of his fixed smile while standing next to the Easter Bunny would haunt him forever.

The country was losing its mind. And surely it was the unreality of it all that was making Dawson lose *his* mind and misunderstand what Joss was telling him, because his go-to expert on the ground could not possibly be telling him that *that* was the plan.

"Let me get this straight," President Dawson said, pinching the bridge of his nose. "We're facing a potentially cataclysmic event that could mean the lives of countless Americans and render nearly a third of the country uninhabitable for generations to come...and your plan is to send a fifty-year-old man whose only scuba training was on his honeymoon twenty years ago into a radioactive pool to underwater-weld—a dangerous, experience-based skill that he has absolutely no training in—a piece of sheet metal to the side of a wall."

"That is correct, Mr. President." Joss's voice came through the speakerphone in the center of the table. *"Our plan to stop a nuclear meltdown is to patch it like a pair of jeans."*

Joss held her sat phone to her ear and listened to the president while watching Steve and several of his firefighters gathered around one of Clover Hill's emergency communications team's satellite computers as some folks from the U.S. Navy gave them a crash course in underwater welding.

George would be the *tender*—the person on dry land who would turn the electricity on and off, a vital safeguard. *Hot, cold*—that's what Steve would say to cue George for when to turn it on and off. The *stinger*—the handheld electrode holder, essentially the tool used to fuse the weld.

Each new vocab word and specialized device made the mission feel more audacious, and she was glad Dawson wasn't there to witness it. If he was skeptical already, seeing it in action would have sent him into orbit.

But she'd mostly tuned him out a while back anyway, somewhere around the time he mentioned something about toilet paper. She didn't give a damn about any of it. Markets in crisis. Misinformation on social media. Traffic accidents, riots, looting as the result of evacuations. None of these were her concerns and she could feel herself growing annoyed with what felt like a lecture from someone who was as safe as could be half the country away in an underground bunker.

"Well, you wouldn't know any of that here," Joss said. "We're cut off. No one's coming in, and most people can't even head out. We're just handling it."

She described how the National Guard had arrived and how the local firefighters were finally able to take a seat and get a drink of water. She explained the virtual communications blackout and how they were using a CB radio system and retro technology to get information and directions out to the community—which made her think of Carla and wonder what she'd found going on at the church.

If Joss knew Waketans—and she did—they'd figured out a way to make something out of nothing, and she told Dawson as much. The president asked her what Waketa needed.

"I don't know, get someone to United Grace Church and find out yourself," she replied, frustrated. "I'm here. I'm at the plant. I'm not in Waketa any more than you are, Mr. President. I know they need help, but come here and ask them. Let them tell you what they need."

The president was silent through all of that and didn't have a response, and if she had to interpret what she didn't hear, it'd be that he was impressed. Which made her proud. She *was* proud. This was what small-town America did. They handled it.

Joss could tell the welding lesson was wrapping up, which meant it was time for Steve to put on the gear and get the mission underway. Joss stood and began telling the president that, but he interrupted.

"Again, surely we can wait for someone, a professional welder, to get to you."

"Mr. President, we're moving to the pool now. This is happening *now*."

"I'm worried it's not safe, Dr. Vance."

Joss blushed. *Doctor.* The word had no business sounding that good. Clearly, someone had revisited her file. "Then let me relieve you of your worries, Mr. President. You are correct. It's not safe."

"Mocking the president. You know, the FBI has been unleashed for less."

"You wouldn't dare."

"What makes you so sure?"

"Because you don't want my answer for who my favorite president is to change."

And with that, Joss hung up on the leader of the free world.

Dawson shut off the speaker, and the dial tone went away. At the end of the table, Tony pretended to read the papers in front of him while doing his best to hide a smirk. He glanced up and saw the president watching him.

"What?" said Dawson.

Tony raised his hands in surrender and went back to pretending to read. "I didn't say a thing."

CHAPTER TWENTY

COUNTDOWN TO ZERO HOUR

12 HOURS AND 59 MINUTES

THERE WAS STILL no foam. There were still no reinforcements. One little boy was still not a priority. The situation at the bridge was dire and there were no next steps.

Levon trudged down the hill, plopping down to sit beside Dani. They both stared into the unrelenting fire. Frankie was right—the wings must have been nearly full of fuel because the blaze had barely let up. It was a steady, constant state of raging heat and taunting flames holding them back from the van.

Dani knew there was a solution, but she didn't know what it was. She eyed the structural reinforcements of the concrete and metal bridge. They seemed to be sound, but what did she know? She wasn't a civil engineer.

"Take a break," Levon said. "I'll stay with him. Go get some water."

"I bet Connor would like a drink. I bet he's thirsty too."

The tone of her voice told Levon it'd be better not to push it so he just said, "Well, you'll be of no use to him if you have to tap out."

They sat there together for a while in the chilly April air, not talking and watching Connor. The boy was lying on his side curled up in a ball, moving and adjusting himself only every once in a while. He was too old for a daily nap, but Dani hoped exhaustion would win out and maybe, just for a little bit, he would doze off. Leave this place and these horrors. Go somewhere warm and bright, where his only concern was which toy he wanted to play with.

"You haven't heard from Marion, have you?" Levon asked.

Dani shook her head, remembering with a twinge of guilt the handful of times she'd turned away from Connor to check her phone. "Carla?"

"Nope," Levon said. "Can't get a call to connect. My texts say 'undelivered.' I'm sure she's got the same on her end. Boggs somehow got a text from his girlfriend. She's okay. Frankie's got nothing."

"I bet Carla has Bri. And I bet Daddy figured out a way to get to them. They're fine."

"We'll probably see them round the corner with our foam here in a bit."

"Carla knows a guy whose sister's friend's brother has a stock of foam."

"Nah. Marion knows the recipe. He's going to make it from scratch."

There was probably more truth to that than either of them wanted to admit. Any qualities of bravery and ingenuity Dani had, she'd gotten from her daddy. Levon would be the first to say that marrying Carla was the smartest thing he'd ever done. Of course Dani and Levon were worried about them. But they were also confident they were fine. The far greater fear lay in thinking of the possibility of a life where they weren't.

Levon stared into the fire, transfixed, as his mind went back to their kitchen just that morning. He'd walked in to grab his coffee thermos before heading to the station and found Carla at the sink staring at the bird feeder in the backyard.

The water was running, but Carla's hands were still. She was looking at a cardinal pecking at the feeder when suddenly the bird flew away. Levon had seen the seed in the bird's beak and assumed she was bringing it back to her babies in the nest.

He knew Carla assumed the same.

Levon cleared his throat now and told Dani, "We lost another baby."

Dani dropped her head. The sound of the river grew louder. "Shit," she muttered finally. "When?"

"Last weekend."

Dani thought back. That had been Brianna's birthday weekend. They'd had a little party. Carla had baked the cake. "I'm sorry, Lee. I am *so* sorry. She was, what, ten weeks?"

"Eleven," he said.

Dani was the only other person who'd known Carla was pregnant. They'd learned the hard way, after the first two, to wait to tell anyone. Fewer questions to field. Fewer gifts to return. Fewer mournful arm squeezes.

"How's Carla?" Dani asked.

Levon considered. He wasn't sure he had an answer.

"I'm not good at it, you know?" he said finally. "I never know what I'm supposed to do. Or what she wants me to say. I don't know what she needs."

"She probably doesn't know what she needs either."

Levon nodded, thinking that was an easy out. "I looked it up. You know the whole *It happened for a reason* stuff people say? All that bullshit? They say don't say that. It invalidates the pain. Makes it like it's a good thing. Like it's a good thing that your child didn't... you know. Didn't make it. Like you should be glad it happened or something."

Levon stared across the river at Connor's dad's lifeless body slumped over the wheel. The last thing Paul had done on this earth was face away from his son to protect the child from the sight of his dead father. As if what the boy couldn't see couldn't hurt him.

"But I just—" Levon stopped short. Eventually, when he did continue, his voice was low. "I don't know, Dani, I just keep thinking, what if she *were* still pregnant? Today, I mean. With everything happening at the plant. The baby would be here in it too. Breathing it. Being around it. Exposed..."

He trailed off, not completing his thought.

He didn't have to.

After a while Dani stood, stretching her back, taking a deep breath of cold spring air. Her eyes were trained on Connor's dad too. In her peripheral vision, the flames danced.

"I don't think being glad your child isn't here to see this means you're glad your child didn't make it," she said before looking down at Levon. "I think it makes you a father."

Dani passed him the megaphone and squeezed his shoulder. "If Connor needs me, I'm just at the truck."

As she made her way up the embankment to the fire engine, she saw Boggs and Frankie going through the tools and supplies they had, trying to come up with something. Dani got her water and leaned against the rig, helmet tucked under one arm. Closing her eyes, she rested her head back, trying to clear her mind.

The cold air pinched at her cheeks. The smell of smoke and jet fuel seeped into her suit. A bird chirped. The river rushed and rambled. Voices, quiet and distant, occasionally came over the radio.

The water in her mouth was wildly refreshing; in this heightened state, she felt as though she could trace its journey through her body. She visualized the path it took: through her mouth to her throat, down her esophagus, and into her stomach.

Dani opened her eyes and slowly lifted her head.

"So, we've been thinking," Frankie said, coming around the front of the fire engine. "If we go through..." He trailed off, seeing her face. "You all right? Dani? What is it?"

Dani kept staring off at nothing, looking out across the distance, across the river. The water, the bridge, the van. Finally, she turned to Frankie, almost surprised that he was there. Her mouth was open and she looked distracted as the pieces in her head moved closer together.

"I think," she said, working it through, "I think I might have an idea..."

Frankie didn't respond; he just looked where she was looking, trying to catch up. In the background, someone on the radio started talking.

"Be advised, travel on I-35..."

"So, what's your—" Frankie began.

Dani's hand shot out as she shushed him.

"...teams have cleared the..."

"Oh my God," Dani said as she scrambled into the truck, turning up the volume on the CB radio. After a few seconds, she giggled. "That's my dad!"

"That's your dad?" Boggs said, joining them. "Dude, he's unreal. He's at the plant and he's relaying all the information over channel seven. Everyone's listening to him."

Dani couldn't believe what she was hearing. "This isn't our comms? This is everyone?"

"Yup."

"Like, anyone in town with a CB? You're shitting me."

"I'm not, I swear. He's literally the only way the town's getting information, since the power's out."

"All of Waketa is hearing him?"

"Well, anyone with a CB."

"So he can get any message to the community?"

Boggs crossed his arms. "Dani, you're starting to make as much sense as Frankie. Why is this so confusing?"

"I just—I want to make sure I understand. My dad, right now, can get messages and warnings and requests—any information—to anyone listening to the radio?"

"Yes."

Dani couldn't believe it. She smiled big.

"I know how to get Connor out."

CHAPTER TWENTY-ONE

COUNTDOWN TO ZERO HOUR

12 HOURS AND 43 MINUTES

STEVE STARED DOWN into the pool at the spent fuel rods.

What happens if he touches the rods?

He dies.

George had asked the question. He'd thought Joss was joking. Steve knew she was not.

The fuel rods were highly radioactive, she'd explained, but the four hundred thousand gallons of water in the forty-foot-deep pool made being near them safe. The water worked in two ways: One, it kept the rods cool, and two, it acted as a radiation shield. The farther you were from the rods, the safer it was. The closer you went, the more dangerous it got. When she said that, *that* was when George had asked his question.

Get in, get out, Steve thought. Just like he'd told his crew earlier in the day. Work fast, and it'd be fine.

Steve sat on the edge of the pool in full scuba gear, the condition of which had been a little concerning when he'd suited up. Brittle rubber, rusted metal, warped plastic; no one had commented on any of it, even though they'd all noticed. What else were they going to use? He adjusted R.J.'s tight wetsuit and watched through the bean-shaped glass of the industrial dive helmet as tiny flecks of black neoprene rubber shed from the second skin.

"Can you check the connection for my air?" Steve asked, hearing his own tinny voice echo through the heavy, hot, carbon-fiber-reinforced fiberglass helmet. George, beside him in full hazmat gear, looked up from checking his own equipment.

"Can you breathe okay?" George asked.

"Yeah. But just—just check it for me, will you?"

It was the piece of equipment Steve was most worried about.

Because industrial divers needed to stay underwater for long periods, they used SSA—surface-supplied air—as opposed to a traditional scuba dive tank. A thick braid of rubber-coated cables called the umbilical ran from the surface down to the diver's helmet, providing a comms line and, more importantly, oxygen. They realized they had a problem once they understood that the topside compressor that supplied the oxygen for the umbilical used ambient air as its source.

Which was a problem if the ambient air of the room you were operating in was radioactive.

Further complicating things, the backup option, the bailout bottle—a small, portable oxygen bottle connected to the helmet for use in emergencies—was one of the few pieces of equipment R.J.

had managed to sell. With SSA not viable and no bailout bottle available, their only option was to retrofit one of the larger firefighter oxygen bottles.

It wasn't a perfect fit. The female end on the helmet was slightly larger than the male connection on the hose. But the use of a rubber O-ring in conjunction with electrical tape wound around the point of connection over and over again created a workable modification.

George leaned over to check the connection. "Looks good," he said after some fiddling. He grabbed the tank strapped across Steve's back and checked to see how secure it was. "Looks real good."

Steve nodded solemnly, staring at the waterline, which was now a solid ten feet lower than it should have been, which meant he would be ten feet closer to the rods than someone should be. "All right," he said. "Let's get this over with."

The whole world went silent the second he went under the water. Acclimating, he let his body drop in the weightless environment while bubbles rose up from his helmet in a distant, muted gurgle. Using his arms, he spun a bit to orient himself and assess his surroundings, and as he turned, he saw beams of sunlight streaming in through the water from the cracks in the wall.

In an instant, he was somewhere else.

Claire. Their honeymoon. Hawaii. Underwater, diving off the coast of Molokai. He could see Claire's hazel eyes peering at him through her mask, her lush red lips pouting out as they circled the regulator. Bubbles rose all around her as rays of bright sunlight streaked down from above, lighting up her bright red hair. It shimmered as it moved around her face in slow motion. Dancing; weightless and free. Like fire underwater.

Steve heard his name called from somewhere far off, *Steve,* repeated over and over until he snapped back. Claire was gone. It was just him, alone in the pool with the rays of light in the undulating water taunting his heart. Steve shook his head, angry at himself. *Stop it.* He had to focus. Compartmentalize. Claire, Matt, the fear, the grief—he had to block it all out.

"*Steve. Talk to me, buddy*," George said through the comms in his helmet.

"I'm good. I'm okay," Steve said, already feeling a coating of sweat on his upper lip under the fitted rubber mouthpiece that covered his nose and mouth.

Steve kicked his fins and swam to position himself in front of the damaged wall where the sunlight was streaming in—or, more crucially, where the water was pouring out. Dropping down until he floated in front of the worst of it, he closed his eyes and took a breath to center himself.

Once that sheet was slipped into the water, the clock would start ticking. It was all on him. He had to get it in place and secure it before the movement and agitation created more damage and made things worse. This was it. This was their one and only shot.

Steve opened his eyes. Gave the go-ahead. And the mission began.

Topside, positioned high above the pool, an operator in the rafters of the gantry crane, wearing full hazmat attire, began to lower the sheet of aluminum into the pool. The crane's claw attachments, typically used for inserting and removing the small, square fuel rods, were perfect for this task. The operator listened to the directions George relayed from Steve and tapped the joystick left. Then right. Then right a little more. Slow. Slower.

Underwater, as soon as the aluminum broke through the surface, Steve swam up to meet it. He placed his hands flat against the center of the sheet and kicked furiously, applying as much constant pressure as possible to keep the lightweight aluminum pressed flush against the wall while he and the sheet slid down in tandem. It was a slow, steady process. But it was progress.

All the while, beneath him, the rods lay in wait. A couple of times, Steve glanced down in spite of himself, almost like he was making sure they weren't coming up after him. He felt like he was swimming with sharks but without a diver's cage—no real protection, only a flimsy agreement that they wouldn't bite.

Steve kept guiding the sheet down bit by bit until it was, to his eye, in place.

"Hold," he said.

The sheet stopped moving. Steve flipped down the tinted welding screen on the front of his helmet, and with that, the clock really started ticking.

"Hot."

On the surface, George, his tender, flipped the knife switch to turn on the power. A moment later, Steve felt the pulse of electricity coursing through the stinger in his hand. As fast as he could, Steve squeezed the tool's handle, and a sudden blinding light of burning electrodes at the end of the stinger lit up the water. Squinting through the light and the roiling mass of bubbles the process created, he placed the tool against the seam where the sheet met the wall and drew a short line across the top, just as the navy reps on the video call had taught him. After a few moments, he released his grip and the light went out.

Flipping his visor up, he quickly checked his work. Not bad, but not great. Good enough for a beginner, but, more important, good enough for what they needed.

"Cold," Steve said.

Floating in the water, his free hand pressed up against the sheet, he waited until the electricity coursing through the stinger's cable to the surface went still before he swam over to repeat the process on the upper left corner. The navy instructors had been adamant: *Do not swim while the stinger is hot.* There was too much risk of electrocution. Even experienced welders followed this guideline, and Steve wasn't merely *in*experienced—he had *no* experience.

Upper left corner. Hot—work as fast as he could. Cold—swim to the lower right corner. Hot—work. Cold—move. Around he went, making quick, dirty spot welds, just enough to hold the sheet in place. Once it was somewhat secure all the way around, he would go back and secure it more substantially. Like tightening lug nuts on a tire.

As he worked, Steve began to notice flecks of black floating through the water. He ignored them initially, assuming they were some sort of by-product of the burning electrodes—until he felt something cool on his leg. The bead of fused metal jagged as, startled, he looked down.

He could see his skin through the suit. The flecks of black were from the deteriorating wetsuit. His heart began to race as he told himself it was only R.J.'s old sun-warped, low-quality suit falling apart. It wasn't that the radioactive water was eating it.

But truthfully, he didn't know.

Focus, he chided himself. *Get the job done. Get out of the pool. Get back to Matt. And that's it. That's all you have to do.*

His welds were getting cleaner. His work was going faster. He was nearly done when out of the corner of his eye, he saw something dark come at him. He swatted at it, reflexively jerking away, before realizing with some embarrassment that nothing was coming at him. It was only the tail of the electrical tape.

...The electrical tape that connected the hose from the oxygen tank to the helmet.

...Which meant the tape was unraveling.

...Which meant his oxygen might be cut off at any second.

"The tape is unraveling," he said, the words coming quick out of his mouth. "This is the last weld. Hot." Moments later, the stinger pulsed to life. Steve started the weld. In his peripheral vision, he could see the tape growing longer as it unraveled. He kept going, nearing the halfway point with this bead of fused metal, when he felt the pressure in his helmet pop as the air disconnected.

Steve immediately took a breath in and held it, his pulse shooting up from a spike of anxiety-fueled adrenaline. He was alone, deep in radioactive water, with mere tens of seconds left to breathe. His hand shook as he tried to finish the weld, but fear won. He decided that would have to do.

Panic rose in his chest as he kicked for the surface, the primal fear of drowning clamping down on his chest, making him feel like what little air he still had was being squeezed out of him. Darkness crept in on the sides as he went into an odd sort of tunnel vision and the anxiety began to cloud his mind. Kicking his fins, he waved his arms, the stinger in his hand vibrating with electricity as he swam in a clumsy, uncoordinated way, tripping over himself, as much as that was possible underwater.

He didn't know how it happened; he didn't know what had happened. All he knew was that the bright light of the burning electrodes suddenly appeared when he hadn't meant for it to.

In an instant, it was practically over before it began. His whole body tingled, went numb, and then there was nothing.

George peered down into the water.

"Steve."

No response.

George flipped the knife switch, shutting off power. Something wasn't right. That last blast of light seemed wrong. It had been too short. Like an afterthought. Nothing like how the rest of the welds had gone.

George watched Steve. What was he doing down there? He was about to call Steve's name again—when it dawned on him that he had no idea what he should do if something went wrong. They'd been so focused on the mission, there had only been time to consider steps for success. They'd never considered what to do in failure. And as this was sinking in, George realized what Steve was doing.

He wasn't floating, nor was he swimming up.

Steve was in free fall, headed for the radioactive rods at the bottom of the pool.

CHAPTER TWENTY-TWO

COUNTDOWN TO ZERO HOUR

12 HOURS AND 29 MINUTES

"WHAT HAPPENS IF *he touches the rods?" George had asked.*

"He dies," Joss told him.

George blinked at her.

"If he were to swim down, touch them, then immediately swim back up," she continued, "that alone would be enough radiation to kill him. If he stayed down there in physical contact with the rods, he'd be dead in minutes."

* * *

Steve's unresponsive body sank headfirst to the bottom of the pool, where the nuclear rods waited to catch him. It was like a perverse countdown; every inch his body descended ticked off the decades, years, months, days, he had left to live. The water temperature rose the farther down he went, but Steve, blacked out, did not notice.

The rods were right there. He was just about to hit them when— *snap*— the stinger's cable, attached to the weighted dive belt around his waist, went taut. Steve's body recoiled, then flipped in slow motion through the weightless environment, doubled over like someone was pulling him up from behind by the belt strap; his arms hung down, and the tips of his gloved fingers brushed against the top of the rods.

There, at the bottom of the pool, Steve floated, suspended, dangling just above the rods as flecks of rubber shed furiously from the suit, dancing around him like he was in the center of a snow globe filled with black snow.

On the surface, the stinger line was slipping through George's trembling rubber-gloved hands. After screaming for backup over the comms, he grunted and looked around, trying to figure out what to do, how to get to Steve. He couldn't dive in after him. If he let go, Steve's body would hit the rods flat and it would be over. And if George or anyone else swam down to him, they'd suffer the same fate and double the number of people needing rescue.

In his peripheral vision, George saw the door to the pool burst open and several firefighters in hazmat gear run in. Up above, the crane operator repositioned the claw attachments over the pool, closer to where Steve was. One of the firefighters dropped to the ground beside George and lay prostrate with his arms reaching over the edge of the pool, trying to grab the line to help him pull Steve up. Another firefighter climbed down the ladder fixed to the side of the pool, heading, rung by rung, toward the water's surface. He stopped, held on with one hand, and leaned out as far as he could to grab the line and help George pull him up. But the line was beyond his reach.

The claw attachment dropped into the pool to grab Steve and drag him back up. But the movement in the water made waves, distorting the visual, making it impossible to get a fix on where Steve was.

"*Someone direct me!*" the crane operator yelled into the comms.

Before anyone could say anything, the firefighter on the ladder hurried down the rest of the way and dropped into the pool with a splash.

George put one hand carefully under the other as he pulled Steve up. Small, meager progress was made—until the wet line slipped through his wet rubber gloves and Steve dropped back down.

The firefighter in the pool, treading water on the surface like a snorkeler, held his breath and peered down to the bottom. Motioning with his arms—*left, left again, up, now back a little more, drop*—he directed the crane operator. The claw was in the water, moving in accordance with the directions. After a moment, the firefighter made a motion with his fist that could mean only one thing: *Grab him.*

Everyone waited. The seconds felt like hours. Then, suddenly, the firefighter in the water gave a thumbs-up and frantically started pointing up.

George felt the resistance on the line in his hands ease as the crane brought Steve up slowly. Slowly. Very slowly. George held on to the line, adjusting his grip as it went, taking up the slack in case Steve slipped out of the claw. The firefighter on the pool's surface nodded, continuing to give a thumbs-up as he watched the progress under the water. *Yes. Good. Keep going...keep going...*until finally Steve's body was close enough to the surface that the firefighter could grab him.

With Steve firmly in the firefighter's arms, George dropped the stinger line and scrambled to the ladder where the other firefighters were already waiting. The man farthest down the ladder hooked one arm under a rung and grabbed Steve with the other. Awkwardly, with difficulty, they relayed the fire chief up and up, until his limp, unresponsive body was finally at the top.

George watched this from all fours next to the top of the ladder. He was the last to grab Steve and drag his boss, his friend, out onto the deck. Everyone circled around the body, breathing heavily from the exertion, as George screamed Steve's name.

Someone rolled him onto his back.

There was no movement, no response.

CHAPTER TWENTY-THREE

COUNTDOWN TO ZERO HOUR
12 HOURS AND 14 MINUTES

EVERYONE IN THE control room wondered if they had just watched a man die.

Ethan stared at Maggie. Maggie stared at the pool's water-level meter. Had it worked or not? Were they okay or, after all that, were they still on the brink of ruin?

There was nothing to do but wait.

In the silence, it all replayed in Ethan's head.

For the rest of his life, however long that might be, he would never shake the panic and chaos he had heard over the radio, the soundtrack to the images they'd all witnessed on the audio-less security feed from the cameras inside the spent fuel pool building. They'd all stared helplessly at the screen as their own fate and the life of one man entwined in one horrific scene. And now that it was over, they didn't even know if it had worked.

The possibility that it could all have been for nothing was almost too much to bear. After all that, they could be right back to where they'd started. And the most terrifying part of all was that there was no plan B.

"Maggie. Where are we at?" Ethan said, pacing.

The controller never took her eyes off the gauge. "Still too early to know," she said.

Ethan grabbed the back of a chair and pushed it forward, banging it into a desk. Everyone flinched and turned.

"Did it work or did it not?" he said, his voice loud and angry.

"Both inflow pumps are on," Vikram said. "They're flowing at max—"

"Yes, but did it *work*? If it didn't, we need to *know* that. We need to know that *now*."

Ethan's face was bright red as he paced back and forth like a caged animal. Everyone glanced at each other, unsure of what to do. That he expected them to know if it had worked was not only irrational, it was impossible. They couldn't have the figures yet. It would take some time to see if the water going in was holding and rising.

"If it didn't work," he said, his voice booming, "then we need to find—"

"Okay, Ethan," Joss said quietly, her hand under his elbow. "Let's just calm—"

"No!" he said, wrenching his arm away. "'Let's just calm down'—no, Joss. How about let's just do our fucking jobs."

"Ethan."

"How about let's just not kill a man for no reason."

"Ethan—"

"How about let's just try to stop a nuclear meltdown from destroying—"

"*Ethan!*"

Joss's final scream worked like a slap across the face. He looked around with a dazed *What just happened?* expression, his mouth moving as if he wanted to say something but didn't know what. Instead, without a word, he left the room, the door closing quietly behind him.

The only one who didn't watch any of this was Maggie. She just kept staring at the water-level gauge, waiting for the needle to go up.

Gloved hands pumped rhythmically on Steve's chest under the bright lights of the decontamination unit. Rapid-fire orders were shouted, muffled beneath thick, redundant layers of protective hazmat gear. The room of medics scrambled, knowing every second meant something.

"He's got a pulse," someone said as someone else unbuckled the dive helmet and slid it off. Steve's eyes were closed, his skin blue, his lips parted; a faint pulse was one of the few indications that there was still any hope. Layer by layer, everything Steve wore was stripped off him and tossed in a pile in a corner of the room. Soap and water washed his bare skin, which was rapidly changing from pink to red. Raw, open wounds on the tips of his fingers were expanding. In less than a minute, Steve was naked, exposed and laid bare in a room filled with people who were completely covered and protected from head to toe.

"Get that out of here! Now!" someone yelled, gesturing toward the contaminated wetsuit and gear. It was shedding radiation, working against their efforts, but in an all-hands-on-deck moment, there wasn't time to dispose of it properly. Someone grabbed the pile, chucked it into the hall, then got back to work.

The gear lay in a puddle in the empty, quiet hallway. Muffled, chaotic sounds of shouted vital signs and running water continued inside the room. From beneath the heap of wetsuit, Steve's personal dosimeter bleated out a steady warning. Down the hall, standing in the threshold of the break room, Matt was the only one who heard it.

Ethan could just make out the Mississippi River through the branches of the trees. The sky had partially clouded over, a gray, monochromatic coating over patches of soft blue. If it were any other day, or even a mere handful of hours earlier, it would have been an idyllic scene.

But it wasn't any other day, it was the day the unthinkable had happened. He watched the rising smoke that came from smoldering piles of crash debris and the flames that still billowed out of others. The firefighters and National Guardsmen down below moved with skilled precision, individuals working as cohesive units. Men and women exposed to the worst of it so that other men and women would be spared the worst of it. He wondered how many of them had thought, *This isn't what I signed up for.* He doubted many had.

Hearing footsteps down the hall, Ethan didn't bother turning. He knew who it was. Joss came up beside him and stared out the window too. Neither of them spoke for some time. They just stood there. Remembering what had been, looking at what was, wondering what would come.

"They're probably close to North Dakota by now," Ethan said finally.

Joss glanced over. Ethan didn't look back. "Your family?"

He nodded. "She knows not to take any main roads, so I'm not worried about I-35. But maybe they're stuck in traffic anyway. I don't know."

Joss didn't say anything. They both just looked out at the destruction.

"We have a code," Ethan said after a while. "It's different depending on which direction to head. But the idea is the same. If Kristin gets a text with the code, she knows. Something happened. Get the kids and get out."

Joss waited. Ethan realized with amazement that even after all these years, Joss knew when he had more to say but wasn't yet able to access it. Impatience was one of her strongest personality traits. But with him, for whatever reason, she'd always had the patience to wait while he found his way to where he needed to go. Today, that grace only made the guilt worse.

"I don't remember what I did first," he confessed. "Did I start a checklist or did I text my wife? I was in charge. I was at the controls when it happened. This was on my watch. And my instinct was to put myself first. My family. I put them first. Over everything."

"You're human," Joss said. "Anyone would do that."

"You wouldn't."

"Yes. I would."

He didn't respond. For the first time, he finally understood what she had always tried to tell him. She wanted to change the world. He wanted to have a family. He didn't understand why they couldn't do both. She didn't get how he didn't see they couldn't.

Today, he got it.

"There's a lot you've been right about," he said. "You tried to warn us."

"Hindsight's twenty-twenty," she said.

"Joss, your dissertation was titled 'Nuclear Spent Fuel Pools: A Problem That Without a Solution Will End Mankind.' That's not hindsight."

"Well. Feels a little on the nose now. But yeah, I tried to warn you."

There was a silence between them that, if they were honest, had started fifteen years ago. After a while, Joss was the first to talk.

"It wouldn't have changed anything," she said.

He didn't know if she meant today or then. "What wouldn't?"

"If we'd stayed together."

She meant *then*. As if the guilt already weren't enough, his mind went back to that day. Driving to her house to pick her up. The look on her face as he put her bags in the trunk and she'd realized his bags weren't there. How hard they'd both cried during the ride. How she'd walked into the airport alone and never looked back.

"If you'd come with me to Washington," she said, "if we'd taken on the suits together, it wouldn't have changed a thing. They won't change unless they have to."

"So that's why you came back."

"I know when I'm beat," she said, her voice tinged with resentment. "Wait—you didn't think I came back for you?"

For the first time since that morning, Ethan actually cracked a smile. This was a filling-in-the-blanks fifteen years in the making. This was what healing looked like.

"At least you tried," he said.

"I tried. Every court needs a jester."

There was something in her voice when she said that—after all, he knew her emotional junk drawer as well as she knew his—something in her tone that said she now understood too. Understood what he was trying to say. That you didn't have to spend your one life saving the world just because you saw the problem. It didn't have to be you. There was also something to be said for just living a life, and that didn't make you a coward or selfish. There was value in enjoying what's here, what's beautiful, what's now. Not overthinking it. Just enough *is* enough. Sure, you could spend your life tilting at windmills, but to what end?

"Joss, the world needs people crazy enough to try to save it."

She smiled ruefully. "But it's only worth saving if it's full of people whose first impulse is to protect the ones they love."

They turned at the sound of running feet coming down the hall. Dwight was breathless, his face unreadable. When he spoke, there was a slight tremble to his voice.

"We got a reading on the water level."

CHAPTER TWENTY-FOUR

COUNTDOWN TO ZERO HOUR
12 HOURS AND 12 MINUTES

ALL AROUND THE WORLD, everyone stopped to hear if the mission to fix the pool had been a success.

A family loading up their car in Iowa paused to watch the president on their teenage daughter's cell phone. Lawyers in a Chicago high-rise crowded around the conference-room TV. Surfers suiting up in LA turned up their truck's radio, exactly like a group of field-workers in Guatemala did. In London, the after-work pub crowds were wall to wall; in Greece, families allowed the TV to stay on during dinner. Antinuclear activists in Central Park stopped their chants as, a few miles downtown, the stock exchange trading floor slowed to a standstill.

And at a hole-in-the-wall bar tucked into some forgotten coastal fishing village, the bartender whistled at the crowd, then pointed the clicker at the small, 2000s-era TV hanging in the corner. As the volume went up, the chatter of thick New England accents quieted down.

The bar was packed, much of the crowd the same people who'd watched that first COVID press conference. Years prior, they'd all sat at the bar trying to figure out what the hell a subprime mortgage was. Not long after that, they were there shaking their heads as they watched oil pour out of a rig in the Gulf. It was there they'd felt closure as they listened to details about SEAL Team Six's raid on Osama bin Laden's compound, and it was there they'd watched that horrible black smoke slash across a perfect blue September sky.

They'd been there for Buckner; they'd been there for the bloody sock. Olympics, elections, scandals, and storms—they'd been there for all that too. The bar hadn't been around when Armstrong first walked on the moon, but it was for the *Challenger*, and with that, as with every other tragedy and triumph, they'd watched together with elbows resting on a beer-sticky bar, waiting to find out what came next.

"Bobby!" the bartender cried. "Shut the fuck up!"

Bobby, drunker than usual (which was saying something, but who could blame him?), held his hands up in surrender just as President Dawson appeared on the screen.

"Good evening, my fellow Americans."

Carla turned up the volume on the school bus's radio, then retook her seat. Principal Gazdecki glanced over from behind the wheel.

They exchanged a look as Marion continued relaying the update from the plant.

"...and as we speak, President Dawson is addressing the nation. He just received the same update I did from the R2 control room and the update is — the mission was a success."

Carla dropped her head in relief. Gazdecki slapped his hand against the wheel.

"The flow of water leaking from the pool has been stopped and it is being refilled. Once Clover Hill gets equipment that can reach high enough, they will reinforce the repairs from the outside. But to reiterate: The emergency stopgap measure was a success. The water in the pool will remain cool enough. A meltdown has been averted."

"Does that mean we can stay home?"

Carla turned around to answer Mr. Wright, the ninety-three-year-old man clutching his cane tightly, but before she could, Marion continued.

"The worst has been avoided — but there are still unhealthy levels of radiation in the air. The evacuation order remains in effect. As we have done all day, we will continue to err on the side of caution."

"There's your answer, Mr. Wright," Carla said as the bus turned and headed for a double-wide at the end of the lane. The trailer's front door opened, and Mr. Lupinsky began the struggle to get his wife's wheelchair out the door and down the ramp to meet them.

Once all the schoolkids had been shuttled to the docks, Carla and Principal Gazdecki took the bus into the community to pick up some of the residents that might have fallen through the cracks — the elderly, the disabled, those with mobility issues, and anyone else simply in need of a ride.

"But even if they *had* lifted the evacuation order," Gazdecki said to Mr. Lupinsky, eyeing him in the rearview mirror, "this is the biggest thing to ever happen to Waketa—you wouldn't want to miss the excitement, would you?"

Mr. Wright harrumphed grumpily. "Seems like a whole to-do about nothing."

"I promise you," Carla whispered to herself while looking out the window in the direction of Clover Hill, "it doesn't seem that way to everyone."

Steve was laid out flat on the stretcher. A clean Clover Hill sweatsuit covered his body, concealing pink skin and blotchy red spots. His hair was still wet. His eyes were still closed. But he was breathing.

He moaned, the kind of sound so soft that you froze, unsure if you'd heard something or not. But a few seconds later, he began to stir, his fingers, wrapped in clean white gauze, slowly feeling their way around, searching in a manner that asked, *Where am I?*

Across the room, George got up from his chair and came to the bedside. He peered down, watching, waiting, until finally, Steve's eyes fluttered open. Squinting into the harsh fluorescent ceiling lighting, Steve's eyes now moved as his fingers had: *What happened, what's going on?* As his gaze made its way over to George, the familiar face seemed to anchor him.

"Did it work?" Steve asked, his voice raw and gravelly.

George smiled.

As George reported the results and gave a status update on the pool, Steve laid his head back on the pillow and closed his eyes, exhaling loudly in relief. It wasn't for nothing. It was for *everything*.

"We did it."

"*You* did it," George corrected.

Steve attempted a smile. "Well. It's done." He grimaced, becoming more aware of his pain. "I remember losing my air. I remember taking a breath. I remember starting for the surface."

"And that's it?" George prompted when he didn't say anything else.

"That's it."

George drew a hesitant breath, then filled him in on what had happened after that. He was direct and devoid of emotion, as if he were giving a press conference, pausing only once to ask Steve if he should keep going. Steve nodded, feeling the tears slip across his face.

When George finished, Steve opened his eyes and asked simply: "How long do I have?"

George looked everywhere but at Steve while making the kinds of sounds you make when you stall, when you don't want to say what you're about to say.

"You know, there's no real consensus," he finally got out. "Once we get you to the hospital, they'll have a better idea."

"Bullshit. No doctor at Minn General will know better than the medics here. What are they saying is the best case scenario?"

There was a pause. A long pause.

"A year."

Steve shut his eyes, a physical rejection of the possibility that he could be dead in a year. *Best* case, a year. The full-body pain intensified as death shifted from an abstract idea to an acute situation with those two words. "And worst case?"

"A couple months. A month."

A *month*! Steve took that in. A month was a handful of weeks. One full moon. One billing cycle. He could be gone before his library books were due.

Steve asked, "Does Matt know?"

"He knows there was an accident. He knows you were exposed. He doesn't know how bad."

Steve didn't say anything for a while.

"Do you want someone to tell him?" George said. "I can if you want me to."

Steve shook his head. No, he would.

The tension in the control room had eased.

There was still so much to be done. They were nowhere near out of the woods—but they were no longer in crisis. Now they could simply do the work.

"I'm going outside," Joss said to Ethan. "I'm going to start measuring radioactivity on the crash debris for the cleanup teams." She held up a walkie-talkie. "If you need me."

"Sounds good," he said, poring over a readout Vikram had just handed him.

Joss turned back. "Hey, do you want to use my sat phone to text Kristin? Better chance it'll get through."

"Ah, thanks. That's okay. Until she hears my voice, she knows to just keep going."

Joss cocked her head. "Okay. Well. It makes calls too."

Ethan waited a beat, shuffling the papers. "Yeah, thanks. Definitely in a bit."

Joss watched the way he didn't look up, the way he refused to make eye contact.

"Right," she said. "I'll be outside."

Matt felt glued to the floor, unable to will himself into the room where his dad lay motionless.

It's not contagious, you know.

His mother's words came back to him with the memory of her on a hospital bed, one like the bed his dad was on now. Her bald head, her pale, emaciated face then. His bandaged hands, his red, blistered skin now.

"See?" Steve said without turning his head. "This is why we don't do stupid dangerous stuff."

Matt forced himself into the room. As he got closer, the familiar smell of soap and antiseptic got stronger, making him nauseated. He knew what those crisp, clean medical smells were covering up. He'd been here before.

His dad's blotchy red skin looked exactly like the first picture. Next, Matt knew, would come the blisters, like in the second picture. He blocked out the thought of the third and fourth and final pictures from the chapter on acute radiation poisoning in the Clover Hill safety manual he'd found in the break room. Those images had looked just like the man he'd seen in this same room earlier in the day—the man Matt later saw rolled out with a white sheet covering his body. Knowing it was all going to happen to his dad made it too much. Knowing how it ended made it unbearable.

"Are you going to die?" Matt said.

He'd meant it to sound tough but it came out scared, and when his dad's eyes flashed a sadness he hadn't seen since the day his mom died, Matt regretted it.

"Yes" was all Steve said.

Matt fought the lump in his throat. He fought the urge to hit him. He fought the urge to climb up in the bed and hold on. "When?" he asked instead.

Steve managed a small shrug. "Too soon."

They stayed there together like that for some time. Matt didn't know what to say or what to do. Neither did Steve. So they just were. Together, they just witnessed the moment.

The concept of time had changed for Steve. He was suddenly so aware of its passing, of its existence at all. He thought he understood after he ran out of it with Claire. But now, he realized he didn't get it at all. If he *truly* had understood what that meant—that time runs out—he would have done it all so differently.

Maybe you can't understand until you're the one standing on the brink. Maybe we're not meant to. Maybe it's some biological trick designed to keep us safe from the saber-toothed tiger, only now it keeps us building big cities and worrying about deadlines. Maybe we're not supposed to get that it will *all* be gone, *we* will all be gone—until it's too late to do anything about it. If life's a joke and death's the punch line, in any good setup, you never see it coming.

Because if we did understand, we would spend it all in the sun with the grass between our toes. What else was the point? We're here, then we're not. And before that and after that, the mountains stay put and the waves keep crashing and the storms come and go and none of any of that is aware that for a brief, fleeting moment, we were here too. We were a part of it too.

It's a relief to know you don't matter, Steve realized. And understanding that brought him the first moment of peace he'd known since Claire had passed. Surely she must have seen that too. After all, she'd walked ahead; he was the one just catching up. None of it, none of us, matter. And once you see it, once you get it, once you're free from the false belief that you think you have time, you can just enjoy it for what it is.

And it is all so, so beautiful.

"What you just said, I never could," Steve told Matt. "I never said that with your mom. I never said she would die. Even after she did. I didn't want to face it. I ran. And I thought I was running from *it*. From the sickness. From death. From her dying. But it didn't change it. And I realize now, all I did was run from her. I was so scared, Matt. So I hid. I hid in all the treatments and all the things we did to fight it. I told myself that if we had a plan, if there was something to do, then it was just the plan we had to deal with. Not what was happening. The plan was real. The protocols were real. The cancer wasn't. Then suddenly — it was too late. She was gone."

Matt kept glancing from his dad to the floor and back, trying not to let the welling tears fall. Steve sat up in bed with a grimace.

"I never let you in. I never let you be a part of it. Even today, I kept you back. Away from me, away from everything that was going wrong. I pushed you away. I did it then, I did it today. I did it to keep you safe. I did it because I didn't know how to get through it with you there too. But it kept you — us — from dealing with what was happening. What was *actually* happening. It wasn't fair to you. And it didn't help you, me, or your mother. But I'm not making that mistake now."

Steve paused; his voice was starting to shake. Any other time he would have turned around, walked away. He would have stopped. But the time for that had passed.

"I am going to die, Matt," he said, giving himself over to the vulnerability. "This is happening. If we got a year, a month, a week — I am here. I am with you. There are no lists. No protocols. It's just us, living the moments we got. You and I know what most people don't. That they're just that. Moments. So we'll spend them together. And it won't be long enough. But it never is."

Matt didn't say anything as he traced the edge of the bed with his finger over and over.

"What are you thinking?" Steve said gently.

Matt's bottom lip quivered until he bit it to keep it still. Eventually, he mumbled something that Steve couldn't understand. Steve didn't ask him to repeat it, though. He just took Matt's hand in his bandaged one and waited.

"We have to fix my fishing pole," Matt said finally, again, letting himself be scared too. "We have to fix it."

Steve reached for his son, and Matt crawled into the bed like the little boy he still very much was and let his dad hold him. They both cried as Steve promised his son that they would fix the pole. Together. He promised.

CHAPTER TWENTY-FIVE

DANI STOOD NEXT to the fire engine mentally preparing herself to do the most insane, most dangerous, most ill advised thing she'd ever done.

It's going to be fine. This is going to work.

Her heart pounding in her chest said otherwise.

"I thought you were afraid of heights," Levon said, pulling the harness's nylon strap taut.

Dani felt the harness cinch around her waist. "Probably not as much as Connor's going to be," she replied.

"He's less than five minutes out" came Marion's voice over the radio.

"Copy," said Frankie. "Any last words of wisdom for your girl?"

The firefighters all looked at Dani, who waited to hear what her daddy had to say.

"She doesn't need wisdom. She needs courage. And we wouldn't be having this conversation if she didn't already have it."

There was a rustling sound and then a moment later, a sweet, high-pitched voice came on.

"Hi, Mommy!"

"Bri!" Dani said, taking a step toward the radio. "Hi, baby. You okay?"

"Yup. Mommy, Granddaddy said we'd probably sleep here tonight. And there's bunk beds. And remember Caycee Williams has bunk beds? But at her birthday party last year, when I slept over at her house? You said I had to sleep on the bottom in case I fell off. But I was five then, and I'm six now. So can I sleep on the top? I promise I won't fall off."

Dani's chest ached. She wished time could just stop. Just always stay right here, right now. Being that oblivious to the true horrors of the world around her—Dani wanted that innocence for her baby forever. *All* children should feel safe enough with the adults blessed to protect them that amid a potential nuclear meltdown, their biggest concern would be which bunk they'd get to sleep in.

Dani swallowed against the lump in her throat. "Six is much older than five, you're right. It's okay with me if your granddaddy says it's okay with him."

Levon heard the crack in Dani's voice she was trying so hard to hide and squeezed her shoulder. Mother and daughter said "I love you" and "Goodbye," and with that, Dani turned and grabbed the megaphone before she could change her mind and headed down the embankment toward Connor, toward the bridge, toward the flames.

"All right, baby," she said to Connor. "I'm coming for you. Now, you need to listen to what I say and do exactly what I tell you to do. I'm your Robin. You're my Batman. I need you, okay? I don't like heights. I'm going to need you to keep me calm, okay? I'm going to need you to hold on to me real tight so I don't get scared. Can you do that?"

The boy nodded solemnly.

From around the corner came a deep rumble. Everyone turned as a massive, heavy-duty tow truck came around the bend, slowing to a stop with a high-pitched whine of the brakes. The driver's door opened and R.J. hung out the side to get the lay of the land.

The fire truck had already been moved, so the firefighters had nothing to do but get out of the way and watch as R.J. threw his rig in reverse and three-point-turned the truck in a manner that not only drove it off the road but also knocked down a mile marker and a sign for the bridge.

With Frankie helping direct, R.J. reversed the truck the rest of the way, placing the back end as close to the bridge as possible. Frankie gave a final thumbs-up and R.J. put the truck in park. Leaning out the window, he looked at the firefighters and said, "Heard on the radio from Marion that y'all could use a lift."

Moments later, the boom swung out perpendicular to the truck and continued over toward the embankment until it came to a stop, hanging out over the firefighters below. R.J. eased down the cable line and Levon reached up, waiting until he could grab the end. Taking the hook, he attached it to the front of Dani's full-body harness and tugged repeatedly, moving it around in all directions to confirm the connection and stability. Satisfied Dani was secure, Levon stepped back, put his hands on his hips, and gave a nod.

Dani looked up and they both paused as if they'd just realized how dangerous this was. How insane this was. She could see it in his eyes, that unspoken *Holy shit*, and she could tell he saw it in her eyes too. But neither acknowledged it because there was no other way.

"Go get him," Levon said finally.

Dani could only nod, too nervous to say anything.

She gave the thumbs-up. Levon gave the call to lift. And slowly, the cable began to rise.

Dani hung on as R.J. brought the boom vertical, her heart

skipping a beat as her feet left the ground. Rising up, she clung to the cable, refusing to look down. She told herself to look at Connor. Focus on Connor. The boy watched with a slack jaw as she continued to rise up and up in the air, suspended by one little cable. The boy was in awe...or maybe it was terror. Dani couldn't tell which.

R.J. made an adjustment, and suddenly the boom was moving out over the river and heading toward the van. Dani could feel the warmth of the fire even through her thick, protective turnout gear. The flames lashed out like an angry mob being held back, ready and waiting for their opportunity to take over, their moment to be unleashed.

"Left," Levon shouted, and the boom adjusted. "More left."

When the boom didn't move, all the firefighters started yelling to move left.

"You'd think I'd found this truck by the side of the road," R.J. hollered back, ignoring them. The boom extended and kept extending until it stopped with Dani positioned perfectly, right outside the open door, not needing to go left after all.

Thirty feet up in the air, Dani and Connor were now mere feet apart.

"Hiya, Batman," Dani said, not having to yell. "I can fly."

Levon jogged to the side to get a different perspective on Dani's position. She was perfectly centered at the door, but there was still a large gap. He waved an arm toward the van. "Extend it," he called out to R.J. "Give her about two feet."

"That's it," R.J. hollered back. "That's all the way out."

Dani heard the exchange and stretched her arms out as far as she could, but the van was still well outside her reach. Clutching the cable again, she swore in her head but smiled at Connor as her suspended body swayed subtly in the wind, her feet dangling over the raging river below.

"Damn it," Levon said, his fingers interlaced on top of his head. He looked from the truck to the bridge to Dani to the van to the truck, over and over, trying to figure out how to close the distance between her and the van, when suddenly there was a creaking noise by the bridge.

All the firefighters heard. And they knew all too well what that sound meant.

Dani's arms shot out to Connor.

"It's almost over," she said, her voice more urgent. "It's going to be okay. But I need you to walk slowly over to me and take my hands."

Connor sat on the far side of the van with his knees to his chest and his arms wrapped around his legs. He didn't move. He was terrified.

Dani studied the scenario. If he stood at the edge and reached out, and if she reached out and leaned in...it might be just enough to close the gap. They could do it. She knew it in her bones.

"C'mon, baby. You and me," she said. "We're getting out of here together."

But Connor refused to budge.

She could see it in his eyes: The thirty-foot drop. The ice cold water below when he couldn't swim. The fireball that engulfed him the last time he went near that opening. His dead mother and father, right in front of him. His dead sister, right behind him. Connor was shaking now, the fear coursing through him. The child had seen more horrors in several hours than most people would in their entire lives. He was petrified by trauma, entirely unequipped to handle the moment; what young child would be? Dani knew there was no chance she would be able to get him to come to her.

Which meant she would have to go to him.

CHAPTER TWENTY-SIX

SUSPENDED BY A single cable some thirty feet above the raging, freezing Mississippi River, Dani began to swing herself back and forth.

"I don't know, Dani," Frankie called as she pumped her legs harder.

"Dani. C'mon, wait," Levon said. "Let's just—Dani! Just hold on."

Dani ignored them, continuing to swing herself back and forth, her fingers *just* missing the inside of the van every time she swung that way.

"Give me a little slack," she yelled to R.J., angling back around awkwardly in the swaying harness.

"Honey, you're doing things even I'm too stupid to think's a good idea," he hollered back.

Dani kept swinging, harder and harder each time, but it didn't matter. She still couldn't make it. She didn't have enough line. But that didn't stop her—and Levon knew it *wouldn't* stop her.

"Give her more cable," Levon called to R.J.

R.J. shook his head. "I really don't think—"

"Just do it!"

R.J. made a disapproving cluck with his teeth but did it anyway. The cable extended, dropping Dani down a foot or two. She pumped her legs again, swinging like a pendulum. trying to increase the arc a little bit each time.

It was clear now that she would have enough line to reach the van, but the extra length had dropped her too low.

"Lift her up," Levon called to R.J., but he was already one step ahead. Hand on the controls, he waited to sync up the lift to her swinging. As Dani's body reached the apex of its backswing, he lifted the boom just enough, and Dani was lined up perfectly with the door's opening. She swooped toward the van, and everyone held their breath. Her outstretched fingers grabbed at the upholstered seat just inside the open door—but it slipped through her gloved hands. Her body jerked, swaying uncoordinatedly.

From inside the flames under the bridge came another metallic screech, this time lower in pitch, stronger in intensity. Boggs dropped to a squat and Frankie swore under his breath. Levon was frozen in place, watching, trying to figure out a way to back her up.

There wasn't one.

Dani held on to the cable, waiting for the herky-jerky motion to still enough that she could start the process over. When it did, she pumped her legs to create a smooth arc. This time she was confident she knew what she was doing and that it would work, so she pumped harder, going higher, and just when it looked like she couldn't go any higher, she swung over into the van, hooked her arm around the seat's armrest, and held on tight.

The bridge might have creaked again, but the firefighters didn't hear it; they were screaming too loud, cheering on their girl while she pulled her legs in and got to her feet.

Inside the van, Dani stood on shaky legs, refusing to look at the thirty-foot drop behind her. When she turned to Connor, she saw the little boy's eyes were open wide in disbelief. "Hi, sweetheart," she said in a soft voice, the dampening acoustics in the small space a disorienting contrast to the megaphone she'd grown accustomed to. What wildly different perspectives they'd both had that day. Connor had looked out and down on them for hours, like peering through a peephole, everything expanded, distorted. By contrast, to Dani, the van felt cramped and closed.

An eerie sense of claustrophobia came over her as she realized it wasn't just herself and Connor in here; there were other people with them. Three bodies. His family. And he'd been alone with them the whole time. Her heart broke all over again.

"We're going to get out of here together, okay?" she said.

And for the first time that day, Dani actually heard his sweet little voice.

"Okay," he said.

She looked around the van, forming a plan. "Can you stand up?"

Slowly, Connor got to his feet.

"Good. You're doing great. Now, can you come to me?"

He hesitated.

"It's okay," she said. "Just take it one step at a time."

After a moment, Connor took one tiny step toward her outstretched arms. Then another. He went for a third—and a low groan came from outside the van, from somewhere inside the flaming wing. Connor panicked. Gasping, he retreated, his back pressed flat against the opposite door.

"It's okay, baby. It's okay," Dani said, ignoring the urgent screams from Levon and the guys telling her to hurry up and get out of there. "We'll do it together and do it fast," she said, unclipping the cable from her harness and clipping it to the doorjamb.

Dani took one careful, small step toward the center of the van. Connor did too. Dani took one more. Connor did too. Inch by inch, they moved together as Dani shifted her balance as slowly and carefully as she could.

"Reach your arms out, baby. Like me."

Connor's skinny little arms reached toward her, his hands shaking. The bridge creaked.

"No, look at me!" Dani cried out. "Look in my eyes, Connor. Stay with me. We're okay."

Connor didn't blink. His blue eyes stayed glued to hers, trusting her. Needing her.

He was right there. Their fingertips were touching.

Dani reached out. Connor leaned in. She stepped forward one more inch and took him under the arms, lifting him up to her body. She wrapped her arms around him, and he clutched her tight, squeezing so hard—as with a loud crack, the bridge gave way and began to collapse into the freezing Mississippi River below, taking the wing, the van, and the woman and child down with it.

CHAPTER TWENTY-SEVEN

THE VAN WITH Dani and Connor inside plummeted down to the river.

Dani lost all sense of direction. Time became meaningless. It felt like a lifetime, but it was probably just a few seconds. She could do nothing—neither fight nor flight was an option—so Dani froze. Even in the violent impact of the van slamming into the water's surface, her body was still.

But clarity—a crystal-clear understanding of what had just happened and what was about to happen—came a split second later when she felt it.

The ice-cold water of the Mississippi River.

Dani's back seized up in the shock of it as her arms tightened their hold on Connor. Instantly, both fight and flight kicked in. *Find the door, find the door,* she kept telling herself. She had to find the door, she had to get them out. But nothing made sense, all direction was distorted. Up, down; she had no idea where anything was in relation to anything else. All she knew for sure was the water was rising.

Instinct took over. Dani took a huge breath just as the water came over her head.

Once she was underwater, everything went blurry. The pain in her ears from the changing pressure told her they were sinking. A soft vibration in her arms as Connor cried out told her the boy was still alive. Bubbles tickled her face and the water got colder as the van kept sinking.

How deep was the river? How far down would they go? How far down *could* they go? Her chest burned. Her face ached. It felt like they'd been sinking forever. And just when Dani began to wonder if she was already dead, the van hit something.

Dani kicked her legs, and her thick turnout boots met the rocky river bottom. *Down. That direction is down,* she told herself as stars began to crisscross her vision in the dark, murky water. She let go of Connor with one hand to feel the inside wall of the van, but nothing was helpful. Her pulse beat in her ears. Her chest felt like it was being ripped open. She had to figure out something. Now.

Dani let go of Connor with her other hand. Both hands free, she felt for something, anything, that would help. She had no idea what that might be, but she had to try. The stars were beginning to fade. She was running out of air. She was about to black out. They were both about to die.

And that was when her hand felt something *different.*

She didn't know what *different* was, but instinct said to go to it. She followed it, and a moment later, her head broke through the water to an air pocket created against the side of the van.

She gasped, spitting out river water, and the sound reverberated through the cave-like acoustics; the relief of the air was nearly transcendent. *Connor!* Dani took a deep breath and dove back under.

Swinging her arms wide, she searched for him. She shouldn't have let him go. She'd told him she had him — how could she have let him go? The burning fear of losing Connor overwhelmed the fear of drowning. Then Dani felt something soft. A limb. An arm.

Grabbing him, she pushed off the bottom.

Breaking the surface together a second later, they both gasped, inhaling and exhaling in greedy gulps of air. She held the boy up, treading water for them both, as he coughed and gasped, spitting water into her face.

She found something to stand on, an armrest or maybe a seat, and clutched Connor to her chest, feeling both their hearts pounding. Dani looked around the dark, enclosed space, trying to suppress her justified panic as, with each passing second, she became more aware of their reality.

Yes, they were alive. Thank God.

But they were now trapped at the bottom of the Mississippi River.

CHAPTER TWENTY-EIGHT

WITH AN AEROSOL hiss from the can, Joss spray-painted a bright red, unmissable, undeniable *X* across a chunk of concrete before moving on to find the next piece of deadly radioactive debris.

As she waved the Geiger counter over the plane parts and rubble, for the most part, the meter's needle rested to the left side of its gauge, like a lion hiding in the reeds, waiting to pounce. But occasionally, the needle would perk up and pop over to the right, and the handheld device's soft, intermittent clicking would grow louder and faster.

That's when she'd paint an *X*.

Crews would soon be coming in to clear the debris. The NTSB and the FBI would be intensifying their investigation. They would all need to know which parts of the debris and rubble were clean and which required a more cautious hand, so Joss walked the plant with her Geiger counter doing the due diligence while the firefighters looked on.

They'd been here all day. They were first responders and there'd been no time to figure out what they should and shouldn't deal with — as if that were even an option. It was their duty to deal with it all. But now, as they watched the sporadic red *X*s pop up around them, the reality of the work they'd done that day began to sink in.

When you can't see it or smell it, when the thing that will kill you is invisible, it's easy to forget about it. They *could* see and feel the flames, so they dealt with that. But now they wondered what they might have to deal with down the road. What kind of damage had they inflicted on themselves just by being here? Damage that, like a ticking time bomb, might or might not go off.

How many years would it take before they felt safe? Or would they always be waiting, wondering when the bill would come due, when they would be forced to pay the hero's price?

To Joss's relief, the *X*s were less frequent than she had feared. She walked the Clover Hill campus alone, listening to the sound of her own breath in the full-body hazmat suit, realizing how heavy the weight of the fear and anxiety of the day had been now that she could set it down. Letting her head fall forward, she rolled her shoulders back. Unclenching her jaw, she inhaled deeply, held it, then exhaled slowly. It felt like the first time she'd taken a breath since that morning.

Joss looked up at a crumbled portion of one of the cooling towers as she rounded the corner of a building — and stopped in her tracks.

There, in front of her, was the towering, intact tail of the crashed jetliner.

She'd seen it on the security feed earlier, but the video had not done it justice. Now she stood next to it, and it was one of the most jarring images she'd ever seen.

The last few rows of the plane and its gargantuan tail lay on the ground in one piece. The fuselage end had crashed into the wall, making it seem like the building itself had a tail. The Coastal Airways logo was level with the building's second-story windows, and behind the end of the plane, unearthed grass and dirt formed an enormous skid mark of a divot where the aircraft had dug in its heels in before colliding with the building.

Joss felt tiny as she approached the aircraft cautiously, as if it were a sleeping beast she didn't want to wake. She told herself to get a grip. The exhaustion was making her ridiculous. Glancing down, she was quickly brought back to reality by the haunting reminders of how the day had started lying there at her feet.

There was an open suitcase. A stuffed pink bear. Someone's cell phone, the screen shattered. A maroon hoodie painted with a cartoon roadrunner, apparently the mascot of Rhodes Junior High, wherever that was, and Joss thought of the teenager it had belonged to.

The passengers of Flight 235 had been the first casualties in a day that had exacted a heavy toll and Joss realized that their friends and family must have found little relief when the plant's crisis was avoided.

Their lives had already melted down.

Joss continued her work, sweeping the device over a laptop, then a shoe, then a plastic carrier of soda cans, their tops already popped, as the crash had happened midflight, midservice. There was the charred fabric on a row of seats. There was someone's sticker-covered water bottle. Each of these things was a tragic reminder of the people who had once claimed them.

But they had no effect on the Geiger counter.

She walked closer, wanding the device over the plane's tail, reaching up as high as she could on the vertical stabilizer. She rounded the tail cone and walked toward the door—but steered clear of its little porthole window. Joss already had a parade of images that would keep her up at night. She didn't need to add to it.

As she absentmindedly ran the Geiger counter over the back of the aircraft, unable to stop herself from envisioning what horrors lay beyond that window inside the plane, the needle suddenly shot to the right and the clicking erupted into a frenzy.

Joss stumbled backward and froze, her heart pounding in shock. Spinning, she ran the device over a backpack lying a few steps away. Nothing. She tried a suitcase. Also nothing. Turning back to the plane, she walked slowly toward it, holding the Geiger counter out as she approached.

The device went haywire.

Hands shaking, Joss stepped up to the door's little window and peered inside.

In the back galley, the body of a flight attendant lay face down, floating. Floating in water that came halfway up the door. Water that had filled the entire plane. Joss held the Geiger counter up to the window, directed it at the water inside, and watched as the needle didn't even move.

It stayed exactly where it was. All the way to the right, as high as the poison-detecting instrument could measure.

CHAPTER TWENTY-NINE

COUNTDOWN TO ZERO HOUR

51 MINUTES

EVERYONE IN THE control room thought the crisis was over.

Joss knew it had just begun.

She swept her arm across the desk, pushing everything off and onto the floor, and unrolled the blueprints. Running her trembling fingers over the plant's designs, Joss mumbled to herself while everyone waited, exchanging glances. After a few moments, Ethan said her name a couple of times. She didn't respond.

"Jocelyn," he said finally. She looked up.

"The—the tail," she stuttered, pulling out the blueprints for

Clover Hill's plumbing system and laying it on the top of the pile. "The plane's tail. It hit. It smashed up against one of R2's outer buildings." She looked directly at Ethan and spoke clearly and slowly: "The tail is rammed into the exterior of the EDG storage building for R2. It's located right"—Joss searched the blueprint, then pointed—"here. Which is exactly where the water main is. The plane's tail ruptured the line."

"Couldn't have," Dwight countered. "The main water line is underground. Buried. Exactly because of a possible attack or accident like this. If it had ruptured, there would have been alarms. We would have—"

"No, not the water line for the reactor," Joss said. "The water line for the building. Your everyday plumbing. Bathroom, break room, drinking fountain. Which is why it didn't set off any of our alarms. Which is why we didn't know it was happening."

"But you said radioactive water," Ethan said. "If it's not the reactor's water—"

"All roads lead to Rome," Dwight said, studying the blueprint. "There aren't separate plumbing systems. It's all connected. Look." He spun the design around to face Ethan. "The building plumbing is like a small tributary off the more substantial line. That's where they merge"—he pointed—"which means the building water is downstream of…"

Maggie helped him shuffle through the pages until they found the right one.

"Here. If it's ruptured like that, the building water would intercept the reactor water *and* the pool, which would mean it would absolutely be radiated."

"You're missing the point," Joss said through clenched teeth. "It's not about how contaminated the water is. That's the least of our problems. Based on what I saw and looking at these designs, I'm pretty sure all day—since the moment that plane crashed—water has been pouring out of those pipes. Which means it's filling—"

"The inside of the building," Ethan said, bent over the blueprints. He looked up at Joss. "The basement."

The room was silent. George, who had been in the control room to relay details from the cleanup, raised his hand.

"Sorry," he said. "Dumb firefighter question. What does that mean?"

"It means," Ethan said, "the building whose basement houses the three emergency backup generators that are connected to Reactor Two and Reactor Two's spent fuel pool—you know, the building practically being held together by duct tape—that basement may be flooded. Which means at any minute, those generators could fail."

"*Will* fail," Joss said. "If they're flooded, they *will* fail, and that will blow the power to R2, shutting off the coolant pumps. When they go down, there won't be enough time to connect batteries or backup generators before—"

"The lower water in the pool heats up and boils off the water, exposing the rods and igniting a fire we have no way of putting out," George finished. "That part I remember."

"But not just the pool," she said. "This time it'd also mean the reactor itself. No power, no coolant pumps. The reactor core will overheat and melt down."

Ethan held up his hand. "Just hold on. Say the generators do fail, and the pumps for the coolant water stop working because of it. How long would we have to get and connect battery power before the water started to boil in the pool?"

Maggie, Vikram, Dwight, and Joss were already running calculations. When they finished, they compared their work, and they all agreed on the answer.

"From the time of loss of power," Joss said, "we'd have less than half an hour."

CHAPTER THIRTY

COUNTDOWN TO ZERO HOUR
47 MINUTES

"IF THE GENERATORS *fail, we're done. We need to start the pump immediately. Get the —"*

Marion turned the volume on the radio up, not wanting to believe what he was hearing.

"Granddaddy, can we —"

Marion shushed Brianna with a wave of his hand. She froze momentarily, then came to his side to listen to the voices coming from the feed to the control room:

"— wait to know if it's flooded or not?"

"We can't take the chance. Turn the pump on now."

Marion stood up so fast, the chair behind him fell. Pressing a button, he yelled into the radio, "Do *not* start the pump system. You cannot start the pump."

Dead air was the only response.

"Hello?" he said. "Does anyone hear me?"

The blinking red transmission light in the control room behind George went unnoticed. Leaning back against the desk, the firefighter listened along with everyone else as Ethan directed the staff's preparations to engage the pump that would remove the water they assumed had flooded the basement where the backup generators were stored.

"All right," Ethan said. "Once we start the pump, we'll monitor the..."

"Sorry," George whispered, moving out of the way so Vikram could get to the panel. He stood up, and at the same time, they both noticed the blinking red light.

"Ethan," Vikram said, hand raised as he pushed the button. Before Ethan could cross the room, Marion's voice boomed through the speaker:

"*—not start that pump!*"

Marion was getting dizzy from screaming into the void, unheard, when finally a voice responded.

"*Marion. We hear you. What's—*"

"Ethan," Marion said, short of breath. "If you start the pump and the subbasement isn't flooded, you'll burn out the motor and blow the pump. It's called dry running. When a pump runs without water, the internal components generate heat due to friction. The bearings, seals, and other parts will eventually overheat and fail. A pump like yours with that much power? You'll destroy it *instantly*. You'll kill one of the most important safety functions you have right now and there will be no recourse once you do."

Brianna didn't say a word as Marion leaned on the desk, waiting, breathing heavily. Impatient, he pushed the button. "Did you hear me?"

"We copied. We're discussing."

"If you're not one hundred percent certain the subbasement is flooded," Marion said, "there is no discussion."

"But if we don't start the pump now and we end up losing power, we'll have limited options to start it after that."

"Start it now and you might not have that pump at all."

"Another dumb firefighter question," George said. "If all this is about whether or not there's water, then why don't we just figure out if it's flooded?"

"Because the pump is in the subbasement," Ethan said as Joss pulled out another blueprint and laid it on top for George to see. "It's a tiny room in our oldest reactor. Nothing monitors the area. No security cameras, no video. We have no way of knowing what's going on in there."

George looked around to see if he was the only one who didn't get it. "Okay...so why doesn't someone just go down and check?"

"Because based on what I found with my Geiger counter," said Joss, "the level of radioactivity in that water will kill you within hours. Anyone who goes in isn't coming out."

Marion glanced down at Brianna, who stood by his side. He'd tried to sugarcoat as much of the day as he could, and thankfully, most of it had been over her head. But that was about as clear-cut as it got, and by the look on her face, he knew she understood. She looked up.

"So...they need to see inside," she said, piecing it together. "But if they send a person into the building, it'll kill them?"

Marion took a seat so he was at her eye level. Running a hand softly over her hair, he gave a small, conciliatory smile. "That's right, baby girl."

Brianna knit her brow, thinking. Looking up at her granddaddy, the first-grader cocked her head.

"Then don't send a person."

CHAPTER THIRTY-ONE

COUNTDOWN TO ZERO HOUR

44 MINUTES

THE WINGTIP WAS all that was left.

It stuck up out of the water like a buoy, marking the location where the river had swallowed the rest of it up. The minivan was gone, the bridge was gone, the wing was gone, and R.J.'s truck was nearly entirely submerged as well, the cable attached to the inside of the van having acted like a boulder tied to the waist of a person tossed overboard. Only the hood and front cab of the massive tow truck were still visible, its front wheels resting on the riverbank.

Levon ran down to the water and began to strip off his boots and outer gear; R.J. climbed out of the truck and started swimming to the shore. Both simultaneously hollered to Frankie and Boggs to call for divers — the National Guard, somebody, anybody, just get divers here. The firefighters ran for the truck, but Frankie stopped, realizing Levon was about to go in after Dani.

"What are you doing?" he yelled. "You can't swim!"

Levon ripped off his turnout coat. "I have to do something!"

R.J. stumbled up from the water, puffing out little clouds that hung in the frigid air, and stripped out of his own coat and boots. Rifling through Levon's discarded gear, he grabbed the oxygen tank and SCBA.

"Stay here, I got it," R.J. said, slipping into the straps of the harness.

"That won't work underwater," Levon said, struggling with his boots. "It doesn't work like scuba."

"It will for about three minutes," R.J. said, twisting open the oxygen release. "After that, it'll vapor-lock and the air won't override the spring-loaded valve on the demand air supply. But all I need is three minutes to find them and see if we even got a ball game. So get us real dive equipment *now*, and how about some people who can actually swim."

With that, he secured the mask over his head and dove into the water.

Damn, that's cold, R.J. thought as he made his way through the freezing, murky water. The mask and on-demand breathing apparatus felt different from the SSA of his industrial-dive helmet, but for him, diving was like riding a bike — second nature.

Swimming to his truck, R.J. made his way to the back and found the cable that was still hooked to the van. Using it like a guideline, he pulled himself down into the Mississippi, equalizing the building pressure in his ears as he went. The water grew darker and colder, and R.J. began to worry if he'd be able to see what was down there at all. As he was wondering if he should swim back up and see about a headlamp, the outline of the wing appeared, like a ghostly apparition.

The cable was coming from under the wing, which meant the van must be under there too. From the side he was on, he saw nothing. The edge of the wing was jammed into the river bottom. Bubbles rose from his mask as he swam over the top of the wing to get to the other side, careful not to cut himself on the charred shredded metal, when suddenly, there was a flash of color in his peripheral vision.

He kicked over and saw the red plastic of a taillight. He'd found the van.

As he pulled himself down, he felt the air in the mask subtly but undeniably shift; it was becoming harder to breathe, as the pressure on the intake had a little more resistance to it. His time was running out. He'd found the van, but now he needed to find out if anyone was alive in there, and fast. If they were still alive, they wouldn't be for much longer.

But could they be alive? R.J. wondered. How? Surely there was no way that little boy and that firefighter had survived the fall. And the sinking. *And* the cold water. Even if they had, and they'd somehow managed to find an air pocket, too much time had passed. They were dead. R.J. knew it. This was going to be a salvage and body-recovery mission. And just as he was coming to that conclusion, he saw the little boy waving from inside the van.

Dani heard Connor call her name, but she was too focused on finding a way out to respond.

The van was lying on its side, the open door flat against the river bottom. The air pocket—approximately ten inches, just enough for her mouth to be out of the water when her head touched the top—stretched across the side Connor had had his back against all day.

Dani had managed to squeeze Connor onto the side of his car seat, which put most of his body out of the water. It was an awkward, uncomfortable position—but it was dry and that was all that mattered. She *had* to keep him dry. In water this cold, they had less than an hour before hypothermia killed them. But if she could keep him dry, his survival time went way up.

Of course, that was only if the air lasted that long.

"Dani! Look!" Connor said.

"Yes, baby," she said without turning. "Hold on."

The broken front windshield wasn't a possibility for escape. Rocks, debris, broken glass, and metal blocked the way out. She could try to move some of it, but she was afraid to move too much. The van's placement didn't feel solid, and the thought of shifting the van and losing the air pocket was horrifying. She'd already tried kicking out the windows and opening the doors—the pressure was too great to do either. And she also knew the harder she worked, the harder she breathed, the more air she used up.

The reality of how much trouble they were in was setting in and the panic was taking hold. As she tried to brainstorm and figure it out, Connor called out her name again, and this time, her patience snapped.

"*What?*" she cried, spinning, her voice booming through the cave-like space.

And that's when she saw the man in the water.

* * *

Levon paced the riverbank in his muddy stocking feet, not knowing what to do. R.J. had been down there too long. Something wasn't right. Levon knew he had to do something, but as he stepped down into the water, Frankie hollered from above.

"You do, and we've got one more person to rescue."

Levon knew he was right, but he felt so helpless just waiting. He looked up to Boggs and Frankie, who were talking on the radio. They spoke urgently but what they were working out, Levon didn't know, because he wasn't about to go up there and ask. If he was going anywhere, it was into the water to find Dani.

The seconds ticked on, each more excruciating than the last. And just as he was about to say screw it and go in, the water began to move.

Bubbles were breaking on the surface, growing more intense by the second. Levon stepped forward into the water, ready to dive under, when suddenly R.J. appeared, shooting up above the water-line. He ripped the mask off his face and gasped for air.

Eyes wide, mouth gaping, he breathed heavily, looking around in a stunned stupor before he focused on Levon. "Get me a crowbar and another mask," he said. "They're alive."

CHAPTER THIRTY-TWO

COUNTDOWN TO ZERO HOUR

41 MINUTES

"**MAYDAY, MAYDAY, MAYDAY!** *Bridge collapse. Firefighter down. Engine Forty-Two calling for assistance.*"

Carla was on her knees at the front of the school bus gripping the handheld mic in an instant. "What do you need, Forty-Two?"

Her voice shook with fear as the memory of kissing Levon goodbye at the kitchen sink earlier that morning flashed through her mind. He'd come up from behind, wrapped his arms around her waist, and whispered his wedding vow in her ear.

I'm gonna love you forever, Miss Carla.

Promise? she had replied there at the sink, just as she had at their wedding.

I do.

The radio was filled with static, but Boggs's voice was clear:

"We need divers. The bridge collapsed. Dani's trapped. We need dive gear. Now."

R.J. was the only person Carla knew who had any diving gear, and his was already in service at the plant. She looked at Principal Gazdecki. He shook his head with a shrug. This was rural Minnesota. No one had their own dive gear. Before she could answer, Marion's voice came over the radio.

"Is she okay? Is Dani okay?"

Carla heard the panic in his voice. She could envision Marion in the bunker, Brianna standing beside him. Carla wished she could take the little girl out of the room. Tell her it would be all right. But Carla was a terrible liar. Brianna would see right through it.

"Marion, she needs help" was all Boggs said back. *"We need divers."*

Suddenly the radio background filled with loud chatter and commotion.

"We got some friends here that might be able to help" came Reverend Michaels's voice.

Carla and Gazdecki were both confused.

Friends?

From the altar, Reverend Michaels nodded to a National Guardsman, who ran off to inform his incident commander of the urgent request for divers.

"We've got this," said the reverend over the radio. "We'll get it done."

Outside on the lawn, a FEMA helicopter was dropping off more supplies: Boxes of potassium iodide pills. Hazmat suits. Breathing masks. Everything they needed. On the other side of the church, a different helicopter was loading up, ready to take the next group of passengers north to Bloomfield, where they'd meet up with the Waketa residents who had already been evacuated by boat. Makeshift short-term shelters were being set up on the dormant fields. Food, water, beds, bathrooms—everything families would need was there or on the way.

Reverend Michaels watched through the window as the National Guardsman yelled something over the sound of the rotor blades to the incident commander; he listened, nodded, and began talking into a radio on his shoulder, presumably relaying the request for divers.

And they would, the reverend realized in awe, get it done.

Reverend Michaels looked around at the scale of the operation that was unfolding before him. All the supplies, all the gear, all the manpower and organization that was given to things at the top of a priority list. It was not a sight he was accustomed to in Waketa. And he deeply appreciated it. They needed it badly.

But seeing the might that came with this kind of operation… it didn't make him feel the way he did when he looked at the pile of sandwiches on the folding table beside the half-eaten sleeve of Chips Ahoy! cookies that came from the McCanns' pantry. The big boxes of new medical supplies were, indeed, crucially needed—but they didn't touch the healing that came from eight-year-old Becky Wallace's Band-Aids with the cartoon butterflies they'd resorted to using earlier in the day.

Reverend Michaels was grateful for the federal assistance. It was desperately needed. But he was also grateful for the reminder that people in crisis need other things too—and only Waketa had been able to provide that for itself.

The National Guardsman ran back into the church. "Coast Guard divers are on their way," he reported breathlessly.

Just like that.

Reverend Michaels smiled and held the mic up to his mouth. "Engine Forty-Two, Coast Guard divers are en route. Tell Dani to hang on, help's coming. And Carla, whoever you told that they could find us all here and that *this* was the place where help was needed? Please thank them. Help has most certainly found Waketa."

CHAPTER THIRTY-THREE

COUNTDOWN TO ZERO HOUR
36 MINUTES

ETHAN COULDN'T BELIEVE he was about to let an eleven-year-old help stop a nuclear disaster.

"You know," Ethan said, "at a nuclear power plant, I never thought a bring-your-kid-to-work day would have them participating."

Steve chuckled as he made his way across the control room, trying to hide a small limp. Taking a seat, he watched with pride as Matt talked with the engineers while they got everything set up. The control-room door opened; Dwight ran in with a remote and handed it to the boy.

Steve jumped to his feet. "Has that been—"

"Yes, it's clean," Dwight confirmed.

"Okay," Matt said, punching a sequence of buttons on the controller. "Tell him to press the button on the bottom of the drone."

"He can hear you, actually," Vikram said, pointing to the radio. And just then, a live video feed of a pair of hazmat-gear-covered boots standing on grass came up on the screen. The feed shook as the engineer outside flipped the drone around and stared right into the camera. Over his shoulder, the tail of the plane was visible.

Matt hopped up and sat cross-legged on the table, the blueprints laid out beside him, as everyone double-checked the video and audio feeds. Matt walked the engineer through the calibration process, and soon the Clover Hill employee gave a thumbs-up.

"Matt? You good too?" Vikram asked.

Matt turned to Steve. Steve smiled. Matt smiled. "Ready," he said to Vikram.

The control room was quiet as they watched the engineer outside on the screen. He swiped his badge on a panel next to the door, then entered a code. A green light lit up on the panel, and the engineer opened the door and stepped inside.

"Okay, set it on the ground," Matt said. A moment later, the camera shot moved down to the floor. Matt worked his thumbs across the joysticks, and the drone lifted off the ground. On the screen, light filled the shot, then disappeared as the engineer went back out the door.

"Okay, you're going to want to go straight down this hallway," Vikram said, hunched over the blueprints, "then take the second right." Matt adjusted the joysticks, and the drone moved forward.

There was no audio. The building was completely empty. Occasionally, it would fly past a blown-out window and over broken glass that covered the linoleum floor. Everyone in the room was rapt as the drone moved through the building.

"Why are the doors all open?" Matt asked as the drone passed through yet another doorway.

"Security feature post-Fukushima," Joss said. "In the event of a power loss, default is for the interior doors to open, not close and lock. People got trapped when the water shorted electronic doors and they wouldn't unlock."

Matt considered that. "But what if the power was cut by bad guys trying to get in?"

No one had an answer.

Just then, static filled the drone's video feed for a split second.

"Does it have enough battery?" Ethan asked.

"I hardly used it today," Matt said. "That's not the battery."

The drone passed through the doorway to the stairwell that led to the basement. The stairwell was lit only by emergency lighting, which gave off a dim and eerie fluorescent glow, so Matt punched a button and the drone's headlight clicked on. The bright white walls momentarily washed out the picture until it gained focus a second later—just as the image went fuzzy again, this time for a couple seconds longer.

Matt guided the drone down one flight of stairs, past an open door, then down another. As the drone approached the bottom, Vikram looked up.

"Okay," he said. "You're almost to the basement. That's where the three generators are. That's where the water cannot get to. The subbasement below that, that is where the pump is. That's what we have to see. We have to know if it's flooded or not."

The drone reached the bottom of the stairwell, rounded the corner, and entered the basement. The headlight shifted with it, shining into the room, illuminating a row of three large generators covered in lit-up buttons. The screen blinked on and off, mirroring the lights on the first generator, which, at that moment, were flashing off and on irregularly. Matt angled the drone down...

And that's when they saw the water.

Not just the subbasement—the basement itself was starting to flood.

Everyone snapped into action.

Check and verify callbacks were shouted and the staff in the control room shifted into a frenzy as they prepared to start the pump. Adding to the panic, the drone footage trembled, then wisps of smoke rose, and the drone began to fly erratically.

"We've seen enough, Matt," Ethan said. "Get it out of there."

Matt shook his head. "I'm trying. It won't do what I tell it to."

The screen blinked on and off, going fuzzy and hazy. Then, with no warning, the whole thing suddenly dropped, and the camera view became a free fall heading straight down. Just before the drone hit the water, the screen went black.

"Fuck the protocol," Joss cried out. "Start the pump!"

But before the words were out of her mouth, a loud alarm went off and a red light began blinking on the panel.

"EDG One is down!" Maggie said.

"Do it!" Joss screamed. "While we still have the other two!"

Ethan flipped the switch. Everyone held their breath, waiting for the pump to start.

It didn't.

CHAPTER THIRTY-FOUR

COUNTDOWN TO ZERO HOUR

34 MINUTES

FOR A FIVE-YEAR-OLD boy, his bravery had held up as long as it could.

"Are they coming back?" Connor asked.

Dani nodded, trying to cover her chattering teeth, but she'd been wondering the same thing. Which was ridiculous. Of course they were coming back.

But where were they?

"They're probably just putting the pizza order in," she said.

"Pizza?"

"Oh, yeah. Making sure we have something warm to eat when we get up there. What kind do you want?"

Connor thought. "Pepperoni."

"Good stuff. I want anchovies. You know. Little fish. I'm feeling one with the fishies."

Seeing his toothy grin in the dim light boosted her. It was just enough. The moment of levity felt good. Necessary. But then it passed, and it was silent again except for their breathing and the soft sounds of water dripping in their little cave-like space.

Her mind went to Brianna. How could it not? Was her baby thinking about her, wondering where her mom was? Boy, would this be an amazing story to tell her. She could see her eyes widening, her jaw hanging down in disbelief. Bri would ask her to tell it over again. Tell the part where they were stuck in the river, and it was so cold. Dani was beginning to smile when Connor's voice brought her back.

"They're not sleeping, are they."

It was more of a confirmation of a suspicion than a question, and it took Dani a moment to understand what he meant. God, it felt like a lifetime ago when Connor's father had told his son to listen to the firefighters. Dani's heart ached anew at the memory of him telling Connor that he was going to sleep for a little while, just like his mom.

"No, sweetheart," Dani said softly. "No, they're not sleeping."

She could feel his grief in the way he didn't say anything, but she wondered what that meant to him. At his age, had he experienced death before? Maybe a pet? A grandparent? Did he understand or was the worst of it still to come? Once he got out of here, was that what waited for him — the excruciating journey into understanding what it was to lose the ones you loved?

"At least," Dani said, "they're not sleeping in the way you think."

In the dark of the van, she saw Connor look at her more closely.

"The way you fall asleep in your bed at night and wake up the next morning. They're not doing that. But do you ever dream while you sleep?"

She felt Connor nod his head.

"I think maybe they're sleeping like that. Wherever that is. You know how dreams sometimes make no sense but also make total sense?"

"I dreamed my cat Riley could talk."

"Exactly. Riley can't talk in real life. But it was totally normal in the dream, right?"

Connor nodded.

"I think maybe your family's sleeping like that. Maybe they're there. But instead of waking up the next morning like we do, they just stay there. And maybe they're doing all sorts of things that make no sense but make total sense. And they're loving it. They're having a great time. And maybe sometimes when you sleep at night, you'll meet them there. And you can have a great time together."

"Can I stay there with them?"

Dani swallowed down the lump in her throat. "No, baby. Not yet. They would want you to wake up and go to school. Play with your friends. Grow big and tall. And while you're doing that, they'll be watching. They'll be with you even if they're not really with you. Because that's how dreams work, remember?"

Just then, over his shoulder, out the back window, Dani saw light. A soft illumination that grew brighter by the second.

"Look," Dani said, pointing. Connor turned to see. "They're back."

At that, R.J. appeared, dropping down from above, with Boggs right behind him. Both wore firefighter SCBA gear. R.J. held a crowbar; Boggs had a crash ax. R.J. turned to Boggs and waved his hand over the side and top of the van, indicating the air pocket.

Boggs nodded. R.J. swam to the wide back window and pointed to the lower driver's-side corner. Boggs nodded again.

"What are they going to do?" Connor asked.

Dani watched them, making sure she didn't miss anything. "They're going to break that back window," she said. "Down there, in that corner. Where it's fully underwater. That way, they don't let our air escape. Once the glass is open, they can come in and we can go out."

R.J. and Boggs began to signal a countdown. Dani held on to Connor, thinking through what could go wrong. Troubleshooting what she would do if it did. Realizing there was nothing she could do.

The countdown ended.

The crowbar came down.

And with a pathetic *ting* of a noise, nothing happened.

Another countdown. Another attempt. And again. Alternating tools, trying the crash ax and the crowbar. Nothing. They tried breaking into a different spot on the glass. Still nothing.

Boggs motioned to R.J., pointed at his mask. R.J. nodded and went up. Boggs looked into the van, gave Dani a *Hold on* hand motion, then pushed for the surface, following R.J. up, leaving Dani and Connor alone.

R.J. surfaced, gasping for air, with Boggs right behind him. They squinted into the air that moved all around them to see a helicopter descending on the scene, landing on a patch of grass not far from the fire truck. Its door slid open, and members of the Ninth U.S. Coast Guard District hopped out, hauling dive gear behind them.

"Glass won't break," Boggs yelled, choking on water as he swam for shore.

The Coastguardsmen were getting into their gear, preparing to dive, conferring with Frankie as Boggs crawled up the riverbank, describing it all to Levon.

"Underwater," he said, breathless, "it's weightless. No...no resistance. No force. It won't break."

But Levon was watching R.J., who was swimming for his truck.

"R.J.!" Levon called. "What are you doing?"

"I got an idea. Get me another SCBA ready," R.J. hollered over his shoulder, water sloshing everywhere as he climbed up to his truck and disappeared into the cab.

Connor's lips were turning blue. Dani knew children his age hadn't fully developed the ability to regulate their temperature, so while he might not seem that cold, he was probably dangerously close to being hypothermic — and she was a few steps ahead of him.

Because, unlike Connor, Dani was in the water. She shivered and her breath hung in the air as little clouds as she tried to kick her legs to keep her heart rate up. But if she was honest with herself, she couldn't feel any of her limbs. She wasn't sure if she was moving at all. Dani's brain was going fuzzy. She wasn't sure of much of anything anymore.

"'...no valley low enough, ain't no river...'"

Dani could have sworn she heard Brianna laughing as Dani sang their song, her off-key voice filling the air pocket. Bri's laugh was so real, so close — wait. Dani looked around. Was she there? No, Bri wasn't there. Of course not. That was Connor. And there were no giggles; it was Dani's own hand splashing in the water.

Dani's thoughts felt scrambled. Her conscious mind was no longer in the driver's seat; some primal survival source deep inside her was calling the shots now, telling her to make sounds and movements that would keep them both awake, alive, hanging on. She obeyed, continuing to jiggle her hand as she sang…but she didn't know how much longer the tricks would work.

It'd been forever since R.J. and Boggs left. Where were they? They had to come back. They had to save them. *Now.* Connor was running out of time. They were running out of air.

She looked at Connor and saw his eyelids were beginning to droop.

"Hey," she said, shaking him with ice-cold hands. "Connor. *No.* Connor! Stay with me."

The boy's eyes fluttered open and he moaned an understanding. But almost immediately, he began to nod off again. Dani flicked water on his face. He flinched, stirring.

"Stay awake, buddy. C'mon."

"But I want to sleep…" he said, his voice trailing off. "I want to see them…"

"No," Dani said, shaking him harder, knowing if he went to sleep, he would die. "Stay with me. You gotta stay with me, Batman!"

But Connor's eyes remained closed.

Dani spun around, trying to figure out what to do. If she put him in the water, the shock of the cold would keep him conscious. But if he got wet, his time for survival would go down drastically. Both were terrible options. But what else could she do?

What would his mom have done? What would Dani choose if it were Bri here instead of Connor? Dani was losing her cool, starting to freak out in earnest. Suddenly, a tapping at the back of the van made her gasp.

Finally! They were back. Connor would be out of there soon. Dani couldn't help but smile as she squinted out the rear windshield, where, to her surprise, she saw only R.J. floating outside—holding a handgun.

CHAPTER THIRTY-FIVE

COUNTDOWN TO ZERO HOUR

31 MINUTES

IT WAS ORGANIZED chaos in the control room. No one knew what had gone wrong in the basement or why the pump hadn't started. Manuals were out as they frantically tried to troubleshoot. Questions were yelled, answers shouted back. Gauges were read, monitors checked.

"Did the power go out completely?" Ethan asked.

"No," Maggie said, scanning the panel. "We're nearly fully operational."

"*Nearly?* Coolant pumps? What about inflow to the pool?"

"Both still functional."

"Then why the hell did that pump not start?" Ethan said.

"Got it," Dwight said, one hand holding an open three-ring binder, the other raised high in the air. "'Emergency-backup generator allocation of power priorities to support critical load. Reactor and pool coolant pumps are number one...'" He read to himself for a few seconds before looking up. "Dead last on the priority list is the subbasement emergency-pump system."

"Shit," Joss said, leaning forward and putting her face in her hands.

In the event of a rolling power loss, there were priorities for which systems remained operational the longest. The pump system — a fourth-level redundancy that would most likely never be used — was at the bottom of the list. With only two of the three EDGs working, there wasn't enough power to run everything, so the pump was one of the first functions to go.

"Which means," said Vikram, "if we lose another generator, we lose even more system functions."

"Correct," Joss said. "And once we lose all three, we lose the whole plant."

"We need more power," said Ethan.

There was a second of silence, and in that moment Ethan and Joss and Steve all looked at each other.

They needed more power, and they *had* more power.

"Get a team," Steve said to George. "Get to the batteries the National Guard choppers—"

"Go with the firefighters," Joss said to Vikram. "The batteries need to move to R2—"

"Let us know the second you're ready to connect," Ethan said, passing Vikram a radio.

The room was a flurry of activity as people ran out the door.

Joss and Ethan watched them go before exchanging a look. Joss began to say something to him, but Ethan clapped his hands for attention.

"All right, people. Let's be ready when they are. Maggie, Dwight, let's walk through connection procedures."

With that, Ethan turned his back to Joss and huddled up with the controllers.

As Ethan led the team through the steps over and over, Joss leaned back against a desk, arms crossed, staring unblinkingly at the floor. She heard them troubleshooting potential hiccups that might arise, making sure everything was ready to connect the batteries as quickly and seamlessly as possible—but her mind was elsewhere. Once they finished, Joss hopped up to meet Ethan.

She spoke low enough that only he could hear. "Ethan—"

"No," he said, cutting her off with an emphatic head shake.

"But we need to be ready for—"

"I said *no.* This will work."

"And if it doesn't?"

"We're not having that conversation now."

"Then when are we?" she hissed. A few people looked over. She dropped her voice back down. "You want to wait until it's too late?"

"Joss, we are *not* having that conversation now." His tone was final. The two stared each other down until the radio squawked.

"We got a problem, boss."

Everyone turned to Steve, Matt included, because he was on comms. Wincing, he pressed down the talk button and held the radio up to his mouth with a bandaged hand.

"What is it?" he asked George.

"Debris," George said. *"Damage from the crash. It's blocking every possible way to get the backup batteries to R2."*

"Are you using the forklift or the tow?" Steve asked.

"Both. We're clearing debris as fast as we can. But until we get this stuff out of here, there's no way to get the batteries over there."

"How long until we lose the second generator?" Joss asked Maggie, who was bent over one of the manuals. The engineer answered but avoided eye contact as she hedged.

"Goddamn it." Joss cut her off. "No one's quoting you. What do you think?"

Maggie looked up. "I'm shocked it hasn't gone out already."

Joss spun. "We have to. There's no other way."

Ethan hesitated.

"Ethan!" Joss stepped around the desk to face him directly. "This is the hard call. This is the tough choice. We can't risk it. We have to move now."

"What does she mean?" Matt whispered to his dad. Steve shook his head, not understanding either.

"We wait until we lose the second generator," Ethan said. "We make no decisions until we lose two."

"If we wait, there won't be enough time," Joss said. "Damn it, Ethan. Find a backbone!"

"The priority is getting the batteries there! We work that problem first. If the second generator goes before that, then—"

"You're stalling. You don't want to make the call. You know it has to be done—"

"Maybe. Maybe not. And if—"

"Ethan, goddamn it! Why are you at the controls? This, right now—*this* is the job."

Everyone in the room watched Ethan and Joss stare at each other in their stalemate—as a loud alarm suddenly went off.

A split second later, the lights went out.

The second generator was dead.

You could feel the collective heartbeat rise as they all looked at one another in the ghostly glow of the emergency lighting and blinking red and white lights on the panels while the alarms blared.

There was only one generator left, the third backup generator. Once it blew, the whole plant would go dark. The pool, the reactor. Total station blackout. Everything would fall into runaway heating until it ignited. And once it did, *everything* burned.

Ethan shut off the alarms. His ears rang in the sudden silence. Joss waited.

"Okay," he said finally.

She hung her head. Not satisfied but, rather, devastated to be getting her way.

"We start the pump system manually," he said.

Someone was going to have to go into the water.

CHAPTER THIRTY-SIX

COUNTDOWN TO ZERO HOUR

29 MINUTES

DANI SQUINTED AT the rear windshield, wondering if she was hallucinating. That *was* a gun, wasn't it? No. It couldn't be—but as she watched R.J. line up his shot for the bottom left corner of the back window and then cock the hammer, adrenaline shot through her system, and she focused up *fast*.

"Connor," Dani said, shaking him hard. "Connor, look up. He's going to shoot out the window. I need you to be ready, okay?"

The boy whimpered and his eyes widened at the sight of the firearm. Dani tried to lift her legs as high as she could so an errant shot didn't hit her feet, but her muscles were so weak and numb, she didn't know where in space her body was. Dani covered Connor's ears with her hands, although she didn't have a clue if shooting a gun underwater would make a loud noise or not—could a gun underwater even fire? Would the dense pressure slow down or speed up the bullet?

Dani had absolutely no idea what was about to happen.

R.J. set the barrel of the handgun directly on the glass. Cocking his head in a *Here goes nothing* type of way, he pulled the trigger.

A loud yet muffled *bang* made both of them yelp as they flinched and turned away—but that was it. Dani looked back quickly and watched the shattered glass sinking in slow motion.

It had actually worked.

R.J. used the crowbar to clear whatever glass hadn't shattered, expanding the opening in the windshield so they could escape. Suddenly there were more lights coming down from above. Within moments, three divers in real scuba rescue gear descended.

"They're here!" Dani said to Connor.

But the boy's eyes were closed.

"Connor. Connor!" She splashed his face and he stirred. Barely. So little, she almost wondered if she'd imagined it. He needed to get out of there, get air, and get warm, *now*.

Dani motioned to the divers to hurry. R.J. passed the crowbar to a diver and headed for the surface, as the limit on his SCBA mask had run out. One of the other divers cleared away the last of the glass until, finally, there was enough room for him to enter the van.

When he surfaced inside the air pocket, Dani could see the alarm in his eyes through his mask. He immediately took the regulator from his own mouth and handed it to Dani. She turned Connor toward her and pressed the mouthpiece against his lips.

"Put this in your mouth. It's air. It's okay, baby. It'll help you."

Connor seemed confused and he resisted at first, so Dani

basically forced it into his mouth and held it there. "Deep breath in through your mouth," she urged.

Connor's eyes grew large as he inhaled, the fresh, pure oxygen hitting his system instantly. The diver passed an emergency secondary air-share line to Dani. It was yellow and smaller, and she put it in her mouth and began sucking air in greedily too, suddenly acutely aware of how diminished their oxygen supply had gotten.

"Here's what's going to happen," the diver said, speaking quickly but clearly. "Connor, you'll go out first with me."

Connor looked over to Dani as though asking if he should do that. Dani nodded enthusiastically, reassuring him with a thumbs-up. The boy nodded that he understood.

"You're going to keep that thing in your mouth all the way up," the diver continued, pointing at the regulator in his mouth. "Keep breathing in and out the whole time. Okay? It might feel weird to breathe underwater, so let's try it out now, okay?"

Together, Dani and the diver moved the boy's head to the water. Calmly coaxing him and talking him through it, they lowered his face under the water and held the regulator in his mouth. Dani felt Connor's body tense as bubbles rose to the surface, and she rubbed his back, trying to calm him as they held him under the water, forcing him to acclimate to the strange sensation of breathing underwater. Add it to the list of traumatic things he'd endured today—but at least this one was for his own good. It was better for him to freak out now than on the way to the surface. When he came back up, Connor rubbed his wide, terrified eyes.

"As soon as we go out," the diver said to Dani, "another diver will come in for you, and it'll be the same deal for your ascent. Okay?" Dani passed the spare regulator back to the diver, nodding.

"Listen, baby," Dani said to Connor as the diver got ready to go. She could see the fear in the boy's eyes. "It's going to be okay. We're going to be eating pizza in no time. Just stay calm, stay with him. I'm right behind you."

Connor's head went up and down, and Dani's eyes filled with tears. How could she have known this child for only a handful of hours? How was that possible? He was as good as her own flesh and blood now, and as she kissed his forehead, pure love radiated through her with an intensity she'd only ever felt with Brianna.

Dani slid Connor off the seat and into the water, passing him awkwardly to the diver in the cramped space. Speed, now, was the priority. They needed to get to the surface before Connor could freak out and spit out the regulator.

The diver and Connor cleared the window seamlessly. Out in the open water, the diver wrapped an arm around Connor's waist and made for the surface, pushing off the uneven rocks on the river bottom—which caused the whole van to shift and roll forward.

The air pocket shifted with it, bubbling up and out of the van through the back window as Dani thrashed in shock, now entirely without air.

CHAPTER THIRTY-SEVEN

COUNTDOWN TO ZERO HOUR

27 MINUTES

THEY WERE RUNNING out of time in the control room—but how do you rush a conversation in which it's being decided which one of you will die? Joss leaned over the blueprints while Ethan laid out the task at hand.

"There are three levels of operation for the scenario of a flooded subbasement," he said. "First option for pump activation is electric. That has clearly failed. The second is a switch inside a panel in the subbasement."

"What are the chances the switch still works?" Maggie asked.

"Virtually zero," Joss said. Ethan didn't disagree.

"The third and final way to activate the pump," Ethan said, "is to open a sluice gate to release the water."

"How?" George asked.

"There's a wheel inside the subbasement. You turn it. Now," he said, standing up and crossing his arms. "Before you all start getting brave and raising your hands to volunteer, you need to understand this water. It's…it's like the water at the bottom of the pool."

Steve stared at the floor in the silence that followed. Ethan's point was clear.

Whoever went in wouldn't come back. It was a suicide mission.

George was the first to speak.

"This is the *only* way?"

"Yes," Joss said. "It's the only way."

The firefighter nodded solemnly for a moment before standing. "I will—"

"No," Vikram said. "It's time for the engineers to share the risks. I'll go."

Before George could respond or Vikram could further plead his case, Maggie said she'd go. Then Dwight. Then the others in the room began to step forward or raise their hands. Just as one person finished explaining why they should be the one, someone else jumped in.

Earlier in the day, when faced with the similar situation of deciding who would go in the pool, there had been some hesitation. A natural, understandable pause as people searched inside themselves to see if they were truly built from the right stuff. The moment now was different. There was no hesitation. Everyone was sincere. Every person in that room was ready to lay down his or her life for the cause. They'd been through too much, gone too far down the road together, for any of them to turn back now.

"Okay, enough," Joss said, straightening up. "We don't have time. Everyone, write your name on a piece of paper. We'll draw."

No one objected.

Paper was ripped into small pieces, pens were shared, a waste-basket was emptied and passed around, and one by one, people put their names in. Almost all the slips of paper had been added when Matt stepped forward.

Ethan regarded the boy with deep respect. "That's very brave of you, Matt," he said. "But you can't—"

"Not me. My dad. It has to be my dad."

No one knew what to say at first, but quickly, murmured variations of refusal went around the room: *No. Steve's given enough. He physically can't. Matt, you've given enough. You two need to be together now.* All the while, Matt and Steve just looked at each other.

After all they'd been through, they needed to make it right, together, with what little time Steve had left. They needed time. To fix the fishing pole. To be together. To set things right for Matt's future, to resolve what had already passed. But here now, in the present, in all there really was, father and son communicated without saying a word. They both understood.

"I'm the reason he's not volunteering and I'm the reason you're not asking him to," Matt said. "No one else should die if they don't have to. My dad can do that. My dad can make sure that doesn't happen."

Everyone in the room was stunned. They looked to Steve, not knowing what to say, taking their cues from him. The father's eyes brimmed with sadness and regret, but he beamed with pride. Steve held his chin up.

"When you hug your children tonight, know that it is because of him," he said with a nod to Matt. "My son. The bravest, most selfless person I know."

It was decided. Steve would open the sluice gate.

CHAPTER THIRTY-EIGHT

COUNTDOWN TO ZERO HOUR

24 MINUTES

DANI WAS ALMOST out of air. Her chest felt like it was collapsing in on itself as she watched the other two divers work frantically to move a rock blocking the way in and out of the van. They pushed and pulled in unison, trying to sway the big boulder, as stars began to dance across her vision. Everything that had been dim was fading to black.

This is it, she thought as everything went dark.

This is the end.

Moments later, the water around her shifted.

Hands were on her body. Something was thrust into her mouth.

That same mysterious something inside her that had tried so hard to keep Connor awake now whispered to her alone:

Exhale. Inhale. Breathe, Dani.

She did as she was told. Her eyes shot open as the oxygen hit her lungs. She grabbed the diver beside her, and he took her firmly by the arm. His message was clear.

We need to go. Now.

Together they made for the rear exit—until something pulled Dani back.

Her pant leg was caught between a rock and a seat.

It wouldn't budge. The diver swam over and grabbed the fabric with both hands, tugging up repeatedly as hard as he could, but the thick, sturdy fabric refused to give. He swam deeper into the van, trying for a different angle—which ripped the regulator out of Dani's mouth.

Gurgling as bubbles escaped her lips, she tried to grab the snaking length of tube now free-floating in the water, but it was just out of her reach. The diver was oblivious, focused only on the pants, but as he swam back to try a different approach, Dani was able to get her hands on the regulator.

She put it in her mouth and, breathing deeply, wondered sincerely how much more her body could take. She was so tired. Maybe she should just go get ice cream like Bri had asked her to. She turned to tell her baby girl that they would go after dinner, but Bri wasn't there. It was the seat's headrest her hand was resting on.

Exhale. Inhale. Just keep breathing, Dani.

The diver flipped open a survival knife he'd drawn from a leg holster, set it to the thick fabric, and started sawing vigorously back and forth.

Dani watched him work. It reminded her of Marion chopping

firewood, how he'd drag a long branch over, saw it into sections, set it upright, then — *thwack!* — down came the ax. Dani smiled.

The fire in the fireplace was warm; this was the only aspect of work she ever brought home with her. Cozy pajamas, the smell of baking bread, Daddy watching his team playing while Bri colored. Love expressed as home. The simple life she'd wished and worked for. Dani felt the warmth. Her life, their life, was all she'd ever wanted.

The diver kept at it tirelessly, sawing back and forth, back and forth, until, with a ripping noise, the knife cut through the last of it and Dani was free. He spun, victorious, ready to signal Dani to move to the back window — and found her floating, motionless, eyes closed, the regulator dangling to the side, out of her mouth.

Levon was on the riverbank, with R.J. beside him shivering in a silver survival blanket wrapped around Frankie's dry turnout coat. Both of them watched the water unblinkingly.

"She should be up by now!" Levon shouted. "What's happening?"

R.J. didn't disagree, and he didn't know. She *should* have been up by now.

Up the hill, Boggs and Frankie and two of the Coastguardsmen worked on Connor, checking his vitals, getting him dry, getting him warm.

"He needs a hospital. Start the chopper," one of them said into a shoulder-mounted radio. Moments later, the engine turned over and the propeller slowly started to spin.

Levon and R.J. both looked at it.

"No, no, no," Levon muttered. He scrambled up the embankment and chased the team rushing Connor's stretcher toward the helicopter. "Wait!"

"We have to move him now," one of the Coastguardsmen said, hollering over the rotor blades. "He doesn't have time—"

"Please! Please wait for her!"

"If we don't go now, this kid might not make it."

"Neither will she if you leave!"

"Hey!"

Levon spun at R.J.'s cry. Bubbles were breaking on the surface.

He ran back down, met R.J. in the water, and they splashed out, knee-deep, to the diver who was dragging Dani's body toward the shore. They laid her on the muddy ground, and Levon checked for a pulse. When he didn't find one, he immediately started CPR.

"I need a defibrillator!" he called out.

Up by the chopper, they were about to load Connor's stretcher in. Boggs left the boy's side and ran to the fire engine for the machine, which cleared the line of sight from the helicopter to the water. Connor's eyes fluttered open. Confused, scared, in pain, he looked over to find Dani's body stretched out on the ground looking very much like she was sleeping. He moved to sit up, to go to her, but his eyes rolled back in his head, and he was out.

"We're losing him," Frankie said.

"We gotta go!" a Coastguardsman working on Connor called out as they slid the stretcher into the chopper. Frankie stepped back, glancing over to see his teammates and R.J. positioning Dani on an orange rescue stretcher.

"No! We're coming!" Levon shouted from the waterside, the desperation in his plea devastating. The chopper's engine began to rev up.

Frankie looked from Connor down to his crew. To Dani—his

coworker, his sister, his family. He spun to the helicopter, laying his hands flat on the cockpit windshield. "Please," he begged the pilot.

The pilot glanced at his copilot, who hesitated, then gave a nod. The pilot looked back to Frankie and mouthed one word: *Hurry*.

Frankie scrambled down the embankment to help carry her up. They flanked her stretcher, grunting as they carried both her weight and Levon's uphill, as Levon was now straddling her unmoving body, refusing to stop chest compressions for even a single beat. Once on flat ground, they ran the rest of the way, barely getting the stretcher into the chopper before it lifted off.

Frankie, Boggs, and R.J. all ducked as the helicopter rose high into the air, peeling off toward the hospital. They stayed there, crouched, on their knees, watching the chopper fly away, getting smaller and smaller, carrying what felt like their whole world.

CHAPTER THIRTY-NINE

COUNTDOWN TO ZERO HOUR

20 MINUTES

IN THEIR FINAL minutes together, Matt and Steve were quiet. Following Joss down the hallway, they simply walked side by side, Matt taking larger-than-usual steps, trying to match his dad's stride. Reaching the end of the hall, Joss gave a nod to Steve and said she'd be right in there when he was ready. Then she closed the door quietly, and father and son were alone.

Steve dropped to one knee in front of Matt, who stared at the floor.

"Take off your shoe," Steve said.

Matt looked up. "What?"

"I need your shoe."

Matt took off his tennis shoe and passed it to his dad. Wincing, Steve started to remove the lace. "Your fishing pole," he said. "Do you remember why it's broken?"

Matt shook his head.

"The reel jammed," Steve said as he continued to unlace the shoe, "because the line was tangled. Do you remember why the line tangled?"

"I wouldn't tie the knot you told me to tie," Matt said, remembering now.

Steve smiled. "You know, the dumb, dangerous ideas you get from me. But the stubbornness?" He looked up with a raised eyebrow. "*That* you get from your mother." Steve set down the now lace-less shoe. "You wouldn't let me tie the knot because you wanted to tie it yourself with a clinch knot. I told you a clinch knot would make the lure swim sideways and eventually tangle the line. But you were so proud of your clinch knot, you refused to let me tie the one that would work." Steve touched his thumb to his pointer finger, making an O. "Do this."

Matt did. Steve took the lace and folded it over. Then, step by step, using Matt's fingers like the eye of a hook, he showed his son how to tie a uni knot — the knot he should have used on the hook that day. The knot that wouldn't have made the line tangle. The knot Matt would need to know the next time he went fishing.

"See?" Steve said, tugging the shoelace knot against Matt's fingers. "Here," he said, untying it and holding his own fingers out in an O. "You try."

With Steve talking him through it, Matt clumsily tied the knot around his dad's bandaged fingers. The son looked up, proud. The father smiled, prouder. "Good," Steve said. "Do it again."

Matt tied the knot again. And then again. Finally, the last time, Steve untied the knot and laid the lace in Matt's hand.

"The reel is still jammed," Steve said. "You'll need my tools in the swing-out cabinet under the workbench. Those are your tools now. You're going to have to take it apart and fix it yourself."

Matt looked down, his voice shaking. "I don't know how."

"I know," Steve said, holding it together for both of them, the last fatherly act he would do for his child. "There's going to be a lot of things you don't know how to do. That's okay. It's okay not to know. Ask for help. People will help you. Let them."

Matt nodded, letting himself be scared. It was the last childlike act he would do for his father. He started to cry. Steve lifted his chin.

"Let them help you. You are already twice the man most men will ever be. You have nothing to prove to anyone, ever. Do you understand me?"

Matt wrapped his arms around his dad's neck and the two hugged for what would be the last time. They held each other for a long time, but it wasn't long enough.

It never would be.

The mood in the control room was somber. Controllers occupied themselves with their own version of busywork—monitoring, checking gauges. Ethan was on the emergency line updating Marion on what was happening so he could then pass the information along to the community. His voice was tired. *He* was tired. The emotional impact of the day was starting to creep in along the edges.

"So," Ethan said with an exhausted sigh, running a hand down his face. "That's the plan."

Marion made a noise of understanding, a promise to pass the

word along, and a statement of gratitude for all he, they, had done that day. As they were about to hang up, Marion asked who they'd chosen to open the gate.

"Oh, I thought I said," Ethan said. "Steve. Joss went with him to swipe him in. He's saying goodbye to his son now." Ethan cleared his throat, covering his emotion, thinking of that moment, imagining what it would be like if he had to have that moment with his own son. Ethan wasn't sure he was that strong. Actually, he knew he wasn't.

"Right," said Marion. *"But who's the second?"*

In the silence of Ethan's lack of a response, he could almost feel Marion sit up straighter.

"There are two wheels. Side by side," Marion said. *"They have to be opened at the same time to release the pressure on the gates evenly. If they're not, the pressure builds to the point that neither will open."* He waited for Ethan to say something. *"It can't be done alone. It can only be done by two people."* There was still no response. *"Are you there?"* Marion said finally.

Ethan wasn't listening. He was staring at the blueprints lying on the table, remembering Joss hunched over, studying them. He was remembering the look in her eyes as she slumped down in a chair and stared off into space. He hadn't understood that look then.

He did now.

Ethan sprinted out of the control room and down the hall, burst through the building's exit, and ran across the campus as fast as his legs would carry him while a stunningly gorgeous early-spring sunset exploded across the sky behind him. He ran past rubble and wreckage, fire trucks and aircraft parts. A stitch in his side intensified as he gasped for air, only then realizing he wasn't wearing any protective gear, not even a mask. He didn't care. He kept going.

Rounding a corner onto the scene of the aircraft tail jammed flush against the building, he saw Joss and Steve approaching the door at the far end. Ethan screamed her name just as she swiped a badge through the door's security panel. Steve turned. Joss didn't.

"Joss! *Stop!*" Ethan cried out as his feet pounded the grass while he watched Joss enter the security code. He was almost there, he had almost caught up—when he saw a little green light on the panel blink on. Joss ripped open the door, pushed Steve inside, followed him in, and slammed the door shut behind them just as Ethan arrived.

"No!" he cried, pulling uselessly on the handle, pounding on the locked door. Inside, Joss, in her full hazmat suit, watched him through the glass pane in the door.

Ethan went for his badge on the retractable lanyard on his hip, but it wasn't there. Patting all around his waist, frantic, he saw movement and looked up to see Joss pressing his own badge up against the window.

"No...no, please. Joss, no!" he screamed, pounding his fist against the door, pulling on the door handle. "Please don't do it. It shouldn't be you. Let *me* go. Please. Let me be the one."

But they both knew he was only saying that because it was already done. It was her, not him. That much had been decided the day he didn't get on the plane and go with her to Washington. Joss held her hand up to the glass on the door; her way of reminding him they'd both chosen their own paths long ago. Her way of saying it was okay.

"No," Ethan said, shaking his head, tears streaming down his cheeks. "It's not. It's not okay."

Joss smiled, her cheeks pushed up by the mask, loving that after all these years, they still didn't have to talk to communicate. She nodded.

Yes, yes, it was okay.

They stayed that way a moment longer, trapped somewhere between what could have been and how it had turned out. Finally, Joss brought her hand down. Ethan kept his up. And just as he had at the airport all those years ago, he watched her walk away and not look back.

CHAPTER FORTY

COUNTDOWN TO ZERO HOUR

14 MINUTES

PRESIDENT DAWSON HAD feared all day long that it would come down to something like this.

"And this sluice gate, it's the *only* way to drain the water?" he asked, flipping through the papers, scanning the Clover Hill blueprints.

"Yes, sir," the chair of the NRC said from a video quadrant on the screen. "It's a two-person operation. Relatively simple. But requiring everything."

"Their sacrifices will not be forgotten," Dawson said as Tony handed him the call sheets with contact information for the two volunteers' next of kin. "They are heroes," he said, looking at the first sheet with the picture of Fire Chief Steve Tostig. "And they will be remembered as —"

The president stopped, the second sheet frozen in his hand.

"Mr. President?"

Dawson ignored the chairman as he studied the image of Dr. Jocelyn "Joss" Vance that stared up at him from the page. A Mona Lisa smirk, a hint of a raised eyebrow. *What'd you expect?* her expression seemed to taunt.

"Tony. Get Dr. Vance on the phone."

Tony cleared his throat. "I tried. I'm sorry, sir. She's already gone."

"Everybody, listen up!"

The church hushed to silence. Reverend Michaels turned up the radio's volume. Marion's voice filled the room.

"Well, ah, this is it. They have left for the R2 auxiliary buildings to open the sluice gates and drain the subbasement. The mission is underway. And, ah, well, the next time I update, I imagine we will know how it went."

The people of Waketa stood side by side with the National Guard listening to the update from Clover Hill. A guardsman held the water bottle Mrs. Shelton had just handed him, waiting to take a drink. Ernie Caro's ankle was almost wrapped, but the military medic had stilled his hands. Outside, the school bus pulled up. Reverend Michaels made eye contact with Carla as Principal Gazdecki put it in park, but everyone stayed on. They, too, were listening.

Everyone paused, to bear witness together.

"The sluice gate takes two people to open," Marion continued. *"Fire Chief Steve Tostig and Dr. Jocelyn Vance are the, ah, the volunteers for that duty."* He cleared his throat. *"Well, I already explained what that means."*

There was quiet. The incident commander removed his hat.

"This is all for now," Marion said finally. *"The evacuation order remains in effect. And...ah. Godspeed to them both."*

The transmission ended. The church stayed silent. Most looked at the floor, unsure of where else to look or what to do next. After some time, Mrs. Jacobs, the mayor's wife, spoke.

"Reverend Michaels," she said. "Should we pray?"

Everyone in the church turned to the altar.

Reverend Michaels looked around the room at the exhausted, the scared, the injured. He saw their fear and their sadness, their trauma from what had already happened and their worries of what was yet to come. He saw need and longing. Desperation and hopelessness.

He also saw homemade sandwiches and butterfly Band-Aids. The parking lot was full.

Reverend Michaels tilted his head.

"Mrs. Jacobs," he said. "What do you think we've been doing all day?"

And with that, everyone went back to work.

CHAPTER FORTY-ONE

COUNTDOWN TO ZERO HOUR

11 MINUTES

BROKEN GLASS CRACKED under their feet as Joss and Steve crept down the same hallway the drone had traveled not long ago. They would trace its path to the basement and, ultimately, Joss realized with a chill, mirror the machine's fate. They too would soon be found at the bottom of a pool of toxic water, gone. Damaged beyond repair. Their duty done.

With sunlight no longer streaming through the windows, the dim emergency lighting cast eerie, distorted shadows. Joss slowed her pace, aware that Steve was trailing her. The effects of the radiation were clearly worsening, but not for one second did she doubt he could get the job done.

Even with the hazmat suit, Joss felt a cold breeze cut through a broken window as they passed. She looked over to the rich navy-blue of twilight painting the sky above a dark and foreboding tree line in the distance. This landscape was home, as simple as it was beautiful. It was the place she had been born and raised—and soon, she realized, would die. She found it comforting that this place, this view, was the last glimpse of this earth she'd ever have.

Clicking on their headlamps, they made their way through the maze of the building, tracing the path of the drone. Down the hallway. Second right. One flight down. Two flights down. Their senses were heightened. Everything felt louder, softer, closer, farther; it was a disorienting state of hypervigilance, like walking through a haunted house.

Joss was in front as they descended the last flight of stairs, and just before they turned the corner, she held up a hand and froze.

They both stood there—not moving, just listening—until they heard it.

Water.

The two exchanged a glance. Joss leaned over the railing and peered down to the last of the steps below; her headlamp reflected off water filling the base of the stairs. The only other sound beyond the soft drips and rush of water was the clicking of the personal dosimeters fixed to both their hazmat suits.

They made their way down the last of the stairs and Joss paused before stepping into the ankle-deep water—yet another psychological point of no return to cross. They carried on, and soon they were standing side by side in the basement looking at the three large emergency generators, only one of which still had illuminated lights on the front. The other two were black and devoid of function. All three sat in water maybe three inches high.

Joss could feel her heart pounding in her chest. It was like standing in front of a mountain lion baring its fangs. You knew you were dead, but if you were brave enough, you could give your friends enough time to make a run for it. She swore she could hear her heartbeat, it was *that* loud—but when Steve ripped off his beeping dosimeter and threw it into the water, she realized what it really was. She followed his lead and the room went silent as their radiation detectors sank to the bottom.

"That way," Joss said, pointing down the hall beyond Steve. She followed him, their rubber boots splashing as they went. The water wasn't hurting them, not yet. The thick rubber of the boots protected the skin. The real damage would happen the deeper they went, when the water rose to where their suits were thinner. They crossed the room to the opening in the floor flanked with handrails: the entrance to the subbasement.

The water coming from the opening subtly bubbled and moved; this was where it was entering the basement. Steve was in front, Joss peered out from behind him. The staircase before them was completely submerged in dark, ominous water.

Steve grabbed the railing and started down into the subbasement. The first step was shin-deep. The next knee-deep. Down he went, each step reducing his life expectancy to nearly nothing.

Joss was right behind him, her hands shaking as she took hold of the railing at the top of the stairs. But just before she started down, there in those final moments, she paused. And in Joss's own way, her life flashed before her eyes.

I am about to die.

Sure, her family would miss her. Yes, her friends would mourn.

But she found relief in knowing she wasn't *really* leaving anyone behind. No husband. No children. No one's life would be catastrophically altered in a day-to-day way by her absence. She thought of all the pain Matt had already endured and all the pain that was yet to come. Joss's heart broke for him. How was that fair, putting a child through that?

Living in this world was painful and scary and unjust. For Joss, she could never really understand bringing an innocent little being into all that pain and trauma just because—

Well…because why?

Because she'd had a crush on the drum major and wondered what their kids would look like? Because baby clothes are cute? Because shopping for her daughter's wedding dress sounded like fun? Because those school photos that, year after year, charted your perfect little human's evolution from child to teen to young adult were as perfect a thing as something could be?

It wasn't that she didn't like kids or didn't want kids. No, her decision not to have children was born *from* her maternal instincts. She wanted to protect them, her nonexistent children, and now Joss felt relief in knowing she had. She had spared her children the devastating pain and confusion of losing their mother. No child would be alone and in pain because she had to go.

Her choice not to have kids had always felt right. She'd never once regretted it. Even now. Especially now. But if she was being honest with herself, here at the end, she found she was sad. Not regretful. She still knew she was right.

But she was sad.

Maybe, she realized, her heart aching as she thought it, it wasn't enough to be right.

No one would mourn her, not in that way. No one left in this world would inherit any pieces of her. Her thoughts, her wisdom, her kindness, her care, her spunk, her fire—it all ended here. And whatever joy and creativity and love her children could have brought to the world over the course of their own lives—it would never exist.

Joss might be remembered; she might be missed. But she would not live on. And there was something profoundly sad in realizing, too late, that inside her—perhaps even as strong as her maternal instinct to protect—was the equally human desire to create.

Joss tightened her grip on the railing and was preparing to step down into the final chapter of her life when suddenly Steve yelled out.

"Wait!" he said, holding his hand out toward her. Joss froze. He bent down deeper into the staircase, angling his headlamp across the subbasement.

"That panel," he said. "The one you said had switches that could be flipped that would turn the pump on. It's down here?"

"Yes," Joss said. "On the far wall. But with it submerged, the wiring would be wet. Not a chance it works and it might electrocute us if we tried to flip it."

"And what if it wasn't submerged?" Steve asked.

Joss was confused. She crouched down, looked under the overhang into the subbasement. Sure enough, there was the panel on the far wall, just where it was on the blueprints.

But what wasn't on the blueprints was the discarded pile of construction supplies, including spare aluminum siding that was diverting the water away from that corner.

The panel was dry.

"If it worked—the switch—would we know?" Steve asked.

"Yes. We'd hear the pump kick on and the water would immediately begin to recede."

"And then we wouldn't have to open the sluice gate? If it worked?"

"Correct."

Steve paused. "So then this would become a one-person job?"

Joss hesitated. She knew where this was going. And she felt tremendous guilt at the massive uptick in hope surging through her body.

"Yes," she said. "That is correct."

Steve smiled. "Then how about we try for one happy ending?"

CHAPTER FORTY-TWO

COUNTDOWN TO ZERO HOUR

07 MINUTES

DANI'S COLD BODY lay motionless on the floor of the helicopter.

"Clear!"

The Coastguardsman drying her torso backed away. There was a soft buzzing windup, then a jolt, as an electric shock went through the paddles and into her chest. Dani's body jerked involuntarily upward in response to the wave of electricity.

"Eighty-one point six," a Coastguardsman working on Connor said, reporting the boy's body temperature. Moderate hypothermia. A temperature up slightly from a minute ago.

Everyone working on Dani glanced over, just as everyone

working on Connor had at the *clear*. The chopper was cramped with three Coastguardsmen, Levon, two pilots, and the two unresponsive bodies laid across stretchers on the floor. Everyone worked in tightly choreographed tandem, passing equipment, calling out readings, thinking a step ahead to anticipate both the patients' and medics' needs.

"We got a heartbeat," said a Coastguardsman working on Dani.

Levon dropped his head in relief while his arms shook with fatigue. She might have a chance.

Warming blankets were thrown over her body. Someone took her temperature.

"Seventy-six point two."

Severe hypothermia. Zero improvement from a minute ago. If Dani didn't get to a hospital soon, to an emergency trauma unit where they could warm her up, she would die.

"Eight minutes out," the pilot flying yelled over his shoulder.

"What?" Levon yelled back over the loud noise of the helicopter's blades. Dani didn't have eight minutes. "How are we eight minutes from Minn General? It's not that far."

"We're not going to General. We're going to St. Paul Pediatric."

"General is closer. They need to be seen *now*."

"The boy needs specific pediatric equipment."

"They'll have it at Minn General."

"We can't confirm that."

"But she doesn't have eight minutes!"

Connor needed the specialized equipment and medical teams they would find at St. Paul Pediatric. For Dani, it was about time. For her, a single minute could mean the difference between life and death.

"Your rescues, your call," said the pilot.

Levon looked from the boy to his best friend. From the innocent, traumatized, orphaned child with no one in the world to advocate on his behalf to the single mother raising a little girl to be just like her: kind, selfless, brave.

"Sir! I need an answer," the pilot barked. "Where am I going?"

On the roof of the hospital, attendings stood by, ready, waiting, two empty gurneys by their side. As the chopper touched down, the doctors and nurses rushed forward.

The door slid open. The patients were transferred out. As they wheeled Dani and Connor in, Levon and a Coastguardsman ran alongside, shouting out vitals and relevant details.

Inside the hospital, people jumped out of the way as Connor and Dani were wheeled through the hallways. Doctors yelled instructions as equipment beeped and the harsh fluorescent tube lighting above them passed like dotted white lines painted on a road. While the doctors worked, Levon ran beside Dani, holding her hand like a vise grip.

"Brianna is waiting for you," he said, his voice bumpy as they ran. "Marion is waiting for you. You got this, Dani. Stay here."

"This is us," the nurse beside him said as the group began to slow. "You can't come in."

"Don't you dare leave us. Please, Dani," Levon pleaded.

"Sir! Let go."

Levon opened his hand and Dani's dropped, splayed motionlessly over the side of the gurney as she was wheeled into a trauma bay. Suddenly, there was a hand on his chest and a nurse blocking his way.

"You can't go in," she said.

He tried to push past, but the nurse was firm.

"I'm sorry. No."

The nurse went in, and through the open door he could see the chaos, could see the scramble, the desperation, as his friend fought for her life — and then it was gone. The doors shut and he was alone on the outside, not knowing what would happen next.

Levon stumbled back across the hall and slid down the wall to a sit. From the floor, he stared at the closed doors in a state of shock while the rest of the hospital hummed on in their never-ending work to save lives. He was wet, bloody, and covered in mud; a stark contrast to the sterility of a hospital. And there above him, at the place where he'd slid down the wall, was a streak of soot and mud across the brightly colored cartoons painted on the bright white hallways of St. Paul Pediatric Hospital.

CHAPTER FORTY-THREE

COUNTDOWN TO ZERO HOUR
03 MINUTES

IF STEVE DIDN'T flip the switch to activate the pump soon, opening the sluice gate would be the only option left.

"Look—"

"No," Steve said, cutting Joss off. "There's no time. You went on this mission because it had to be done. And I respect the hell out of you for it. But don't disappoint me now and try to talk me out of it like you're some hero martyr. We both know I'm going to do it."

There was a beat when neither of them spoke. Then, deadpan, Joss said, "I was just going to tell you which switch it was."

One wouldn't think laughter was possible in the bleakest of times in the darkest of places, but for a very, very brief moment, it was.

"There will be three switches," Joss said, her smile quickly fading. "*Off, auto,* and *hand. Hand* is the one you want. Flip it."

"That simple?"

"That simple."

There was another beat where it seemed like someone should say something, but neither knew what that might be. So Steve turned with a deep breath and started down the stairs. The water rose higher and higher on his body, and just before he got to the point at which he would have to let go of the railing and start swimming, Joss called his name. He turned.

"Are you sure?" she said.

"I knew you weren't so tough."

Joss was crying. "I'm so sorry. I'm so sorry it had to be you."

"I know," Steve said. "Look after my boy."

Joss nodded that she would, and with that, he dipped fully into the water.

As he made his way over to the panel, an all-too-familiar sensation hit him, but this time, he didn't need to look down. He knew the radiation was eating through the hazmat suit as the cold shock of water on his skin immediately transformed into searing pain. His radiation burns came alive at the fresh dose, far more potent than the last. He let out a cry as the intensity of the pain robbed him of control of his movements and his body began to drift.

"Steve!" Joss called.

"I'm fine!" he managed as he slowly trudged back in the right direction. "Stay there!" The construction siding holding the water back like a dam started to wobble in the moving water as he approached.

"Easy!" Joss yelled.

Steve slowed his progress, smoothing out his strokes. He was getting there...he was almost there...steady...steady. Everything was looking good.

Taking hold of a pipe on the wall to anchor himself, he planted both feet and reached out to the panel. It swung open easily, and there they were. Three switches, labeled clear as day: OFF. AUTO. HAND.

Steve reached out, groaning in pain, then paused to reposition himself. As he leaned far over the siding, his grip on the pipe slipped, and his elbow smacked into the top of it. The siding slipped out of its hold, releasing a torrential flow of water where all had once been dry. The panel was now soaked.

Steve lost his grip on the pipe. The world went quiet as his head dipped under the water.

Sunlight across Claire's weightless red hair. Matt's little fingers tying the wrong knot.

Hearing Joss calling his name from a distance, he popped back up.

"No! Stop!" he yelled to Joss as he reached for the panel. He could still get there before the wires got wet. It could still work. The switch labeled HAND was right there, and just as he went to grab it, sparks shot out from behind all three. Grabbing the switch, he flipped it up—

And nothing happened.

Joss watched him flip it up and down several more times to see if anything would happen. Nothing did, but by that time she was already swimming toward him. He cried out in pain as she took him under an arm, then with her other hand, grabbed the pipe on the wall to hold them both up.

"Steve!" she said as he coughed under his mask until he ripped it off entirely—what was the point now anyway? As he came to, realizing what had just happened, they looked at each other and for a split second, they shared a devastating moment of disappointment. Before he could say anything, she spoke.

"Let's finish this."

Together, they swam to the other side of the subbasement where the wheels were. The plastic of her hood's face shield was beginning to fog over and Joss became aware of a dull tingling sensation across her skin. Soon, the tingling turned to burning. Her head started to pound. She was shocked at how quickly it had set in, far faster than she had anticipated. And if this was how she felt, she couldn't image how Steve was still managing.

Glancing over, she saw that he barely was. After helping him to the wheel, she positioned him against the wall with one hand holding on to a pipe and made sure he was secure before taking the wheel opposite him. It was now, right now. They had to get this done. Soon, neither of them would be able to.

The wheels were under the water at what would have been waist height had they been standing. She lodged her feet between the pipes so there would be something to resist her movements underwater. Steve adjusted himself similarly, anchoring his feet like hers.

"On the count of three," Joss said, ripping the mask off her face so he could hear and see her more clearly. "One. Two. Three!"

They both screamed as they twisted. Screams of pain. Screams of exertion. Screams of grief. They tried again. Over and over, she counted down and they'd twist together—but it didn't feel like the wheels were budging. And the water wasn't moving. Or was it? She couldn't tell. Or could she? She didn't know anything anymore. There was only pain.

Everything moved in slow motion. She could hardly hear her own voice yelling over and over as she and Steve stood across from each other twisting and twisting. She stared at the waterline against the wall. Watching it, praying for it to go down.

But it stayed. Right there. Rising.

Joss had no choice but to admit that this might be it. Not only were they not going to survive, but this whole plan might not work at all. Which meant all of it would have been...for nothing?

After all this. After all the work and effort and sacrifices this day had seen, the fire was still going to start. They wouldn't be able to stop it. It would mean ruin for millions of people. Families. Friends. Communities. All gone.

Joss's thoughts began to drift to places elsewhere. Right now, right that moment, what were people in those other places doing? While right now, right at that moment, she and Steve were deciding what their fate would be.

She thought of the engineers in the control room watching the gauges, waiting for the open-gate light to come on. President Dawson standing by the phone. Marion tucking Brianna into one of the bunk beds. Carla at the church with the community. *Their* community. Their home.

She also pictured the people she didn't know but could imagine. In hospitals, in traffic jams, in prayer groups, in protests. The masses huddled around their TVs, the individuals scrolling on their phones. The firefighters at the plant, the firefighters in the community. The people they saved, the people they lost—the people for whom the jury was still out.

Matt, alone, staring out the hallway window at the now pitch-black campus down below, the occasional glow of dying embers a reminder of his father's life's work. As they went out, a tribute to his father's life's end.

Ethan at the back of the control room, remembering everything said from today to years ago—and thinking of everything not said at the door minutes ago.

That, Joss thought as her hands tightened their grip on the wheel, was what their sacrifice was for. All that life, all that love. That was what was at stake. And now, in their failure, what would happen to it all? This moment was the last chance for all those lives, all those hopes and dreams. It was all in their hands.

Joss stared at the waterline. Rising. Holding.

Holding…holding…

CODA

AMERICA HAS SUFFERED *tremendous losses and faced countless crises throughout its history. What was remarkable about what happened in Waketa was how a nation — perhaps more divided than it had ever been in its history — set aside those differences and worked together to save one another, a small community, and ultimately the world.*

It is written in the Talmud, "Whoever saves a single life is considered by scripture to have saved the whole world."

That is what happened in Waketa.

The double doors opened. Everyone stood. President Dawson took his position behind the podium. The youngest president in American history, he'd navigated the largest homeland crisis the nation had ever seen while keeping the public informed and safe the entire time. He'd earned the respect of millions—even those who hadn't voted for him. In his first few months in office, Dawson had already secured a legacy far beyond his age.

The president looked at the teleprompter where the carefully crafted message his speechwriters had prepared waited for him to begin.

America has suffered tremendous losses and faced countless crises throughout…

Dawson blinked at the monitor, at the message he'd approved. It was a good speech. Presidential. But it wasn't what he should say. Dawson knew this moment required his own words. Clearing his throat, the president ignored the written speech.

"It seems impossible that it's been over a year since that day. A day that brought out the best of humanity. And make no mistake, we are only here because the best of us stepped forward. Today, we honor them."

At that, the cameras began to click wildly as Marines in their dress blues joined the president at the front of the room. While everyone was getting into position, Dawson looked over at the large easels holding the large pictures: Steve Tostig in his bunker gear, sweaty and covered in ash, the smile of a man who *knew* he was doing exactly what he had been put on this earth to do. Joss Vance, in a soft black turtleneck, leaning forward on crossed arms, hint of a smirk, eyebrow raised in a perpetual state of *I'd like to see you try.*

"I'm told Dr. Jocelyn Vance found herself at gunpoint not once but twice that day," he said. "I understand she got into it with just about everyone in the control room, refusing to give an inch on what needed to be said and done. And I can personally verify that she argued with, poked fun at, and hung up on the president of the United States."

A murmur of soft laughter rippled through the crowd.

"In a crisis, success or failure can come down to the person making the calls. You pray you have the right person in that position. Someone unafraid to ruffle feathers and be unpopular if that's what it takes. Someone who doesn't care about the status quo or how it's always been done. Someone unfazed by power and prestige. Someone who can not only *see* the tough call but is courageous enough to *make* it."

Dawson paused, giving himself a moment to regain his composure. He knew no one would think twice about it. It was natural for him to be emotional right now. But only he and Tony knew the truth, and he and Tony had never discussed it and never would. He glanced over at her picture, that damn, beautiful arched eyebrow. She'd changed the world, and in a handful of hours over just a few phone calls, she had cut an indelible path through his.

"In our time of national crisis, we *did* have the right person making the calls. We are only here now because of it. We owe Joss a debt that cannot and will not ever be repaid. But we *can* honor her sacrifice. Therefore, it is my honor to award the Presidential Medal of Freedom to Dr. Jocelyn Vance for her expertise, bravery, and selflessness."

The room erupted into applause as one of the Marines handed President Dawson an open box displaying a white star with a blue center surrounded by gold eagles hanging from a bright blue ribbon. "Accepting on behalf of Dr. Vance is former Clover Hill plant manager Ethan Rosen."

Ethan rose from his seat in the audience and joined the president on the raised platform to receive the medal with a handshake held just long enough for the photographers to get their shot.

As the applause died down, Dawson returned to the podium. "We also owe a debt of gratitude to Ethan Rosen for his actions that day. In the time since the accident, Mr. Rosen has created the Joss Vance Foundation for a Nuclear Future, a research-based non-profit whose sole purpose is to continue Dr. Vance's mission to create safe, long-term, viable solutions for nuclear waste. The foundation is meticulously preserving and archiving her research, and it spear-headed the landmark bipartisan regulatory legislation Congress passed earlier this year. It also set up a grant for women in the field of nuclear engineering research who look to continue the crucial work Joss started. This will ensure a safe future for generations to come, and this foundation will enshrine her name, her legacy, and what she did for and meant to this country."

The crowd applauded again. Ethan looked down at the medal in his hand, which was the place he wished everyone else would focus too. He glanced up into the audience to see Kristin smiling proudly, sitting next to the kids, who did the same. He had to believe Joss would be happy to see his family there like that and that she too would be proud and pleased with his work now. He would finish what they had started as undergrads. It was time for him to do his part.

While the applause died down, Dawson considered where to go next. He wished he had notes to rely on and wondered if maybe he should just jump back to the prepared speech. The president looked to the teleprompter—but found himself glancing instead at the front row of the audience.

Matt stared at the floor. The suit he wore looked brand-new and it fit him perfectly. His hair was combed neatly, and his shoes were shined. This was a child who was cared for. Protected. Loved. Not only by the aunt and uncle who had taken him in but by an entire town, an extended community that had declared that Matt was one of them and that he would never have to go it alone. But as the president looked at the boy, he knew that there were missing pieces in him that no person, no medal, no words, would ever fill. Dawson cleared his throat.

"That day asked a lot of us," he said. "But for a few of us, it asked *everything*."

Hearing the passion in the president's voice, Matt looked up to find Dawson talking directly to him.

"It wasn't fair. What your dad had to do. It wasn't fair. We all get to stay here. Live long, happy lives. And he's gone. A good, decent man is gone. And that's wrong. And it hurts. And it's not fair."

Something flickered across the boy's face. Something like recognition. Dawson wondered if anyone had said anything like this to him before or if, being well intended, they'd only emphasized what a hero Steve was and how much his sacrifice meant. Had Matt heard only the hopeful, positive, future-facing sentiments meant to create meaning and purpose out of his pain? Had no one looked this boy dead in the eye and acknowledged the truth?

Dawson looked Matt dead in the eye. "This sucks."

A look of relief broke onto the boy's face — then he laughed.

"It really does," Matt said, his eyes welling with tears.

More laughter mixed with tears as Dawson motioned for Matt to join him on the platform. The two hugged to applause before a Marine handed a medal to the president and he presented it to Matt. Wiping his eyes, Dawson returned to the mic.

"I never knew my father. Growing up, I used to dream of the kind of father I wished I had."

He turned to Matt.

"It was always a man like your dad. Stable. Confident. A decent, kind person who looked out for others and protected not only his own but those he didn't know. You were lucky to have him. And we are grateful you shared him with us. His character will be emulated by all the inspired little boys and girls who will grow up hearing stories about who he was and what he did. He will live on in them. He will live on in you. And when you look at this medal, I hope you remember how proud we are of him and how grateful we are for what he did."

Matt smiled at the applause, glancing up at Ethan, who applauded hardest of all.

After a few moments, Dawson cleared his throat. "The scope and scale of what was dealt with that day at Clover Hill and in Waketa is, even now, difficult to comprehend. The fate of a nation hung in the balance. The lives of generations to come were in the hands of a few. The sacrifices we honor today and all the actions taken that day were for the benefit of countless scores of people we don't know and will never meet. That day last April, it was declared in every way that it *isn't* about the individual. It's about the whole. The collective. The greater good."

President Dawson thought for a moment. He cocked his head.

"But it's a paradox. Because what is the whole without the individual? If we do not care for the life of one person, how do the lives of millions have meaning? The firefighters of Engine Forty-Two understood that. And in a moment when their logic, their superiors, their fears, were all pressuring them — they said *no.* They stood firm in their convictions and said the life of one little boy *does* matter. That is a different kind of bravery. One of quiet conviction that says, *This is who we are, this is what we stand for, and that matters.*"

He paused, standing up straighter.

"For this final medal, it is my honor to have someone else do the honors."

Connor came up to the stage, and the president positioned a chair next to the podium. He helped the boy up, made sure he was stable and facing the front, and took the medal from the waiting Marine. He placed the ribbon in Connor's little fingers and held the back of the chair steady as the boy lifted the medal up and over Dani's head.

After helping Connor with the clasp, Dawson said, "It is my honor to present the Medal of Freedom to Dani Allen of Waketa Township's Engine Forty-Two. Dani is the Golden Rule personified. If any one of us had been in that van, we would have prayed for someone to fight as hard for us as Dani and her crew fought for Connor. That was bravery; that was sacrifice."

"Damn right it was!"

Everyone laughed at R.J.'s outburst. Frankie let out a loud whistle as the rest of the firefighters led the cheering. Levon pumped his fist, proud tears filling his eyes, before he placed his hand on Carla's growing belly and gave her a kiss.

She was due in June. It was a girl. They would name her Jocelyn.

Dani's eyes welled with tears as she looked out at Marion and Brianna, both of whom beamed with pride. Bri's seat was next to Connor's. Marion sat beside Connor's grandparents. Their little family had grown, albeit through tragedy, but they'd decided together that *love* would be the takeaway.

Dani turned to hug Connor. Ethan put his hand on Matt's shoulder. And the president shook his head at that damn arched eyebrow.

* * *

Reverend Michaels's footsteps echoed through the empty chapel as he walked up the aisle toward the altar blowing on his cup of tea when a flash of color to his right made him turn.

Stepping closer, he peered out the window down to the cemetery and saw the newly placed flowers resting against Claire Tostig's headstone. He smiled, hearing the bike whiz by through the church's open front door.

The crickets chirped in the early-summer sunset and he knew the bullfrogs would join them soon. The air was warm, the crops were growing. The reverend closed his eyes and took this all in, from the heat of the mug in his hand to the smell of the fresh-cut grass in his nose.

Bowing his head, Reverend Michaels said a prayer.

And then, he continued on.

The bike's wheels spun over the cracked asphalt of Main Street. The bank's secretary waved to Matt as she got in her car to go home just as the neon sign at Kline's frozen custard clicked on. The door to the hardware store chimed as someone went in, and an Elton John song poured out the window of a truck going the other way.

Matt looked up to the town's new water tower, smirking as he passed the spot where he knew his name was carved. Mom would have been pissed. Dad would have laughed hard—after all, his name had been up there once too.

He rode past the fields, the cornstalks growing just barely faster than he was. He rode through the woods, beside a doe and her frolicking spring fawn. He went the way his dad's truck used to drive, the secret way, the way no one else knew, the way to their spot.

The river rambled noisily as he hopped off his bike. Grabbing his pole, Matt let his bike drop into the underbrush and made his way down to the water. He unzipped his backpack, grabbed his small tackle box, and crouched as he got out what he needed.

His fingers worked with practiced ease as he tied the knot tight. The correct knot. The knot that wouldn't tangle. The knot his dad had taught him. Then he took his pole—no longer broken after Mr. Levon had helped him fix it—swung back, and cast it out to the water.

Matt slowly reeled the line in and cast it back out.

Then again.

They'd never talked much when he and his dad used to come here. They just sort of hung out. They were just together. So now, when he came here alone, the silence didn't feel weird. It felt like maybe they were still just hanging out. Like they were still just together.

He'd give anything to talk to him, though. He had so many questions: *Did it hurt? Where are you now? Are you with Mom? Can you guys see me? What do I do?*

Matt knew enough to know questions like that didn't come with answers, so he'd learned to stop asking. Most of the time he was okay with it. Sometimes he wasn't. And when he wasn't, when he got too angry or too sad or it hurt too much—he'd go see them. He'd bring Mom flowers at the cemetery, but because he knew his dad's tombstone was over nothing since his body was too dangerous to be buried there, he'd come here to be with him.

Matt cast the line, and the lure hit the water with a rippling *plop*. A breeze picked up, bringing with it the smell of a campfire some-one somewhere was burning. Matt closed his eyes, breathing deeply the scent of his father. He let it all fill him—the anger, the pain, the love, all of it. The scrape of his beard, the sizzle of pancakes hitting the griddle, the truck pulling into the drive, his boots on the back steps. It was all there; it was all *still* there.

Matt's eyes closed tighter against the tears, the pain unbearable. "I love you, Dad," he whispered. "I miss you so much."

Suddenly, his eyes shot open and he gasped.

As fast as he could, Matt began reeling in the big fish tugging on his line.

ACKNOWLEDGMENTS

Thanks to the team at Little, Brown: Sally Kim, Craig Young, Helen O'Hare, Sabrina Callahan, Anna Brill, Brandon Kelley, and Tracy Roe. I'm so excited to build and grow with you.

To the colleagues who gave this book an early read: Don Winslow, Steve Hamilton, Eric Rickstad, Reed Coleman—much of the evolution that occurred from those rough first drafts to this polished final one are because of your feedback. Thank you.

At my agency, The Story Factory, thank you, Deborah Randall, for running support in innumerable ways. And Ryan Coleman, thank you for not only keeping the wheels on but making every project we do better by your notes and ideas. (Oh, and the laughs. Lord knows, if we're on the phone, they're probably needed.)

Thanks to Lindsey Sayers of Southern California Edison for educating me on all things power and electricity (pumpkin, pecan, or a little of both?). And to Cousin Jer, Captain Jeremy Newman of Roanoke County Fire and Rescue, for educating me on all things fire.

To my family: Mom, Pop, Dog, Jertybird, Weasel 1, and Weasel 2. You support me, and trust me, and give me space when I need it, and are right there when I need that, too. I have people, and you are the greatest blessings of my life. I'd be nothing without you.

And last but not least…

Okay, look. Here's the deal.

I love this book, right? I love the characters, I love their stories, and I'm quite proud of how it all turned out. But if I'm being honest, writing it and getting it to this point was *extremely* tough for myriad reasons. I remember one particularly rough day during the process when my mom came over to lend support, and somewhere during my long-winded, tear-filled rant, I half-jokingly told her: "I'm not writing acknowledgments this time. I'm writing grievances."

Writing a book is hard. Publishing a book is harder. Having a bestseller is damn near impossible. All the late nights. All the frustration. All the stress and anxiety. Draft after draft after draft after draft of the manuscript, the marketing copy, the cover, the… the…the…

We could have avoided it all if you just hadn't opened that manila envelope, Shane.

I would've gone on being a flight attendant. You would've carried on making deals. Maybe another agent would have signed me. Maybe another author would have delivered you a different bestseller. We would've continued on in our separate lives, never knowing what could have been.

Except you *did* open that envelope.

So here we are. Four years since our lives crossed. A million emails, a billion phone calls. Multiple bestsellers, multiple movie deals. We've laughed, we've cried, we've celebrated the wins, and we've mourned the losses. None of it has been easy. A lot of it has left a mark. And all of it, I blame on you.

All the times I've made my family and friends proud. All the opportunities I've had that I never dreamed were possible. All the ways I've evolved as an artist. All the ways I've grown as a person. It's all on you, Shane Salerno. You, who just had to open that envelope, call me up, and change my life. If I'd known then what I know now—how hard the work is, how scary it can be, how uncertain it often feels—would I have answered?

Only if it was you calling.

My phone is on, Shane.

ABOUT THE AUTHOR

T.J. Newman is a former bookseller and flight attendant whose first novel, *Falling*, became a publishing sensation and debuted at number two on the *New York Times* bestseller list. The book was named a best book of the year by *USA Today, Esquire,* and Amazon, among many others, and has been published in more than thirty countries. Her second novel, *Drowning*, was released in May 2023 and also became an instant *New York Times* bestseller. Both books will soon be major motion pictures: *Falling* with Universal Pictures, and *Drowning* with Warner Bros. Newman lives in Phoenix, Arizona.